SHAMAN

FRIEND

ENEMY

———— ∞∞∞ ————

OLIVIA LAWSON TECHNO-SHAMAN BOOK TWO

mterrygreen.com

ISBN: 1466463007
ISBN-13: 978-1466463004

Text set in Garamond by Monotype Typography. Titles set in Cochin by Linotype. Headings set in Myriad Pro by Adobe Type. Ornaments set in Type Embellishments One LET by Esselte Letraset.

SHAMAN FRIEND ENEMY

OLIVIA LAWSON TECHNO-SHAMAN BOOK TWO

M. TERRY GREEN

Los Angeles, California

DEDICATION

For Cheese.

ACKNOWLEDGMENTS

It takes so much more than a writer to create a book. Jesse Steele, of The Editorial Department, brought a critical editor's eye to this story. Her sense of reader expectations was crucial in the final stages and allowed me not only to take a more distanced view of the big picture but also a closer look at some of the finer details. Her work was indispensable.

In the latest version of this book, author and designer Keri Knutson of Alchemy Bookcovers & Design completely re-envisioned the cover concept and artwork for the entire Techno-Shaman series. Her beautiful work is a perfect fit and I'm excited for readers to see it.

Copy editor David Drazul, after lending his talents on the third book in the series, could hardly be left out of the others. From the paragraph down to the comma, there doesn't seem to be a sentence he can't improve.

My husband and I often call ourselves a team but the word becomes insanely applicable when it comes to this book because he occupies a whole raft of positions: reader, critique partner, editor, engineer, programmer, and designer. He's also mastered that mysterious math of life that makes my burdens less than half because he shares them but my happiness more than double. Go team.

CHAPTER ONE

SK SCOWLED AS the pulse at Livvy's jugular vein jumped to life. He leaned forward, staring at it, and furrowed his dark eyebrows. Lately, all of her healings were like this.

He leaned back far enough so he could look up at the client, who was lying in an ornate four-poster bed. As usual, he hadn't stirred. SK looked back down at Livvy, who hadn't moved since she'd lain down on her mat and put on the goggles.

Her diaphragm began to rise and fall at a faster rate. He slowly shook his head and pressed his lips into a tight line.

Get in, get done, get out. It was one of the first things that shamans learned. What was she doing?

Despite the fact that he knew she wouldn't hear him, he urged her on. "Come on, Liv," he whispered.

Except for her, the client, and himself, the well-appointed bedroom had been vacated. Electricity was almost guaranteed now. Her shamanic power had grown quickly. He glanced around the molded baseboards although he knew nothing was plugged into the outlets. When she called down her spirit helper in the Multiverse, he'd know in the real world. In his entire career as a shaman's intercessor, he'd never seen anything like it. Then again, he'd never met anybody like Livvy.

He looked down from where he sat cross-legged on the floor next to her. Again, he leaned forward. Above the silver goggles that she wore, he lightly brushed a lock of gleaming white hair from her forehead. Tiny beads of sweat had started to form.

What was taking so long in the Multiverse?

• • • • •

In the Underworld, Livvy watched the clouds streaming by overhead.

"Yeah, I know," she said. "I *know*."

Her spirit helper was trying to guide her to the client. The only trouble was she didn't want to see the client. Not just yet.

She stood in the central plaza of the Underworld, a downtown district that appeared much like her real-world home of Los Angeles. In the distance stood the pyramid-shaped roof of city hall. The high-rise buildings that surrounded the plaza towered above it, the clouds seeming to skim their roofs. The water of the fountain that had conveyed her there gurgled gently behind her.

A rumble of thunder slowly rippled through the mass of boiling clouds and internal flashes of lightning reflected off the myriad windows nearby. Livvy ignored them and crouched down to examine the small group of objects on the ground in front of her.

Something was wrong with the setup: a clear crystal pyramid, the engagement ring hanging from the tip, the ankh, a heptagram carved from amber, an amethyst heart, a soul catcher amulet, a kila dagger plunged into the ground, and a small polished garnet in the shape of a human skull.

"Why doesn't this work?" she muttered. "It *has* to."

A different arrangement maybe? She bit her lower lip. The descriptions had been so vague.

Again, thunder rumbled overhead. She glanced skyward and then glared at the objects, trying to think. Maybe it was something about the process, not the artifacts. What else needed to be done?

A quick burst of lightning arced across the sky, from one end of downtown to the other, and sent harsh shadows skittering along the ground.

Damnit, just a few more minutes!

The following peal of thunder reverberated through the Underworld, echoing endlessly and vibrating nearby windows.

"Fine!" she yelled.

She frowned at the objects on the ground before she scooped them up and put them back into the inner pockets of her jacket.

If it didn't work, it didn't work—*again*. She wasn't going to be able to figure it out here.

She stood, hands on hips, and looked up at the clouds. "All right," she grumbled. "Let's do this."

The clouds streamed away, the entire sky moving in one direction—the direction of her client. She took off at a jog that quickly turned into a run. The longer you stayed in the Multiverse, the harder it was to return to the real world. It was a fundamental rule of shamanism. You delay, you stay. It was time to find the client and get out.

It was past time.

Spirit traffic appeared normal. Various animal guides roamed to and fro—a number of birds perched on the surrounding ledges, a lion that could have been from the plains of Africa sprawled on the sidewalk. A large elk stalked slowly past it. There were also the occasional ancestor spirits, though not many. Two men crossed the plaza together, small but wiry with jet-black hair cut in bowl shapes, wearing only thongs. Each carried a large staff and each had a white bone labret through their lower lip. Neither they nor the animal spirit guides took any notice of Livvy. Their business wasn't with her. Only her own spirit helper had anything to do with her, and her spirit helper was impatient.

At the end of the block, the clouds took a new direction. She turned right to follow them, keeping up the sprint. She passed buildings and streets, spirits and ancestors, running as fast as she could—which was fast. Her power as a shaman was directly reflected in her abilities in the spiritual realm and, the way that power had grown in recent months, it seemed as though it had no upper limit. She nearly flew down the middle of the street, her speed only hampered by the need to change direction. At first, it had taken her by surprise but now she found she liked it.

What had been wrong with the object arrangement in the plaza? Everything was there now. As far as she knew, she wasn't missing anything.

Suddenly, the clouds stopped streaming. Livvy skidded to a stop, her boots grating and skipping along the pavement. She had almost missed the client.

"Fletcher," she said.

He sat at a small table on the sidewalk, outside what appeared to be a small café. He might have been waiting for a latte except that he was dressed in pajamas. Of course, the latte would never come no matter how he was dressed or how long he waited. The look of the downtown landscape was just that—a look, a means by which

Livvy could navigate the Underworld.

As Fletcher raised his gaze, he cocked his head at her. "Olivia?" he replied, in a thin, dry voice.

Fletcher Mosely was eighty-one years old and in dire health despite a liver transplant. Although it wasn't typical for an octogenarian to be the recipient of a replacement organ, Fletcher Mosely wasn't your typical guy. He was a multi-billionaire. When he had learned of the recent motorcycle death of one of his employees, someone who had already agreed to be part of an organ donation program, he immediately contacted the family. The young man was brain dead but his liver was in excellent shape. Although there was nothing to be done for the boy, at least the family was never going to have to worry about money again. Fletcher's story had raised outcries from other families whose members were waiting their turn for a liver transplant. It had mattered little to him. At this point, only one thing did–survival.

Unfortunately, the new liver wasn't working as advertised. The operation had gone perfectly, as expected from the top-notch doctors he had hired. His body had accepted the organ with very few complications and was not rejecting it. And yet, the liver was not doing its job and nobody had been able to tell him why–except Livvy.

"Yes, Fletcher," Livvy said, as she approached and stood next to him. "It's me and we're in the Multiverse, the spiritual plane. We won't be staying long because we're gonna get you healed and get you out of here. How does that sound?"

He smiled much as he did in the real world, without mirth. Mostly, it was a look of satisfaction. "Most excellent," he said.

Livvy and SK had both thought Fletcher's symptoms sounded like a case of bad energy, leftover from the body of the donor. That energy needed to be extracted.

"All right," said Livvy. "I need you to take off your pajama top."

He smirked as he stood and undid the buttons. "You're sure just the top?" he said, eyeing her. "For a good looking girl like you, I'd be glad to–"

"Thanks," said Livvy, trying to smile pleasantly. "Just the top will be fine."

"Sure, honey, sure. Never hurts to ask."

He tossed the pajama top to the chair and Livvy had her first view of the area around his liver. It was bad energy all right and in a big way. The skin there was completely purple, like the worst deep bruise that could be imagined.

Apparently seeing something in her face, Fletcher decided to look too. "Oh my god," he said, the smug tone gone. "Oh my god."

In the real world, the bad spiritual energy was undetectable, even to a shaman. This was Livvy's first time seeing it and Fletcher's too.

"Turn around for me," she said.

Without a word, he raised his arms slightly and began to turn his tall but frail frame, shuffling in place. There, on his back, was a matching mark, just like the front but mirrored. The bad energy had gone clean through.

Fletcher craned his neck to see. "Is it back there too?"

"Yes, it is."

He turned to face her. "You can fix it though, right?"

"Yes," she said simply. "Let's step out here."

She took him by the hand and led him to the middle of the street. Already the wind was starting to pick up. The clouds above swirled as lightning arced back and forth, faint thunder tracing its course. He glanced up and then back to her and gripped her hand.

"Okay, Fletcher," said Livvy, moving around to his side. "I'm going to need you to stand absolutely still. It's very important." He turned his head and stared at her. "No matter what you see or hear, you mustn't move. Can you do that?"

He only nodded.

"I need you to let go of my hand now," she said.

Instead of letting go, he grabbed harder. She felt the warm slickness of his grip as he squeezed.

"Fletcher, it's going to be all right. I promise but you need to let go of my hand."

Slowly, he released her hand, let his arms drop to his sides, and faced forward.

"Good," she said. "Here we go. Remember not to move."

She reached her left hand in front of him and settled it directly over the black spot. The skin there was cool and smooth. Slowly, she reached her other hand up to the sky.

"Lightning," she said.

• • • • •

This part always made SK nervous. Although glad to have reached this point of the healing and despite having been through it hundreds of times, he knew it was still unpredictable, still dangerous. A dim blue luminescence formed in the power sockets. He kept them in his peripheral vision. He had positioned himself at a point in the room where he was not directly between any of the outlets.

The glow brightened and a faint reflection of the strange light was caught in the highly polished silver of Livvy's goggles.

Her breathing grew quicker.

Any moment now.

He glanced at each of the sockets, now glowing bright blue. A small white tendril of electricity snaked out of one. He smelled the faint odor of ozone.

This is it.

• • • • •

A white-hot bolt of lightning zigzagged from the center of the whirling clouds above and exploded onto Livvy's hand. Its energy raced down her body and into the ground with a buzzing and crackling that made her teeth vibrate. Violet sparks poured off her upraised hand like falling water, completely surrounding the two of them.

Fletcher did his best not to move, although he had flinched at the explosion. Now his eyes were squeezed closed against the bright light and sparks, his mouth clamped shut, and his hands rolled into fists, waiting.

Livvy kept her left hand on the black spot on the front of his torso and slowly lowered her right hand behind his back, still channeling the lightning strike, bringing it lower. Then, smoothly and without hurry, she placed her right hand on the black spot on his back.

Fletcher convulsed between her hands as the energy traveled through him. His hair lifted as did hers, swirling in the surrounding static discharge field. Livvy looked down at her glowing hands, light blue sparks dancing around them like tiny, erratic fireflies. She watched the black spots beneath them begin to shrink.

"Just stay like that, Fletcher," she yelled. "You're doing fine."

• • • • •

With a bright blue flash and a loud crack, the outlet with the tendril of electricity popped out of the wall and tumbled to the floor, blackened and smoking. Then another did the same.

SK heard a scream from somewhere beyond the closed bedroom door, in the hallway where the family was waiting, but he dared not take his eyes away from the wall.

Two writhing snakes of electricity had made their way out of the empty sockets and were inching toward one another. With a sudden start, SK stood. They were leaving scorch marks behind them and he could smell ozone.

"Oh no," he said as he glanced down at Livvy. "Control it, Liv— and hurry."

• • • • •

Livvy pressed her hands together, squeezing Fletcher's torso between them. He grimaced but kept his eyes shut and body still. The wind swirled around them, carrying some of the tiny blue points of light from Livvy's hands. Like a slowly turning dust devil, the breeze carried the sparks with it as it rustled their hair. Fletcher's pajama bottoms ballooned and the long tail of Livvy's jacket began to rise. She pushed her hands together with one final effort and then released them.

In an instant, the lightning receded and the wind died. Their hair and clothing fell as though normal gravity had been restored. The two of them stood in complete silence.

Livvy slowly leaned to the right to see Fletcher's back. It was clean. The purplish black spot that had marked the bad energy was completely gone. She gently took Fletcher by the shoulders and turned him to face her. The spot on the front was gone too. Only smooth clean skin was there. She looked at his face, which was still grimacing with his eyes shut tight.

"It's okay, Fletcher. You can open your eyes."

He opened one experimentally and peeked at her.

"We're done," she said smiling.

He raised his eyebrows and opened the other eye and looked down. He ran a shaky hand over the skin. "You did it," he murmured. He looked at her, grinning madly. "You did it!" he yelled and hugged her.

"Yeah," she managed to get out.

"Of course she did it," said a voice from the sidewalk. "She's the Lightning Shaman."

Livvy spun around nearly toppling Fletcher.

Was someone else here?

A young raven-haired woman stood watching them. Her long silky hair matched her flowing black leather duster and black, mid-calf utility boots. She wore a gleaming pendant of onyx on a silver chain and she seemed at ease. This was another shaman.

Impossible!

"Yes," replied Fletcher. He had no clue that anything was wrong, his voice elated. "Yes, she is!"

For her part, Livvy was speechless. She gaped at the woman, who simply stared back, her face not showing a hint of any emotion, good or bad, and yet somehow very threatening. Her stance was wide but her hands were in her jacket pockets, relaxed.

Livvy's mind raced. The only other time she had ever seen another shaman in the Multiverse was when she had broken centuries of rules to work with other shamans using networked goggles. As far as she knew, no one else had done it since. No one had so much as tried, not even her. The problem was that she knew she wasn't networked. She was working solo. How could this possibly be happening?

"Did you see it?" asked Fletcher, as he started to approach her.

Livvy quickly grabbed his arm and jerked him back.

"I did indeed," said the woman. "And I would really like to stay and chat with you about it," she said, staring directly at Livvy, "but I think I'll take my leave."

With that, a bright flash of light took her place, and she was gone.

Livvy blinked before checking left and right. The woman had not needed the fountain to leave the Multiverse.

By all the gods, what was going on?

Fletcher looked down at Livvy's hand on his arm and up to her face. "Friend of yours?" he asked.

Livvy didn't answer. She had never seen the woman before, never even heard of a shaman who looked like that—the jet-black hair, darkly glinting eyes, olive skin, and full lips. No, this was not a friend of hers and, like the woman had said, it was definitely time to leave.

Still gripping Fletcher by the arm, she started a brisk walk up the street, back toward the plaza and the fountain.

"Let's go," she said, tugging him along and glancing backward. "We're getting out of here."

CHAPTER TWO

DOMINIQUE SLOWLY SAT up and removed the goggles.

"Water," she said hoarsely, eyes still shut, and held out her hand.

A chilled bottle was immediately slapped into it. She raised it to her lips, but the cap was on. She quickly twisted it off. Then she drained the entire bottle, opened her eyes, and threw it at the woman who'd handed it to her.

"Next time make sure the cap is off," she snarled.

"Yes, ma'am," said Pip as the bottle bounced off her and landed on the floor. She quickly retrieved it. "Um, how did it go?"

Dominique gave the redheaded, freckled girl a sideways look.

"It went well," she said.

Very well.

The Lightning Shaman had obviously been surprised. Then again, so had Dominique. For once, the reports had been true. The Lightning Shaman's power was immense–palpable, even at a distance. The lightning had been staggering, and the shaman herself, stunning: her white hair shining like glass, her skin glowing with vitality, as pretty as the rumors.

Dominique remembered the quizzical look on her face.

She snorted.

Pip looked at her, puzzled.

"Never mind," said Dominique, waving her off. No time for this.

She stood, took off her leather duster, and tossed it into a nearby chair.

"Phase one complete," she said.

CHAPTER THREE

IN THE REAL world, Livvy sat bolt upright and yanked off the goggles.

"Whoa," said SK. "Not so fast."

She quickly turned them over in her hands, examining the front of the lenses and the small jack that would accept a network connection. No, they were not networked. She had known that, of course, but what other explanation could there be for what she had seen?

"Is there a problem?" asked SK.

She jerked her gaze over to his worried face. "No," she said quickly.

He sat quietly and waited, an open water bottle in his outstretched hand. She took the bottle and started to drink.

"Another long one," he said.

She finished drinking the entire bottle. "Yeah," she breathed. "Another one."

She knew SK must suspect something, but there was no way she could explain what she was doing. She didn't *want* to keep secrets from him. In fact, she hated it, but no one could know. *Especially* SK.

Did that shaman in the Underworld have something to do with her secret? How in the Multiverse had they been able to see each other?

And she knew who I was.

She was aware SK was watching her, and she didn't dare meet his eyes yet. Instead, she looked up at Fletcher in his bed. He seemed to be taking a nap.

"He's going to be fine," she said.

"There was never a doubt," said SK, standing up. He kicked out his short legs, a little stiff from sitting.

Because SK was a dwarf, Livvy only saw him from this angle at moments like this. She turned and looked up into his face. His ensemble today was a deep forest green. Lately, he had also added a solid-colored tie to his tailored suits. Livvy had decided it was probably due to all the media attention, but the formal look worked well for him.

He tilted his head toward the wall with the scorch marks, motioning with his eyebrows. She looked over. A dark brown discoloration surrounded two rectangular holes near the bottom of the wall. Livvy saw the electrical outlets lying on the floor where they'd landed. Brown burn marks emanated from the holes and reached toward one another. Livvy's eyes widened.

"Me?" she asked.

He nodded as he tightened up his necktie.

Scorch marks? That was a new one.

These days, SK had the clients sign a waiver in case of damage. Generally, it amounted to burned out light bulbs or melted electrical sockets.

"I don't understand," said Livvy, as she slowly got up. "I was totally in control on this one."

SK immediately came over to help her with a steadying hand. Her recovery time had improved quite a bit over the past year. Most of the time a bottle of water and a few minutes did it. As she stood upright, though, a flash of pain in her temples made her suck in a breath and duck her head.

"What is it?" he asked.

"Headache," she hissed. She massaged both sides of her forehead.

"Let me get some aspirin," said SK.

Livvy nodded a little and leaned against the bed. She carried them for the client's family, along with tissues, in her shoulder bag. SK found the aspirin and shook out a couple of tablets. Then he opened a new bottle of water.

"Thanks," she whispered.

She quickly downed them and finished the second bottle. SK glanced at the door.

"They can come in," said Livvy, standing up straight.

"They can wait a little longer," he said, frowning a little and searching her face.

"Really SK, I'm fine, just a little headache. I'm sure they're anxious."

"Are you sure?"

"Yeah, I'm feeling better already," she replied and it was true. Maybe it had been the second bottle of water but she was definitely feeling much less pain.

"All right then," he said and went over to the door.

He opened it and stood aside.

First through was Fletcher's young wife, Simone. Her worried look didn't detract from her supermodel good looks. Tastefully accessorized and coiffed, wearing makeup that didn't look like makeup, it didn't hurt that she actually *was* a supermodel. She went immediately to Fletcher's side. As Livvy rolled up her mat, the adult children came through as well, two men in their mid-to-late fifties. One wore a polo shirt and looked as though he'd just stepped off a yacht while the other wore an understated business suit. Their expressions, which reminded Livvy so much of Fletcher, said they weren't quite sure what to expect.

"How is he?" asked Simone, taking one of his hands.

"He's going to be fine," said Livvy as she handed the mat to SK. "It was definitely a case of bad energy from the new liver."

"Really," said the son who had come in first, without an ounce of mockery.

In fact, Livvy couldn't remember the last time she'd heard someone disparage shamanism. Fletcher's private nurse came in and started to take his vitals. When Livvy spoke, they all turned to listen.

"There'll be nothing noticeable in his appearance or behavior for a while. I wouldn't look for anything to change for at least a day as the liver gets used to its new environment."

The nurse nodded and returned to measuring his pulse.

"Thank you, Miss Lawson," said the second son. "I can't tell you how much we appreciate this." He looked at SK. "We've already transferred the money to your account."

"Thank you, Mr. Mosely," said SK, inclining his head.

Livvy sniffed a little. First a headache, now a sniffle? She wasn't prone to either. Maybe she was coming down with a cold. She bent down to retrieve her bag and saw a red drop appear next to it on the white Berber carpet. She quickly put a finger to her nose. It was bleeding. Before anybody came around to her side of the bed, she took out a couple of tissues, wiped the carpet, and wiped her nose. She couldn't remember the last time she'd had a bloody nose. Maybe when she was a kid? Although Fletcher's family hadn't seen what happened, SK had. She stowed the tissues in her bag.

"I think we'll be going then," he said smoothly.

"Oh, of course," said Simone, coming around the bed. "I'm sure you're busy."

SK held the door for Livvy as Simone approached her with her hand extended. Livvy lightly grasped it as a bright blue spark jumped between them. Rather than appearing surprised, Simone seemed pleased.

"Thank you, Miss Lawson," she said.

"I'm glad I could help," Livvy replied.

"Best of luck to you," said SK as he ushered Livvy out. "And regards to Fletcher."

In the cavernous and high-ceilinged living room, a few dozen of Fletcher's closest friends quietly milled and waited. The sunken floor and two-story windows gave it the feeling of a cathedral. Dressed formally, the various couples and small groups gave the impression that a wake had yet to begin, except that no one held a drink. A hush came over the various conversations as Livvy and SK entered. Min immediately stood and came over.

Soo Min and Livvy had been friends since their early days as shamans, although they had kept it secret back then. They had broken centuries of prohibitions that dictated shamans be kept apart out of fear for their awesome powers. But after Livvy had networked goggles together and managed to work with other shamans in the Multiverse to defeat an ancient god of Sumer, many of the old traditions had fallen away. Not only were they friends, Min was now her personal assistant. She dressed in her usual long, black velvet shaman robes and black boots, an ornate jade choker at her neck—a complete contrast to Livvy.

Livvy wore a double-breasted, full-length coat of linen that shimmered with real silver thread. Underneath, white leggings blended into a formfitting knit top with a V neckline that paralleled the V of the buttoned jacket. Below, where the linen coat flared open, she wore knee-high white boots. The only splash of color came from her amethyst pendant.

"Several people have asked for a blessing," Min said quietly.

"I'm not sure Livvy's really up to it today," SK whispered quickly.

"Oh?" said Min, looking concerned and examining Livvy's face.

"Just a little headache," Livvy whispered.

"And a bloody nose," insisted SK but careful to keep his voice low.

Min scowled a bit as Livvy glanced at the crowd. Although all the faces in the room were turned toward them, everyone kept a respectful distance.

"I'm fine," Livvy said. "It'll just take a minute. They've been waiting."

SK frowned and looked at the crowd. "Let's make it quick then," he said to Min.

Min nodded and turned toward the crowd. It had taken her months to get over her shyness, but she finally seemed at ease dealing with people. Once she had relaxed, they seemed to respond to her naturally. Although her high-pitched voice would never have a commanding ring to it, it had acquired an air of authority.

"All right, everybody, if I could have you line up, the Lightning Shaman will greet you as she leaves." She smiled and motioned toward the front door. "We'll start the line here."

The crowd promptly organized themselves, moving around the areas of large furniture and past the grand piano. Min went to the end of the line, furthest from the door, followed by Livvy and SK, and then glanced back at Livvy.

"Whenever you're ready," said Min, smiling as though for a photograph.

SK managed a small smile as well. Sandwiched between them as they made their way down the line, Livvy looked at the first person she would greet. The young woman seemed overcome with emotion, her eyes glistening and her smile radiant. Livvy couldn't help but smile in return.

"Olivia," breathed the woman, like a prayer, and bowed her head.

Livvy reached out her hand and a small spark jumped out to the woman's hair.

Each one in turn either bowed their head or extended their

hand. Some said her name, some said 'lightning shaman.' To each one, Livvy imparted a spark. Occasionally, someone would touch SK as he passed. Early on, people had requested lockets of Livvy's blindingly white hair. Although she had been born a blond, her hair had become white immediately after her vision quest, the first encounter with her spirit helper. Although she had unwittingly obliged the first few requests, she quickly realized it was something she couldn't keep doing.

Near the front door, one woman extended her hand and looked longingly into Livvy's eyes. "Please, Lightning Shaman," she said. "I have a daughter who needs your help."

Min took a step backward and smoothly interceded.

"I've taken all her information," Min said, nodding to the woman and smiling gently. "I assure you, we'll be in touch."

"Of course, of course," said the woman bowing.

Livvy reached out and touched the woman's hair with a spark. Finally, they were at the front door but the worst was yet to come.

"Ready?" asked Min over her shoulder.

"Never," said Livvy.

SK smirked.

"Right," said Min.

She opened the double doors of the grand entry to the sound of whirring cameras and a barrage of flashing lights.

"Livvy!" Came the calls from the assembled photographers. "Livvy, just a quick look!"

The attention of the media was a recent development that Livvy didn't particularly welcome. It spoke well for shamanism, SK had said. It helped shamans everywhere. For that reason she did her best to be responsive to them, although what she really wanted to do was run.

"The car is this way," Min said into Livvy's ear, pointing past the crowd.

The sound of cameras whirring and clicking jumped a notch. Livvy nodded.

"How did it go today?" yelled someone. "How is Fletcher Mosely?"

"He's going to be fine," yelled SK as he kept Livvy moving forward behind Min.

"Just a touch," said one man, who didn't have a camera as he reached out his hand to Livvy, jostling for position with the photographers.

Livvy quickly reached out to him as they passed and a spark popped between their hands. Again, the cameras mass-clicked and the flashes fired furiously. Finally, they were at the curb. Min held the back door open.

The Porsche Panamera was silver, but the windows were tinted an impenetrable black. Livvy quickly ducked in, sliding easily on the leather, followed by SK. Min immediately shut the door and moved around to the driver's side. The sudden quiet was interrupted when her door opened and she got in.

"Where to next?" someone asked.

"The Multiverse," said Min, with a mischievous grin, then she shut the door and started the engine.

Livvy slumped down in the back seat and exhaled. "It's worse than the black lake," she murmured.

SK laughed a little.

The black lake was the passageway between the Middleworld and the Underworld. Although he'd never seen it, Livvy knew he had heard plenty of shamans complain about it. Cold and inky black, shamans had to submerge beneath it in the Middleworld to emerge from the fountain in the Underworld.

As Min carefully pulled away from the curb, the crowd finally faded behind them. With the spots of the camera flashes still floating in her eyes, Livvy recalled the healing. She secretly touched the small cache of objects in her inner jacket pocket and pretended to look out the window.

Who had that other shaman been? She had addressed her as the lightning shaman. She knew Livvy, though that was no surprise given all the media attention. But how had she appeared with her in the Multiverse without their goggles being networked?

"Are you okay?" asked SK.

Startled, Livvy looked over to him. "Yeah, I'm good," she said, a bit too quickly.

She saw Min glancing at her in the rear view mirror.

"I'm fine. Why?"

"You were just kind of quiet," he said.

"Just that headache," she lied. "It's almost gone."

"All right," he said, watching her for a few more seconds. He took out his phone. "Before I forget." He punched a couple of buttons and then held it to his mouth. "Fire extinguisher," he said, enunciating.

"Did you say 'fire extinguisher'?" asked Min.

Livvy thought of the scorch marks on the walls of Fletcher's bedroom.

"Yes," said SK, putting the phone away. "A new addition to our work kit."

CHAPTER FOUR

DOMINIQUE THUMPED ON the door three times, waited a few seconds, then thumped again. She repeated the pattern until she heard the deadbolt and then the knob being unlocked. The door opened just enough for the chain to be taut.

A heavyset, middle-aged black woman with short-cropped hair, a round face, and big hoop earrings to match appeared in the gap, her face angry and then surprised.

"Are you crazy, woman? Comin' here like this?" said Tamara in a Haitian accent.

"Open the door, Tambourine," Dominique ordered. She snapped her fingers twice. "Make it quick."

The woman closed the door then opened it all the way. She stood to the side and Dominique entered.

The dingy little flat was barely furnished, but various piles of trash helped to fill up the space. Dominique recognized the Papa Legba statue, with its straw hat and cane. Originally from West Africa, he was a vodun spirit who had crossed the Atlantic and been incorporated into the traditional religion of Haiti. A simple offering of cooked rice on a piece of tinfoil lay at his feet.

Like Tamara, Dominique had fled Haiti for a better life and brought her shamanism with her. Unlike Tamara, Dominique was of mostly French descent, though the light caramel coloring of her skin hinted at something more than French. Also unlike Tamara, and most importantly, Dominique had been in Los Angeles for years and had worked hard to eliminate her accent and blend in. Tamara was a recent arrival, fleeing the devastation of the earthquake and still an outsider.

"Afraid to be seen with me?" Dominique asked.

Tamara shut the door and locked it. "You know the rules," she said, glumly. "And my name is Tamara not Tambourine. I do not like Tambourine."

Which is exactly why I do it.

Of all the shamans that she used, Tambourine was her least favorite–a vivid and unwelcome reminder of the past.

"Well," said Dominique, fishing inside the pocket of her leather duster. "What you like hardly concerns me. And the rules?" She took out a small plastic packet of pills and white powder and tossed it at the woman. "The rules are changing."

Tamara made a futile grab as it flitted erratically through the air. It landed on the ground between them. Tamara quickly bent down to retrieve it, but Dominique stepped forward, planted her heel on the ground, and hovered the front of her boot over it. "Not so fast," she said.

Tamara slowly straightened up.

Dominique recognized the tense pinch of the mouth and the darting eyes as Tamara tried to look at her but couldn't help staring at the drugs. She needed her fix. Like many shamans who had learned their profession before the advent of goggles, Tamara had entered the Multiverse with the use of drugs.

Dominique had also used drugs in the beginning, since techno-shaman goggles in Haiti were almost unknown, but some shamans slipped into drug use even when they didn't need them for the Multiverse. Tamara was one of these.

"I'm putting together a network," Dominique said. "You'll be in it."

"What 'network'?" said Tamara glowering, her attention finally on Dominique.

"I mean a network of techno-shamans," replied Dominique, impatient. "With goggles hooked together."

Tamara shook her head quickly. "Nobody does that. Not since–"

"I know," said Dominique.

There was a brief silence.

"Why do such a thing?"

"I didn't invite questions," Dominique snapped. "I'm not asking for your opinion either. You'll report to this address on Friday and you'll keep it to yourself."

She handed Tamara a small slip of paper.

Tamara's forehead furrowed deeply. Then she shook her head but with less conviction. "I do not–"

Dominique began to lower the boot.

"No!" said Tamara, gesturing for Dominique to stop. "Wait." She licked her dry lips and stared at the packet. Then she glanced at the slip of paper.

This is taking too long.

Dominique slammed the toe of her boot down and crushed the pills.

"No!" wailed Tamara, lurching forward. Nearly doubled over, her hands stopped just short of the boot.

Dominique ground the packet slowly and turned toward the door.

"Friday," she said over her shoulder. "There'll be plenty of *that*," she motioned to the packet that Tamara had retrieved and was opening.

Dominique unlocked the door and stepped out. It closed immediately and the locks clicked into place behind her.

Doesn't want to be seen with me? Fine.

That would change soon enough.

CHAPTER FIVE

THE WEATHER WASN'T right.

Livvy gazed up at the dark sky. When was the last time they'd had a truly sunny day?

The tinted windows in the back of the sedan acted more like mirrors than glass, especially on a day like today. Even though she lived on the Westside now, to be centrally located for clients all around L.A., her location change didn't really explain the lack of sun. El Niño, the cyclical weather pattern brought about by changing temperatures in the Pacific Ocean, was being blamed for it. Even for an El Niño year, this amount of rain and cloudy weather was unusual.

As they sat in traffic, Livvy tried to recall the last bright day. Although the clouds sometimes made for spectacular sunsets, the middle of the day was often gray. She had never been a morning person. Maybe a fabulous sunrise was something people on the east coast enjoyed.

Her eyes unfocused and SK's reflection came into view. He was wearing his hair the same as he always did, with a bit of tufted texture on top, but he'd added a small, thin beard at the line of his jaw. Livvy thought it suited him. It highlighted his mouth a little more. She watched his reflection. He was typing something on his phone, as usual. He had never been so busy. In fact, none of them had ever been so busy. Lately, the three of them were almost always together.

In reaction to something he was reading, he smiled a little to himself. Livvy smiled too. She watched the curve of his lips slowly fade and wondered what it'd be like to kiss them.

She suddenly sat up and looked straight ahead at the back of Min's head. That was the second time she'd wondered that in as many weeks. Her face flushed hot, and she stared down into her lap.

"Is something the matter?" he asked.

Oh no, he's noticed.

Min was looking at her in the rear view mirror. "Your face is red," she said.

Thanks.

"Do you want more air conditioning?" Min asked.

"No, I'm fine," Livvy replied.

All of a sudden, the ride home in rush hour was taking forever.

There was silence again, but SK put his phone away.

Livvy felt her heart racing and realized her hands were sweaty too.

Good grief. It's like high school.

Her feelings for SK had steadily grown over the last few months. From the time they'd met, he had been her mentor, the first one who had believed in her ability. She had looked to him not only for work but also approval. If not for him, she and the other shamans who had networked with her would never have defeated Tiamat–the Sumerian monster of the Underworld. She owed SK everything.

From time to time, she thought maybe he felt something for her as well, but he had never said anything.

It was only natural, she had told herself. People who worked together, who spent a lot of time together, to the exclusion of others…well, sometimes they ended up together. She had questioned whether that's all it was.

Somehow in the last few months, though, he had seemed more accessible and less remote. Maybe it was her newfound notoriety. Or maybe it was how well they worked together.

Or maybe, I'm just getting to know him better–except for his name.

'SK' was the only thing she'd ever heard him or anybody else say. Even when she'd asked him point-blank his only reply had been to smile and say, 'It's SK.'

Livvy looked out the window, careful not to look at his reflection, and sighed. She had wanted to say something about her feelings for weeks, but the moment never seemed right.

Face it. You're nervous.

Actually, chicken was more like it.

Her private doings in the Multiverse didn't help. Afraid that she might accidentally let something slip, she had become more quiet than usual.

Well, maybe that would be changing.

CHAPTER SIX

THE LITTLE BELL at the top of the door tinkled its melodic greeting as Livvy came through, folding her umbrella. The familiar smell of a hundred types of incense and candles mixed together and surrounded her. She paused, inhaled deeply, and then slowly exhaled, as though she were leaving the worries of the world behind her. Tonight the smell of sandalwood seemed the strongest. She smiled as the bell tinkled again and the door closed behind her. She stowed the umbrella in the receptacle next to the door and was careful to wipe her feet on the colorful mat.

Wouldn't want to slip on the terra cotta tile.

It had taken her, SK, and Min a solid hour to sort through all the business at the end of the day but she was finally here. Something about Mamacita's place felt like home, even with the recent expansions. Livvy passed the aisles of shelves with their strange combination of New Age paraphernalia, electronics, and religious icons, into the new area with racks of velvet robes. At the far end of the store stood the massive book, CD and DVD collection. Mamacita had expanded the store twice in the last year to accommodate all the new business–business caused by Livvy.

As word of her, her friends, and what they had accomplished, spread through the shaman and non-shaman world, Mamacita's place had become the navel of the universe for every shaman and wanna-be in the western hemisphere–and then some.

"Livvy, honey," said Mamacita.

Livvy turned to see her emerging from one of the aisles of clothing, a robe in one hand and a duster in the other, a big smile on her face, her plump arms flung open. She wore a dark blue, one-piece dress that had a square neckline bordered with bright embroidery. Over that she wore a matching blue cardigan sweater, buttoned at the top. At the billowing bottom of the dress, the complicated stitching was repeated. When the weather had started to turn chilly, she had taken to wearing thick gray socks inside sheepskin slippers. A small blue spark jumped between them as they hugged. Livvy closed her eyes and held her tightly for a few moments.

"Mamacita," she whispered.

"Well I just never know when to expect you anymore," said Mamacita.

Livvy gently let her go and grinned down at her.

Her round face seemed a little more round of late but time never seemed to touch her. Her dark hair was pulled back under a large, flat barrette. Her shop had been legendary among shamans even before Livvy, rumored to have been in the same location for sixty years. Now with the lightning shaman a regular customer, it was famous.

"And I just always expect you to be here," replied Livvy. "Don't you ever go home?"

Mamacita chuckled. "And miss a visit from the Lightning Shaman?" she said, moving toward the back of the shop. "You know, a couple young ones waited for hours earlier today, hoping to catch a glimpse."

"Really," said Livvy following Mamacita.

"Really," replied Mamacita, shelving the duster behind the counter.

"Really," squawked Pete, Mamacita's pet cockatiel.

Livvy glanced around but the shop was empty. She breathed a sigh of relief. People trying to meet her, like the media attention, was an unexpected and unwelcome consequence of defeating Tiamat. At first, Livvy had been surprised, then flattered–then followed, hounded and even stalked. She adored seeing Mamacita, but it had become more and more difficult.

Livvy took a peanut from the bowl and unshelled it. She tossed the nuts into Pete's cage, and he responded with, "Thank you," before descending on them.

Mamacita settled down on her stool behind the massive counter. "What brings you here this time of night?"

"Oh, maybe another book and just to say hi."

"You're turning into my best customer lately," said Mamacita, cracking open a peanut.

There had been a time, not long ago, when Livvy had been far from Mamacita's best customer. She had been Mamacita's favorite charity case. Now, it was Livvy's turn to give and it was nice.

The bell at the front door tinkled.

"Maybe I'll just…" Livvy whispered, tilting her head toward the books.

"Sure, honey," nodded Mamacita, with a wink. "You just take your time."

Livvy quickly and gratefully ducked into the book section. That was lucky. She was sure Mamacita was going to ask what kind of book she wanted, and Livvy was tired of lying to her. Actually, she was sick of it. The sooner things were back to normal, the better.

Mamacita's melodic voice drifted in from the background along with the gentle rattling of a rain stick, probably being tested by a customer. Livvy ran her fingers over the spines of the books on the shelf in front of her and then crouched down low to examine the books on the bottom shelf.

I have to be missing something, some important piece of the puzzle, some last little detail. But what?

It wasn't easy to find information on this topic. In fact, it was next to impossible. She'd already bought all of the books that had seemed like good candidates–mostly dry academic treatises from cultural studies that touched on different indigenous peoples throughout the world. The books that were left would only have a mention, if that. The title of one caught her eye. She glanced behind her to make sure no one was looking. Mamacita was still busy with her customer.

Livvy immediately flipped to the index and ran her finger down it. There were a couple of references here. She heard the bell at the door chime and no more conversation. The customer must have left.

As she stood, she randomly picked out a couple more books. As usual, she tried to mask her true purchase with other items. A small statue of Ganesha, the Hindu elephant god, caught her eye on a nearby display table, and she picked that up too before taking the entire lot to the counter. Mamacita was already there. She picked up the half-circle reading glasses that hung from a beaded chain around her neck. Perching them on her nose, she looked down at the books, turning them around to see their titles.

"You're turning into quite the student," she intoned.

Livvy felt her face starting to flush. She absently picked up a peanut and cracked it open. Pete came down in his cage in anticipation.

"And Ganesha," Mamacita said, tapping his little elephant head. "Always popular."

Livvy popped the peanut in her mouth as Mamacita looked up and lowered her glasses.

"Shall I put it on your tab?"

"That'd be great," Livvy said around the peanut.

She resisted the urge to spit it out. She didn't like peanuts. It's not that she was allergic but the taste was just revolting. She quickly plucked another from the bowl, shelled it, and tossed it to Pete, who was still waiting.

"Thank you!" he squawked.

Mamacita took a plastic bag from under the counter and put the books inside. She wrapped Ganesha in some tissue paper and placed him inside too.

"Well," said Mamacita, holding out the handles of the bag. "I don't suppose you'll stay for tea."

"I can't," said Livvy, finally swallowing the peanut.

"I'm sure you're busy as ten shamans put together," nodded Mamacita with a smile. "I'm happy for you, honey."

Livvy knew her face must be glowing by now and could barely look at Mamacita. Then something occurred to her. "Mamacita, can I ask you a question?"

"Oh you sound *so* serious. Goodness. You can ask me anything, child."

Livvy hesitated but then decided to plunge ahead. "Do you know SK's real name?"

Mamacita chuckled, a quiet bubbly sound that put Livvy at ease. "It's SK."

Livvy arched her eyebrows. "Seriously. That's it? Just SK?"

"Mmm hmm," Mamacita said, nodding.

Same answer that SK had given her.

"Okay," Livvy said, a bit deflated.

Who would name their kid SK? What kind of name is that?

She shrugged and smiled and then came around the counter.

She remembered to touch Mamacita on the sleeve first to discharge the spark, then hugged her.

"Thanks, Mamacita."

"Don't be a stranger," Mamacita replied. "You hear?" she said, emphasizing the last with a squeeze. "And stay out of trouble."

"Promise," said Livvy, with an imperceptible sigh.

It was a promise she wouldn't be able to keep.

CHAPTER SEVEN

"THAT'S THE LAST one, Ursula," said Tony, drawing the door closed behind him.

"The *last* one?" Ursula thought.

She checked the clock. It was barely nine.

"Humph!" she said, sitting down. Business had never been so bad.

"Damn earthquake," she muttered.

Watts had been seeing a small but steady trickle of Haitian refugees after the earthquake. Once the poorest country in the western hemisphere, Haiti was now also the embodiment of destruction, disease, and death. Anyone who could get out was getting out. A number of refugees ended up in Los Angeles, some of them in Watts, and a few of them were shamans.

It was competition.

Ever since Ursula, Livvy and the rest of the networked shamans had defeated Tiamat, Los Angeles had become a shaman mecca. It hadn't hurt Livvy's business. Ursula knew that SK, Livvy, and Min were incredibly busy. She couldn't help but know, thanks to the television. Alvina, the woman in Palm Springs, was far enough away that the influx didn't affect her. Wan-li wasn't even in L.A. most of the time but was touring through China, famous there for her part in Tiamat's defeat. The Nahual from Central America had vanished as quickly as she had appeared. Of all the shamans who had finally agreed to help Livvy in the Underworld, Ursula was the only one who hadn't reaped a benefit. In fact, it had been the opposite.

'Past years are always better.'

The old proverb was true.

Many of her former clients had been lured away by the ridiculously cheap prices the refugee shamans charged. To the patients, it must seem like the bargain of the century. To the shamans, it must seem like a gold mine. It was a classic win-win.

"Lose-lose for Ursula," she said, her smooth deep voice filling the room.

She stood and paced in the dim light. Thick draperies prevented streetlamps in the alley from intruding. A large crackling fire provided the only light in the room but it was more than enough. On the far wall, psychedelic portraits of vodun spirits seemed animated in their gilt frames as the flickering glow washed over them. Ursula turned slowly in front of them and stepped back toward the fire. The myriad beads sewn into her deep burgundy velvet robes glinted with reflected sparkles. She reached a hand up and began to unwind the bright pink head wrap but stopped.

'What happens to the turkey can happen to the rooster too.'

"If they can do it, Ursula can," she said.

She tucked the hair wrap back into place and glided to the small glass table crowded with bottles. These were her own herb mixtures, passed down through generations of shamans before her. They had been a significant part of her business until the Haitians had arrived.

She picked up one of the large bottles, its contents gently clinking against the glass.

With a little help from the right person, they might be a staple again.

She set it back down on the table amongst the others.

It could not hurt to ask.

CHAPTER EIGHT

LIVVY DROPPED THE book on the hardwood floor.

That *had* to be it.

She looked at the collection of artifacts on the glass top of the coffee table and picked up each one in turn before carefully placing it into the soft leather pouch.

The amethyst heart stood in for her own.

The seven points of the amber heptagram represented the seven chakras, the energy centers of the spiritual body. Even the amber itself held the remnants of ancient life.

The ankh was the symbol of Osiris, the green-faced Egyptian god of the dead and also rebirth.

The soul catcher amulet was a bone tube with bear heads carved at both ends, mouths open, intricately detailed with the totem symbols of the Pacific Northwest and inlaid with mother of pearl.

The three-sided Tibetan kila dagger looked more like an ornate nail than a knife. Impaled in the ground, it brought stability to the ritual area and harmonized the energy of it.

The clear crystal pyramid lacked any impurities or internal fissures. Since it had to work as the channeling device, it had to be perfectly transparent.

Her mother's engagement ring–of course.

And finally, the human skull made of garnet. Nothing was more emblematic of death. Garnet wouldn't have been her first choice, but ruby was simply out of the question.

She sat at the front edge of the sky blue leather couch, hunching over the suede pouch in one hand and the small skull in the other.

Maybe it *was* the garnet. She turned the grim little face toward her as she bit her lower lip. She shook her head and tightened a fist around it. No, it was the shape and the color that were important in this case, not the material.

"Why doesn't this work?" she said, louder than she'd intended.

On the outside of her calf, a little orange tabby rubbed the entire length of his body, then quickly swiveled and rubbed the other side.

She had been so focused on the artifacts that she hadn't seen him. She nearly jumped but caught herself in time and exhaled.

"Nacho," she said, letting some tension go. She placed the skull in the pouch before reaching down to scratch him behind the ears. It sent him into a fit of purring.

Nacho had been the building cat at her old apartment downtown. When he showed up every night at her place, she'd started to think of him as hers. Although she'd been nervous about making him an indoor cat after the move, he seemed content so far. His favorite place was the perch next to the sliding doors that led to the rooftop garden. He watched the outside world with interest, particularly the frequent bird visitors.

Although it was too dark to see, Livvy heard the muted ringing tones of the wind chime in the garden. It had belonged to her parents, but she'd never had a place where she could hang it without disturbing neighbors. So she had saved it and waited. On moving day, she had put it up before the movers had even finished. It was the last time she'd been in the garden. The lush greenery and box flowers had really sold her on the penthouse condo, and she did enjoy looking at them, but she never made the time to venture out. Work always came first.

Nacho had seemed 'wind chime deprived' as well. Livvy often saw him staring at the tubes of metal as they swayed in the breeze. At the moment, however, he seemed much more interested in scratches. She gave him a last gentle tousle of the head and turned her attention back to the leather pouch.

She felt the soft suede exterior, aware of the different shapes inside. There was only one way to find out if she could get them to work. She cinched it closed and kept it in her hand while she reached for her goggles. A gentle click turned on the power and they began to quietly hum.

She glanced around the living room. This one room was larger than her entire previous apartment. She'd had an interior designer recommended by the building's homeowners association do the decorating. Although she'd chosen the color scheme, approved all the purchases, and knew that the place was modern, sleek, and comfortable, it never really felt like home to her. Tonight, there was an extra feeling of unease.

It made her nervous to make a journey to the Multiverse without someone standing by–without SK standing by–but she couldn't keep using the time with clients. The only other time she'd gone solo was at the beckoning of Tawa, the Hopi kachina.

She paused. It'd been months since she'd thought of him–the giant feather-fringed face, the rattle and flute. She couldn't help but smile. He'd saved her life more than once. She glanced down at the leather pouch in her hand and the smile faded.

He wouldn't approve of what she was doing. Even so, it *had* to be done.

She tightened her grip on the pouch and looked down at Nacho. "Wait here?" she said.

He signaled his interest by heading to the kitchen.

"Right," she said quietly.

Livvy brought her legs up onto the couch, took in a deep breath, and lay back on the small pillow stuffed with wheat kernels and sage. Then, she put on the goggles.

The symbols of the entrance to the spiritual realm were already playing in vivid 3-D: spirals, handprints, crisscrossing lines, dots, and sunbursts. They swam in and out of view, cycling in hues of yellow and red.

As Livvy put her hands down to her sides, still holding the leather pouch, she slowly and deliberately inhaled and then exhaled. The smell of the fragrant sage had its usual soothing effect. The cycling of the symbols increased until they were a glowing blur that grew transparent. Beyond them, the familiar landscape of the Middleworld began to take shape. She stepped through.

• • • • •

The clouds were so dark they were almost a solid black, covering the sky from horizon to horizon. Although Livvy knew it was always high noon in the Middleworld, she hadn't seen the sun here for months. She sensed that something was changing, something fundamental about the Multiverse. She had felt it for some time but, remembering how sunlight used to suffuse the Middleworld, the current scene was a stark contrast.

She walked up the dirt path that led from the edge of the thick pine forest to the shore of the black lake. Without hesitation, she strode directly into the water. Overhead, thunder pealed and echoed from the mountains that circled the lake. Anxious to get to the Underworld, Livvy ducked under the water as it began to swirl around her.

In moments, she was expelled from the fountain and jumped lightly to the pavement next to it. She turned to see the bright blue inverted funnel of water splashing back down. Up above, the clouds were already boiling, as though her spirit helper had somehow sensed her anxiety.

"This won't take long," she said, as if in reply. *It better not.*

With no client to find, the clouds had no direction to take. A crack of thunder and flash of lightning within the dark mass lit the plaza in a stark white light for a few seconds. The shadows between the buildings were thrown into deep blackness, where no light could penetrate. She'd never noticed that before. A shudder ran down her spine.

Get in, get done, get out, went the shaman's maxim. *Especially if you're working solo.*

Livvy quickly knelt down and opened the leather pouch. She drove the kila dagger into the pavement and then placed each of the items around it. She finished with her mother's engagement ring, slipping it over the apex of the crystal pyramid.

It had taken months to figure out this much and she knew she had to be close now. With the last bit of information clicking into place, it almost seemed obvious.

Livvy stood, raised her hand to the sky—and hesitated.

She stared down at the artifacts, letting her hand drop while her stomach did a flip-flop. She ran a hand through her hair and then both hands.

The whole thing felt wrong.

Probably because she knew it *was* wrong. It was exactly the opposite of what shamans were supposed to do. She had already learned that flouting shaman prohibitions could have a terrible cost. Min had almost died as a result. Would there be unforeseen consequences to this?

Her eyes landed on the ring.

"Mom," she quietly moaned as the familiar tightening in her chest began.

That's what this was about. That's what everything had been about from the time she had become a shaman. It had all led to this moment but, now that it was here, she was unsure. She bit her lower lip.

I have to do this. I have to at least try.

Before she could change her mind, she thrust her hand to the sky. "Lightning," she said.

An incandescent bolt shot from the center of the whirling clouds directly on to her hand with a buzzing crackle. The energy surged through her making her skin tingle and the soles of her feet vibrate. She looked down at her mother's ring and slowly raised her other hand to point at it.

"Elizabeth Lawson," she yelled over the crackling and the wind that had begun to rise. Electricity leapt from her finger, through the engagement ring, and onto the tip of the pyramid. "I summon you!"

Overhead, thunder pealed furiously as the lightning strike grew brighter. A dazzling beam emerged from the pyramid, pointing upward like a searchlight. It too grew brighter.

"There she is!" Livvy heard someone yell behind her.

She immediately dropped her hand and spun around.

CHAPTER NINE

THE LIGHTNING STRIKE receded into the sky, and the wind died abruptly as Livvy stared at the new arrivals. The fountain lay between them, calm and shining blue. There was no inverted funnel or splashing of water because they hadn't come through it.

Livvy knew she was lying alone in her living room in the real world. But if that was true, how had these shamans gotten here?

The one from before, the tall girl with the long black hair, onyx pendant, and leather duster stood in the back. In front of her stood two new shamans.

A young freckled girl, just a slip of a thing, was on Livvy's left. Her short, red hair was done in lethal looking spikes. She had a keen look, something quick and furtive. The other woman was black and heavyset, her hair cropped close, with a big round face. Both wore the robes and pendants of shamans. Something in their stance told Livvy they weren't paying a friendly visit.

"Who are you and what do you want?" said Livvy.

"I'm in charge from now on," said the one in back. "That's all you need to know."

The two women in front didn't turn to look at her. They kept their eyes on Livvy.

"In charge?" asked Livvy. That didn't even make any sense.

"Now!" ordered the one in back.

The two shamans in front separated to come around each side of the fountain. Livvy backed up and raised her hand to the sky. Their spirit helpers hadn't appeared, and she had no clue as to what their shamanic powers might be.

"Stop where you are," Livvy cautioned them both. "Don't make me do something you'll regret."

It wasn't a threat; it was a simple fact. Because it had the clear ring of truth, Livvy's warning stopped the two in front. They looked at each other.

"Don't listen to her," yelled the third. "I said *now*!"

As though pushed from behind, they resumed their advance.

Livvy looked up to the sky. "Whirlwind," she said.

The three other shamans looked up too. A spinning funnel of clouds started to descend over them.

"Do it!" yelled the one in back.

The small redhead reached up both hands toward the lowering funnel. "Wind," she screamed.

A giant rush of air flowed from every direction toward the redhead. Livvy felt it surge from behind her, sweeping her hair forward. The wind seemed to grow from the ground around them and when it reached the redhead, it rushed upward. Her robes seemed to levitate in the invisible stream. The wind met the descending funnel of clouds midway and flattened the tip.

Livvy concentrated, gathering power, seeing the whirlwind in her mind and the tip descended again.

By all the gods, why are they doing this?

Meanwhile, the heavyset woman reached both her hands toward the ground.

"Quake," she yelled. The ground bucked violently beneath them all. The tip of the funnel had flattened again.

"Quake," she yelled again. The ground rumbled and a groaning sound could be heard over the growing gale. The pavement suddenly mounded and cracked open. A long, gaping black scar appeared in the asphalt and ran past the fountain, directly at Livvy. With one arm still raised for the whirlwind, Livvy leaped sideways to avoid the opening seam.

The funnel of the whirlwind stopped descending again. Livvy looked over at the redhead, who had begun to pant. She had probably never had to sustain her power so long and wouldn't be able to manage it much longer. The heavyset one, however, was preparing another attack. The one in back only watched but seemed poised to unleash her own power. Livvy wasn't going to wait to find out what that was.

She thrust her other hand to the sky. "Lightning," she yelled.

The bolt sliced through the funnel cloud, obliterated the redhead's column of wind, and crashed onto Livvy's hand. The two shamans in front froze; Livvy didn't know if there were frightened or mesmerized. They had heard of the lightning shaman, but they had never seen her in action.

Livvy slowly lowered the arm that had called down the whirlwind and aimed it at them.

The two in front flinched but stood their ground.

"Separate," yelled the one in back. "Get some distance between us!"

Yes! Distance was exactly what she needed!

She pointed at the growing space between the three of them, just on the other side of the fountain, and let loose. A booming blast ripped through the air as lightning leaped from her hand. A deafening peal of thunder sounded overhead as the ground between the three other shamans exploded in a bright flash of white-hot energy. All three of them were thrown several yards back.

"Please," Livvy yelled. "I don't want to hurt anybody!" She kept her hand raised, though, and readied herself to point again.

The heavyset woman and the one in back were already on their feet, but the redhead was having trouble getting up. The heavyset one ran over and helped her to her feet.

"Retreat," yelled the one in back and, in moments, all three blinked out in flashes of light.

Livvy immediately dropped her hands. The lightning retreated and the wind died down. She stared at the smoking crater she had created and then at the jagged crevasse that ran by her.

Those shamans had come to the Underworld to attack her.

But why?

· · · · ·

In the real world, Livvy sat up quickly, swung her legs off the couch, and pulled the goggles off. She knew she wasn't networked but she couldn't help but check. Her heart beat furiously and she wiped perspiration from her forehead. She dropped the small leather pouch, now soaked with sweat, onto the coffee table.

Abruptly, a searing pain lanced through her head, from left temple to right, as though an ice pick were being driven through. She closed her eyes and groaned, slumping forward.

Gods, another killer headache.

She opened her eyes slowly and found that she was hovering over the open book. A bright red spot appeared on the page and then another, landing with small plops. Livvy reached a hand to her nose. Her fingers were quickly covered in blood. She pinched her nose closed, teetered into the hallway bathroom and hung her head over the pedestal sink.

After several minutes, the pain began to subside. She turned on the water and watched as streaks of blood rushed toward the drain, swirling at the last second before disappearing.

It reminded her of the whirlwind in the Underworld–and those three shamans. She grimaced at the thought.

'I'm in charge,' the dark one had said.

In charge of what?

CHAPTER TEN

"YOU SOUND LIKE you've got a cold," said SK.

He gazed down at the fog-enshrouded coastline below his condo balcony. A few runners went by along the curved jogging path. A bicyclist, who was being pulled by his Great Dane, passed them. SK had been about to go out for a walk himself when Livvy called.

"No, I'm fine. Just a little stuffed up this morning."

He heard a pause, a slight hesitation that no one else would have noticed. There was something she wanted to say.

"I saw another shaman in the Underworld," she said.

It took him a second to process it. "Wait," he said, turning away from the window. "*What?*"

"I saw another shaman—"

"In the Underworld," he said, his voice rising.

"Right," she said quietly.

He stared intently at the floor, not seeing it. *Another shaman? In the Underworld?* "When?" he demanded.

"During the healing with Fletcher Mosely."

"*With Fletcher?* By all the gods, Liv, why didn't you say anything?"

"Well, I didn't really know what to think."

Didn't really know what to think? He scowled. *How about thinking of mentioning it. Is that why the healing had taken so long?*

"SK?"

"Look," he said. "The only time you can see another shaman in the Multiverse is by networking goggles, and you weren't networked." He thought back on the healing. "Are you sure it wasn't an ancestor spirit?"

"No," said Livvy. "I don't think so. She dressed like a shaman. Contemporary too. No, she was a shaman."

"Did you recognize her?"

"No. I've never seen her before. I think I'd remember."

SK considered that for a moment. "Did Fletcher recognize her?"

There was a pause.

"No, I'm pretty sure he didn't know her."

There'd be no point in asking him, either. Clients never remembered the Multiverse.

Why had it taken her so long to say something about this?

SK went over to one of the overstuffed and lowered chairs and sat down.

"What did she look like?"

There was another pause—a long one. He could almost picture her hesitating.

"Rather than go through this on the phone, can we have dinner?"

He blinked at the sudden turn in conversation. "Dinner?"

"Yeah, tonight," she said. "How about I pick you up at six?"

"Um, sure, sure," he managed to get out. "That'd be fine."

"Great," she said. "Dress fancy."

CHAPTER ELEVEN

CLEARLY, SHE WAS going to need a bigger squad.

"Pipsqueak," Dominique barked. "When is this going to be done?"

Startled, Pip jumped and nearly dropped the soldering iron. Her spiked, red hair jutted up from behind the enormous magnifying goggles, and her eyes looked as big as baseballs.

"I...I don't know, ma'am," she stammered.

Dominique glared at the three pairs of networked goggles.

Livvy–no *Liver*, as in chopped–Liver had easily handled Pipsqueak and Tambourine. If she hadn't been holding back, who knows what might have happened? Dominique had underestimated the enemy–a mistake she wouldn't make twice.

"Tonight," Dominique said.

"*Tonight?*" Pipsqueak involuntarily glanced down at the spool of solder she held over the green circuit board.

Dominique slowly circled behind Pipsqueak, her boots quietly squeaking on the polished concrete. She placed a hand around the back of Pipsqueak's neck and she flinched.

"I have," Dominique said, squeezing, "every confidence in you." She let go with a push. In fact, Dominique already knew it'd be impossible to have it done tonight, but it never hurt to press for more.

Pipsqueak had been expanding the network box since they had come back from the Multiverse. It was starting to look like a rat's nest.

"Yes, ma'am," said Pipsqueak, her head low. "I'll do my best, ma'am."

Dominique turned away and paced to the tall windows on the other side of the studio. It was essentially one big room with a small bathroom at the far end and a kitchenette in one corner. Pip was working at a junky, wooden table Dominique had found on the curb. A couple of white plastic chairs were the only other furniture in the place. Three yoga mats were neatly rolled and stacked in a corner. A box of water bottles was against the wall next to them. A metal storage cabinet was next to those. The place was bare but it was neat–everything squared away.

Dominique had rented this loft in a small industrial park near LAX, not only because it was cheap, but because she could keep an eye on her own place. The floor plans were identical, but in hers she had security windows. She looked across the alley at it and saw a dark shape moving on the other side of the frosted glass.

She glanced at the oversized black watch on her wrist. *Time to check.*

She turned away and paced back to Pipsqueak, stopping in front of the table. Pipsqueak kept her head down, working furiously.

They didn't have to fear Liver's lightning if Liver never got the chance to use it. It was all going to come down to numbers. Big numbers.

In order to work on the network box, Pip had set the nkondi on the floor next to the table. Dominique stopped and stared down at it. It was a bit of the old country–and truly hideous.

Carved of wood, the nkondi was a small statue about a foot high. Although it had arms and legs, these were unimportant. The head and torso were overly large in comparison. The face seemed stuck in a moment of horror, with its gaping circular mouth and protruding lips. The nose was barely there but the eyes were important. Small almond-shaped mirrors seemed to stare into infinity.

Dominique squatted down and gazed into them, seeing her boots reflected there.

The blond wig from some child's doll had been Pipsqueak's idea. It was too small by far but it didn't matter. It gave it the right look. A single large nail held the hair in place on top of the oval head. Around its shoulders was draped a scrap of material that was safety-pinned at the front. Despite the tattered edges, the silvery sheen of the linen glimmered.

The statue held what appeared to be a drum over its stomach. It wasn't a drum, though, as Dominique well knew. It was the reason this bit of vodun worked. Sealed inside the rough protruding cylinder was a single lock of gleaming white hair.

Dominique scanned the ground in the vicinity and saw what she was looking for. She picked up the hammer and flipped open the cardboard box of nails. She pounded another nail through the wig; the hammer blows echoed from every direction in the spartan room. Then she added another and another. She set the nkondi on its back and pounded in some more. She didn't stop until it was nearly covered, studded in gray nails—some of them bent, some at strange angles—all over the torso and the face.

Satisfied, she stood and realized Pipsqueak had taken off the magnifying lenses and was staring at her.

"I thought you said it didn't do any good to add more nails?" Pipsqueak asked.

Dominique tossed the hammer to the floor with a clatter. "It doesn't." She shrugged. "I just like it."

CHAPTER TWELVE

AS THEY WAITED for the restaurant host to return to his small podium near the door, Livvy took off her overcoat while SK closed up the umbrella.

"Liv," he said. "You look fabulous."

She hoped so since she had gone all out for this date. It had been years since she'd worn a dress and she had gone frantically shopping for it only that day. It had taken hours and, in the end, she'd bought three. At home, she had changed from one to another, looking in the mirror, turning from side to side, seeing them with the shoes. She'd decided against something with a low heel in favor of elegant high heels. SK was going to be shorter than her no matter what.

At first she'd thought to wear a simple black dress. It was timeless and safe but her pure white hair was too much of a contrast. She'd probably never be able to wear black again. Eventually, she had settled on the shimmering, green wraparound dress.

The saleswoman had called it sea foam green and said it was an almost perfect match for her eyes. Sleeveless with a V neckline, the loosely bunched material at her shoulders led down to a clinging fit at her waist and then flared out to create a light draping effect that fell from her hips to just above the knee. To Livvy, it had seemed almost Grecian and perhaps a little too plain. Plain would be fine, the saleswoman had said. Nobody would be looking at the dress anyway.

A little makeup and peridot earrings had finished off the look. She'd decided to leave the amethyst pendant at home.

"Your table is ready," said the host. He held out his hands for the coat and umbrella. "I'll take these for you," he said.

SK handed him the umbrella without taking his eyes off Livvy. The host took it from him and nearly did the same thing.

"Follow me," he said.

All eyes turned their way–first as they proceeded through the softly lit bar, then into the dining room, and finally toward the single row of candlelit tables near the expansive window. Conversations died while the sound of scooting chairs resounded off the tiled floor. Livvy knew they must make for an interesting pair–the willowy white-haired woman and the dapper dwarf.

SK had not had to dress much differently than he always did, but this evening he wore the royal blue outfit, her favorite.

"Here is your table," said the host as he started to pull a chair out for Livvy.

SK deftly stepped around her and cut him off. "Thanks," he said to the host, placing his hand on the back of the chair. "I've got it."

Without a word, the host took a step back with a little bow. Livvy couldn't help but smile as SK held the chair.

She took in the view as she sat. From here, they could see the entire pier and much of the coastline's twinkling cityscape. Even through the rain spattered window and light drizzle, the lights of the storefronts and the amusement rides were bright. The ocean was nearly black, the moon covered by the clouds, but it seemed perfect.

When she looked back to SK, he was already seated and quickly lowered his eyes. He had been staring at her.

He cleared his throat. "So, this other shaman," he said. "What did she look like?"

Livvy described her, with as many details as she could remember.

She paused as the waiter came for their drink orders. Knowing that Livvy no longer drank, SK asked for two sparkling waters.

"Well, from a description like that," said SK, "you'd think it'd be hard to miss her." He shook his head. "I don't know a shaman who looks like that. Nor have I ever heard of one."

"How can that be?" said Livvy. She had always assumed that SK knew most everybody involved with shamanism.

He shook his head again. "L.A.'s a big territory and there are other intercessors. Let's just say that I know all the important healers. There's a whole other sub-culture of shamans out there–shamans who fly under the radar, as it were. Shamans who don't particularly want to be known for what they're doing."

"And what are they doing?"

Despite being the lightning shaman, Livvy had never had a proper mentor–another shaman who would have taught her about the Multiverse, guided her vision quest, and passed on something of the history of the practice. Instead, Livvy had learned on her own. She had received her first pair of goggles as a gift from a patient in medical school, and her vision quest had happened immediately. The more that Livvy learned about shamanism, the more she realized how little she knew.

"Typically, those shamans practice the dark arts, create hexes, work to *make* people sick, so they can heal them."

The sparkling water arrived and, as the waiter poured their glasses, she looked at SK and their eyes met briefly.

"Shall I come back for your order?" asked the waiter.

"That'd be good," SK said.

He considered the water for a few moments.

"I don't know the woman you describe, so I'm kind of jumping to conclusions but I think it's a real possibility that she's one of these dark shamans."

Dark shaman had the right sound to it. She hadn't exactly been Miss Sunshine.

"This gets back to the old rules," he said. "The prohibition against shamans working together partially came about to avoid the type of situation where one shaman might secretly create an illness only so their partner could cure it. In that she's working alone, that doesn't seem likely."

He took a sip of water.

"Well," said Livvy, staring at the stem of her glass. "She wasn't exactly alone."

SK sputtered a bit and then coughed. He put his napkin to his mouth and, before he could ask, Livvy answered his question.

"She had two friends and I think she was looking specifically for me."

The waiter chose that moment to check on them.

"Not now," SK said to him as he neared.

The man quickly changed his course and passed their table.

SK swung his gaze back to Livvy. "*Three* shamans?"

Livvy nodded. "The one with the leather jacket was the one 'in charge.' I didn't recognize the other two shamans either."

She gave their descriptions and also related what they had done–the whirlwind and the earthquakes–but that there had been no spirit helpers.

"Whoa, whoa, whoa. Wait a minute," said SK, pushing his glass away. "They attacked you?"

"I guess so," said Livvy. "I don't know any other way of saying it."

"Liv," he said, suddenly stern. "Why didn't you tell me? Why didn't you mention this?"

This was the tricky part. She had lied about there being only one event because he couldn't know about her mother.

"I wasn't sure they were shamans," she said. "I wasn't sure what had happened at all. It might have been a mix-up of some sort."

"A mix-up?" said SK as he frowned.

The waiter appeared from nowhere and deftly poured a little sparkling water into each of their glasses. "Do you have any questions about the menu?"

Livvy quickly opened hers and focused on the larger type at the top of the second page. "Two of the house specials?" she said and looked at SK, but his menu was closed and he was holding it out to the waiter, clearly waiting for him to leave.

"Excellent," said the waiter, taking it. "We are, of course, known for our lobster." He took Livvy's menu as well and smartly turned on his heel.

"Three shamans together," said SK as soon as the waiter was out of earshot. "They attack you with wind and earthquakes and you think it's a mix-up?"

"Well, it's not like I've ever been attacked before," she said quickly, trying to defuse his growing anger. "I've never even seen another shaman there without being networked. I still don't understand how that can be."

He seemed about to say something else but paused and sat back for a second. "No, I don't either," he replied. "Three together…"

"Only two attacked," said Livvy. "The other one, the one with long dark hair, she hung back and was giving the orders."

"Even so, three together," he said. "They must be networked."

"I didn't think anybody was doing that," said Livvy. "Not after...you know."

The first time she had networked goggles she had nearly died, and Min had gone into a coma. The risks could be high.

"I didn't think anybody was doing it either," he said. "But the fact that I don't recognize any of these three says a lot about what may be going on that I don't know."

He seemed to be calming down and analyzing the situation. "Three dark shamans, then—working together," he said as if to himself, staring at his glass. "How and why?"

As much as the appearance of the three shamans worried her, it wasn't the real reason Livvy had asked SK to dinner, and it certainly wasn't the reason she had shopped all day for a killer dress. It was time to be honest about her feelings.

Since becoming a shaman, she hadn't managed to date anyone for any significant length of time. With the strange hours, let alone the strange work and sometimes the strange clients, it was almost impossible to develop, let alone keep, a relationship. The last time she'd had a boyfriend was probably the last time she'd shopped for a dress.

Still deep in thought, SK gazed in the direction of the pier though Livvy could see the gears turning behind his intense eyes.

She lifted her water glass, still watching him, and then slowly but deliberately set it back down.

"SK," she said.

He turned to her as she leaned forward slightly.

"I–"

"Here we are," said the waiter, as an enormous plate passed in front of her. She quickly sat back. "The house lobster."

Another waiter behind him set an identical dish in front of SK. "Is there anything else that I can get for you?"

Both she and SK shook their heads, partly in answer to his question but also in bewilderment at the heaping piles of food.

"Bon appétit," said the waiter.

SK put his hand on the fork but instead of picking it up, he looked at her. "No Multiverse," he said.

"What?" said Livvy, surprised.

"No Multiverse until I can get some answers."

"But we've got–"

"I'll have Min cancel everything tomorrow," he said.

"But, SK, I can handle this—"

"Liv," he said, reaching across the table to put his hand over hers. "I'm dead serious on this. We're not doing anything in the Multiverse until we find out who those shamans are and how they're doing what they're doing, including how they're finding you."

She stared down at his hand. His touch was warm and soft.

"I know it's hard," he said. "But I'm not going to let you take a risk. Please, just go with me on this."

She gazed into his eyes, deeply set and dark. He was concerned and now a little on edge. She reluctantly nodded.

Her gaze wandered between his soft brown eyes and then down to his lips. His sideburns and beard were starting to get a few gray hairs, a look that she thought lent him a dashing air. The flickering candlelight danced in his eyes, almost hypnotic.

"Okay," he said, nodding once. He squeezed her hand for emphasis before letting go. Then he picked up his fork and looked at his plate.

"SK, I—"

He looked up, his fork poised in midair, and waited for her.

"I love you," she blurted out.

He froze and then slowly put the fork down without looking up. Livvy watched intently as several emotions seemed to flash across his face, the first one clearly shock.

Uh oh. Shock? Could it be that much of a surprise? I shouldn't have said it like that.

All day she'd searched for a better way. All day she'd played this moment out, over and over, and had never come up with anything that seemed right. So, she'd decided to just come out and say it.

And he was *shocked*, although he was doing his best to cover it.

A smile began to curl the corners of his mouth. Livvy realized her heart was pounding but then his smile vanished.

"Liv," he started. "I…" He paused but *still* didn't look at her. "I don't know what to say."

The thing she hoped he would say—the thing she'd heard him say when she'd envisioned this moment—was that he loved her too.

But that's not what he had said. And it didn't seem like he was going to.

CHAPTER THIRTEEN

THE ONLY SOUND in the car was the rain and windshield wipers. SK sat silently in the passenger seat.

I have so screwed this up.

She gripped the steering wheel and wished she could bash her head into it.

Idiot!

He had barely touched his dinner after her 'confession.' Just wanting the awful evening to be over, Livvy had quickly asked for their meals to be wrapped up. The waiter had been speedy about it, likely sensing this was a date that had gone wrong.

So wrong. What an idiot.

You know, he might even have a girlfriend. It's not like you ever asked. Then again, we're together so much, where would he find the time?

Or maybe he just didn't feel that way about her. Why would he?

Gods, what was I thinking?

He was the ultimate power broker of the shaman world. SK knew hundreds of shamans. All of them craved his attention. One word from him could make or break a career.

But it wasn't the power that had drawn her to him; it was the way he never used it. He treated everyone the same. She had never seen him lose patience with a client, and he had never complained about the long hours. In fact, there were no complaints of any sort, even in the difficult circumstances in which they sometimes found themselves. The thing that fascinated her, though, was no matter how many onlookers or cameras were present, he never pretended to be anything other than himself. He seemed at ease, comfortable in his own skin. It was as though some deep place at his center grounded him. It was a place Livvy needed to know more about.

Thankfully, they were at his condo in only minutes. She pulled the sedan to the curb and waited, the engine idling, the windshield wipers still slapping from side to side. He didn't open the door but he didn't say anything either. He just sat and stared out the passenger window.

Finally, she couldn't take it any more.

"I'm sorry, SK," she whispered, barely audible. She looked down at the console between them. "I somehow thought you might feel the same way. I—"

"That's the problem, Liv," he said, looking at her. "I do feel the same way."

Her eyes blinked to the point of fluttering. "Well but—"

"But I'm the go-between, the intercessor," he said firmly, as though he were trying to remember the fact. "I'm the impartial one in the middle." He shrugged. "At least I'm supposed to be."

"But if you…love me—"

He shook his head. "I can't, Liv," he said, biting off the words. "I can't. It's wrong." His voice was so strained.

"Is this a rules thing? Because if it's rules—"

He shook his head again, slowly. "No, it's not a rules thing. It's just the way that shamanic power and my skills as an intercessor work. Most intercessors are simply shaman go-betweens, business people who mediate arrangements between shamans and clients. Hopefully they're people who've gotten into the business because they have a sensitivity to the work. For people like me though…"

He looked back out the windshield and his eyes seemed to be following the rivulets of rain that ran down it. He shrugged.

"I don't understand," Livvy said. "People like you?"

"I was born with a talent, same as you. In different cultures I'm called different things: water baby, master of animals, or simply the dwarf. When I work with a shaman, I'm more than a go-between— all dwarfs are. We have the ability to amplify a shaman's talent."

"You amplify—" Livvy repeated, trying to understand. "Wait a minute. Do you amplify my power?"

He turned back to her. "Not often, but yes."

A thousand questions ran through her mind: *Which healings? How does it work? How much amplification?*

But only one question was important right now.

"Why can't we be—"

"Not we. Me. It only works if I'm in the middle, in balance. I can't become…attached…to any one shaman." He considered that for a moment and shook his head. "But that's exactly what I've done, in more ways than one. I can hardly deny it now."

He clenched his jaw and she watched as he took in a deep breath and slowly let it go.

He opened the car door.

"SK, please…"

He paused but didn't turn around. "I've got to go, Liv," he said. Then he got out and closed the door.

CHAPTER FOURTEEN

LIVVY SNIFFED, CAUSING Nacho to freeze and stare at her as though she'd yelled. She smiled a little before reaching for the tissue. She'd been crying on and off since she got home. The pretty green dress was a lump on the floor on top of the perfect shoes. She'd immediately switched to the flannel comfort pajamas and gotten into bed. Nacho had hovered around her the entire time.

Now he sprawled on his back while Livvy scratched his stomach. The little tabby was lying in her lap, in the soft, aqua-colored, chenille hammock created by the bedspread over her crossed legs.

Her eyes drifted over to the altar in the corner of the room as they often did when she was here. It had been a while since she'd added anything to it. Even so, it was three tiers tall and crowded. Like every other shaman Livvy had ever met, she had collected items of ritual or religious significance since she could remember. The objects were drawn from all sorts of religions in nearly every part of the globe. As always, she focused on the items of the top tier, the gifts she'd received from her shaman friends: the sage bundle from Alvina, the small vodun doll from Ursula, the mala beads from Wan Li, and the kachina doll of Tawa from…she didn't know who. It had simply appeared with the other objects and she'd assumed it was from the Nahual, although that didn't really make sense, since the Nahual was from Central America and Tawa was a pueblo god.

With his one foot raised in dance and his enormous shield-like face turned toward her, she frowned at him. More and more she found herself worrying about solo trips to the Multiverse and more and more she thought of Tawa. She knew, even at this moment, why her eyes lingered on him yet again. She looked back down at

Nacho who was limp in her lap, still on his back, still enjoying scratches. Livvy sighed and wiped her nose with the tissue.

Only the small Tiffany lamp on the nightstand was on, and the curtains were drawn in front of the sliding glass door. Although she couldn't hear the light rain, she heard the runoff dripping in a metal gutter.

"What a botched date," she whispered.

What an evening.

Oh gods, the look on SK's face when she said she loved him.

A few tears slipped down her cheek, and one fell onto Nacho's stomach. He immediately patted the spot with his paw, as though he might have trapped something, and took a quick peek.

"Sorry, Nacho," she said, rubbing the warm soft fur there.

As bad as the restaurant had been, his reaction in the car had been worse.

You couldn't have worked up to it? Somehow let him see it coming? Maybe asked him on a second date?

"Oh stop it," she muttered. "Stop going over it. It was done."

Her eyes landed on the silver goggles on her nightstand.

SK had said no Multiverse, when he was still talking to her, that is. No Multiverse, until he could find out who those shamans were. The last time in the Underworld, though, she had been very close to making the summoning work. She'd have pulled it off except for being interrupted. They had fled immediately when she'd called down lightning. They might not come back so quickly–if there even was a next time. Maybe they'd never show up again.

Livvy stared at the goggles and felt a tiny pat on her hand from Nacho. She had stopped scratching. She gently rubbed him with the one hand but picked up her goggles with the other. Nacho looked up at the shiny silver of them but was quickly bored and looked away.

Sk had said no Multiverse, but he didn't know what was at stake. He didn't know how much he was asking. She leaned back toward the nightstand and opened the drawer. Nacho rolled out of her lap and into a standing position.

Livvy withdrew the small leather pouch and felt the artifacts inside clunk together.

Later, she promised herself. She would explain everything to SK later.

• • • • •

Livvy couldn't help but glance around the plaza one more time. The fountain gurgled, clouds filled the sky, and the tall buildings towered. A spirit helper in the shape of a tortoise wandered by in the distance, while a baboon strolled in the opposite direction. An ancestor spirit dressed in long robes and some type of tall, cylindrical hat crossed in the middle of the plaza. The Underworld looked as it always had.

Then why does it feel so different? Guilt?

She shook off the uneasy feeling, crouched down and opened the leather pouch. As before, she placed each of the artifacts on the ground, drove the kila knife into the pavement, and finished with her mother's engagement ring on top of the crystal pyramid.

That should do it.

She stood and scanned the plaza, unable to stop herself. Both times the dark-haired shaman had shown up there'd been no sign. Whatever she was doing to find her, Livvy was not able to see it coming.

She focused on the small arrangement at her feet then looked up to the sky.

No time to waste.

She thrust up a hand toward the boiling and swirling mass of dark clouds. "Lightning," she said.

The glowing bolt shot down and landed with a crash on her hand. Livvy felt the tingle and buzz of the energy flow through her as it rushed toward the ground. She raised her other hand while still channeling the energy and pointed at the tip of the pyramid. A thin arc of electricity leaped between her finger and the clear crystal, causing it to glow. In moments, a beam of purple light erupted from its tip and shot upward. Livvy followed it with her gaze and saw a faint purple circle of light on the underside of the clouds above. She looked back down at the source of the beam.

"Elizabeth Lawson, I summon you!" she yelled.

There was an enormous and elongated peal of thunder as the beam brightened. Slowly, as the lightning that Livvy channeled from the sky intensified, the beam grew even more brilliant. Her hair floated in the static and her teeth vibrated from the energy, but she kept her hands in place.

There, in the most radiant part of the purple light, at the tip of the tiny pyramid, a ghostly figure emerged. Small at first, it steadily grew taller and also more substantial, expanding to fill the widening beam. Although the figure was facing away from her, Livvy could see that it was a woman and that she was blond.

The ground at Livvy's feet sizzled and blackened as the energy poured through her. The charred blackness seeped toward the artifacts but stopped short of the kila dagger. Heat was building up around her ankles and spreading up her calves. It was becoming difficult to breathe.

The beam from the pyramid cast a shimmering lavender light onto every building that bordered the plaza. It was as though a small purple sun had risen near the fountain. All of the spirit helpers and ancestor spirits turned to look, their faces awash in the strange light. Beings who normally took no notice of shamans or each other now stood still and watched.

As Livvy looked at them, she realized her vision was starting to blur. No wait, not blur. Her eyes, her whole body was actually vibrating with the sustained lightning strike. Even through the tremors, though, she could see someone in front of her, someone who was no longer ghostly but solid. Like the others in the plaza around her, Livvy watched as that person stepped out of the beam.

Livvy dropped her arms to her sides, exhausted and out of breath. Gods, she had never sustained lightning for so long. She bent over to keep from falling and tried to catch her breath.

"Livvy?" she heard a familiar voice say.

Livvy froze as a sudden pang of recognition flooded through her. As often as she'd dreamt of this moment and had visualized it from every angle, she had never thought of hearing her mother's voice.

"Mom," she whispered, slowly straightening up.

Only a few feet away, almost close enough to touch, stood her mom. Stunned, Livvy could only stare. Her mom's eyes were searching her own. Then, she tilted her head in just that certain way Livvy remembered all too well.

"Livvy, it *is* you!" She began to smile and hold out her arms but then stopped. "But how are you…Oh gods. Livvy, are you–"

"No, no, no," Livvy stammered. "No, Mom, I'm not dead." She

took in a deep breath. "I've summoned you."

Livvy watched as her mom tried to understand. First, she looked down at the small group of artifacts on the ground. Then she looked at the ancestor spirits and animal helpers, who were still staring. As her mom turned her head, Livvy stared at a glint of light in her green eyes, the same exact color as her own.

"Oh no, Livvy," said her mom as realization dawned. "What have you *done*?"

Livvy couldn't help but wince. "I needed to talk to you?" she said.

Her mom looked into her face and her eyes softened, and then she smiled and held out her arms. "Oh I know, honey," she said. "Come here."

Livvy immediately closed the distance and fell into her arms. "Mom!" she said and immediately choked up. She buried her face in her mom's shoulder.

"Ah, my poor baby," her mother said. "I know. I know." She rubbed Livvy's back and kissed her hair.

"I missed you," Livvy managed to get out.

"I've missed you too, honey. Here, let me get a good look at you."

Livvy wiped her eyes, sniffed and stood back.

Her mother beamed at her and moved a strand of hair at her forehead. "That's my girl," she said smiling. "All grown up." Her eyes lingered on the hair and she touched it. "I like it."

Livvy gave a small laugh.

Then her mother's face became serious. "We have a lot to talk about," her mom said, lightly grasping her arms. Then she frowned. "Livvy, honey, you're trembling."

Whether it was the exhaustion from the lightning strike or the emotion of the moment, Livvy didn't know, but she hadn't stopped shaking since the summoning.

Her mother noticed the artifacts on the ground and the scorched pavement next to them.

"Livvy, how long have you been here?"

"Just a little while," said Livvy quickly. "I can stay a bit longer."

Her mother shook her head. "You know the rules, honey. You delay—"

"You stay," Livvy finished, then realized what they'd said.

"But Mom, how do you–"

"Next time, honey. Seriously, I'm worried about you."

"But Mom," Livvy whimpered.

More than anything she wanted to stay–be with her mom, look at her, listen to her–but the sustained lightning strike had been more difficult than she wanted to admit.

"Olivia," said her mom, using the warning tone that always accompanied her proper name.

Livvy sighed.

"I'll be here when you get back," her mom reassured her and glanced around the plaza. Then she looked back at Livvy and smiled. "There's time for talk later. Really, honey, it's going to be all right."

Livvy felt a lightness in her chest as though a great weight were lifting, a burden she had never acknowledged and yet had carried for years, but she knew her mom was right.

"Okay," she finally said.

She bent down to gather the items back into the leather pouch but swayed a bit with a slight sensation of vertigo. Hoping that her mom hadn't noticed, she crouched down and started putting the artifacts into the bag, but something was missing.

"What happened to your ring?" Livvy said.

"Oh," exclaimed her mom. "Looks like I'm wearing it."

Livvy looked up to see her mom gazing down at the engagement ring on her finger. Even without the wedding ring, it looked right.

Livvy put the remaining items into the pouch and carefully stood. They looked at each other for several long moments until her mother gently took her by the arms and gave her a soft kiss on the cheek.

"I'll be fine, honey," she said. "Take your time. I'll see you when you get back."

"Okay Mom," said Livvy, automatically returning the kiss. She already couldn't wait.

CHAPTER FIFTEEN

"DAMMIT!" SK SAID as he slammed the front door. He spun around to glare at the dark front room of his condo.

"Dammit!" He paused, hands on hips as he lowered his head.

"*I've got to go?*" he mimicked himself. "That's all you can think to say!"

Like a pitcher with a wicked sidearm, he hurled his keys at the couch and they buried themselves with a thud between the cushions.

He stalked to the panoramic window on the other side of the living room. Through the rainy darkness, the lights along the boardwalk gave off an eerie glow. There was no moon in the sky and some of the shops and concession stands on the pier had already shut down for the evening. He closed his eyes, not seeing the dark landscape anyway. Instead, he saw the restaurant.

He leaned his forehead on the cool glass. Every man in the restaurant would have traded places with him in a heartbeat. Any one of them would have been thrilled to hear the words that she'd said to him.

Particularly that one word.

He squeezed his eyes even tighter against the sound of her voice.

She had laid her heart on the line and he…he had pushed it away.

He banged his head on the glass. Everything had seemed to be going so well. It felt so good to be with her and not on a job.

He should have seen it coming.

He raised his head and saw himself in the glass. "Oh come on," he challenged his reflection. "You *did* know and you lapped it up, you ass." You let her put herself out there when you already knew you couldn't–or wouldn't.

He turned away from the window unable to look at himself.

His eyes landed on the couch, the place where she had slept–was it only a year ago–when her place had been vandalized. Ursula, Alvina and the rest of the shamans had called him on his feelings for Liv even then. They needed him in the center and in balance. He was their intercessor and the one who stood between the power of shamans and the power of the Multiverse. He had been born to his role in the same way shamans were born to theirs. In that role, he had become the most powerful broker and intercessor in recent memory.

Then came Liv.

He went over and sat down on the couch, touching the spot where she'd been.

Liv had changed everything. She had risked her life for her clients. She had allied with other shamans. She had created the first network of goggles and been the first shaman in thousands of years to actually work with others in the Multiverse.

SK looked back in the direction of the pier.

The network of goggles.

Now someone else was trying to do the same thing, but that someone was trying to hurt her. He stood and paced back to the window. He didn't know who they were and how they were doing it but he was going to find out–and quickly. They might be flying under the radar but someone somewhere would have to know something. There wasn't time to canvas the city, though. He needed a shortcut. Luckily, he had one. Once it was morning, he knew where he would start.

Until then, there would probably be no sleep. He exhaled loudly, put his hands in his pockets and stared into the blackness of the Pacific Ocean. Although the view hadn't changed, his world had.

CHAPTER SIXTEEN

I TOOK OFF my goggles didn't I?

Yes, I distinctly remember taking off my goggles. I went to the kitchen for water and then I went back to bed. Nacho was already asleep.

So what am I doing in the Multiverse?

Livvy looked around. This was definitely the Middleworld: the dirt path, the forest, and the black lake. There was a distant sound of lapping water, and the chirping of birds came from the surrounding trees.

"Back so soon?" asked SK, behind her.

She jumped and spun around. "*SK?*"

He nodded, hands in pockets, looking as elegant as ever. "In the flesh," he said. "Well, so to speak."

"What are you doing…oh," said Livvy, relieved. "Okay. I get it. It's a dream."

"You think so?" he said. "Really? You dream about the Middleworld?"

Livvy thought about that. "Well, actually no," she said. "I don't think I've ever dreamed about the Middleworld."

Suddenly, she remembered the only time she'd ever heard about shamans dreaming in the Middleworld. Indra and Min had both dreamed of being buried there and found it hard to wake up. Indra had then died.

"I think I'd better get going," said Livvy.

"But you just got here," said SK, smiling.

She adored that relaxed and easy look of his. It was almost tempting to stay.

"I don't know why I'd dream about the Middleworld, but I know why *you're* here."

"I'll bet you do," he replied, nodding his head. "That was quite the date."

"Uh, yeah," she said.

What would be the point of talking to SK about it in a dream? Shouldn't she just wake up and talk to him in person?

"There's my beautiful girl," said Livvy's mom.

Again, Livvy spun around. *Oh no, Mom! SK can't know this.*

Livvy paused and took a deep breath. *Okay, stop it. This is your dream. You're doing this.*

She let the breath go. "Hi Mom," she said.

"Livvy," she said. "I really do love the hair."

"I was the one who convinced her not to color it," said SK.

"Good call," said Mom. She paused and waited, looking at Livvy. "Livvy, wouldn't it be polite to introduce us?" she said finally.

Her mom and SK waited expectantly.

Livvy shrugged. "Okay," she said. "Mom this is SK. SK this is my mother."

They politely shook hands.

"I've heard so much about you, young man," said Mom, smiling, with a pleasant conversational tone to her voice.

"Well, I've heard next to nothing about you," he replied, also conversational.

"I guess that's not too surprising," replied her mom.

"Right, I think we're done," said Livvy, wondering how to leave. She looked up and down the path. She could leave, couldn't she?

"Honestly, Olivia," said her mom, a sudden anger in her voice. "I think that's rude."

As she turned back to her mom, she found herself being jerked forward. She stared at her mother's angry face and realized her mother had grabbed her with both hands by the neck.

"What is it with the young people these days?" asked SK.

"SK," Livvy managed to get out. "Help."

Her mother's grip grew tighter.

Livvy grabbed her arms but couldn't move them. Her mother was strong, incredibly strong. Frantically, she tried to back away, turn, move in any direction but her mother's grip was like a rock. Finally, she started pounding her fists on her mother's arms. Her mother responded by squeezing harder.

She's going to break my neck.

She clawed at her mother's fingers but did more to scratch her own throat than dislodge the grip. She tried to scream but her vocal cords were being crushed. No air could flow.

"You know, you could just wake up," said SK calmly.

Livvy flicked her eyes down to him but couldn't utter a sound.

"Go ahead, Liv," he said a bit sadly. "Wake up."

He cocked his head and stared at her, as though he were waiting for her to disappear. When she didn't, he screamed in her face, making her blink. "Wake up!"

• • • • •

Livvy heard someone screaming, a cross between a wail and a cry.

"Wake up!" someone else yelled.

Livvy's eyes flew open and she caught herself in mid-scream. It had been *her* wailing.

Something was hovering in front of her and she tried to back up, scoot away, until her head hit the headboard.

"Livvy, it's me," said Min. "It's okay."

Was that Min's face hovering in midair? Livvy's chest heaved but she managed not to scream. With wide eyes, she finally brought Min into focus.

"Livvy," said Min. "Gods, you were screaming."

Livvy slowly sat up, still breathing hard. "Sorry," she said.

Min sat lightly on the edge of the bed, still tense. She rested a hand on Livvy's leg. "I heard you from outside the front door," she said, looking intently into her face.

Livvy sucked in a huge breath and closed her eyes, trying to slow her heartbeat, calm down.

"You were having a nightmare," said Min.

Livvy only nodded. *That was putting it lightly.*

It had not been one of the garden-variety nightmares to which she was prone. SK had told her that dreaming and shamanism often went together but the nightmares seemed above and beyond, especially this one. She had *never* dreamt of the Multiverse before, nor of her mother. Suddenly, she shivered and her teeth made a small clattering sound.

Min took one of her hands in both of hers. "You're freezing," she exclaimed as she tried to rub some heat into it.

She ran an experienced eye over Livvy's face, slipping into

shaman mode. She put the back of her hand to Livvy's forehead. "And you're covered in sweat," Min said, looking at Livvy's eyes for any clue.

"Just a bad dream," Livvy said, right before another shiver began. Again, her teeth chattered.

"Maybe more than that," said Min. "Okay, a hot shower for you. You need to get out of those damp PJs."

Livvy nodded.

"You do that and I'll get some tea on," Min said.

Livvy got up and headed to the bathroom. "Just a bad dream," she whispered.

• • • • •

Reassured by the sound of the shower, Min turned away from the bathroom door and toward the bed. She saw the green dress in a small pile on the floor on top of high-heeled shoes. She bent down to pick it up.

"Very nice," she murmured. Then she glanced back at the bathroom door. She had never seen Livvy wear a dress. What was the occasion?

"Hmm." She hung it in the large walk-in closet and put the shoes there as well.

"Nacho," she called. Normally he greeted her at the front door.

When she had become Livvy's assistant, she had given her a set of keys—the car, the apartment, the mail. They had slipped into a pattern quickly. Virtually every day, Min would let herself in, make tea, feed Nacho, and start checking the schedule she and SK shared. Then SK would arrive and they'd leave for their first appointment. Min took care of the business side of the work. SK took care of the client side. Livvy took care of the Multiverse.

The three of them had worked nearly non-stop for months now. Normally Livvy was ready to go when she arrived.

"Nacho," Min called again.

A small meow came from under the bed.

Min went over, lifted the white ruffle at the bottom, and looked underneath. Two glowing orange eyes greeted her, and another meow.

"Nacho, what are you doing down there?" Then Min realized

he'd hid himself from Livvy's screaming. "Come on out," she coaxed. "It's okay now."

He didn't budge.

"Aunt Min brought you a new toy. Catnip. Your favorite."

He just stared at her.

"It's breakfast time," she tried. "Aren't you hungry?"

He meowed again but didn't move.

"Well, we'll see about that," said Min, getting up.

Down the hallway and past the front door, Min went directly through the swinging, half-height, café doors into the kitchen. She passed the island with gas cooktops and proceeded to the cabinets of frosted glass. On her left were the built-in refrigerator and oven and, below the oven, was Nacho's rug.

She took his dry food from a bottom cupboard, making as much noise with the bag as possible. Then she poured some into his bowl and rattled it slightly. She waited a few seconds and then rattled it again. Sure enough, he came trotting in under the swinging doors. She scratched his back as he crunched away.

"That's better," she said.

Once she stowed the food, gave him fresh water, and put on a kettle for some tea, she slid into the upholstered breakfast nook in the corner of the kitchen and opened her netbook.

"What?" she said out loud. "All appointments canceled?"

SK hadn't left any notes as to why. A former client of Carmen's plus two new clients had been scheduled today. They were all canceled. Min would need to start making phone calls right away. She scrolled to the next day. Same thing. Only one client was left for the rest of the week—one that could hardly be canceled. Min shook her head. *All the rest though?*

The teakettle whistled.

Min took the glass teapot from the cabinet, filled the built-in strainer with loose Genmai-cha, and then poured in the hot water. She heard the shower in the bedroom stop. Livvy would know what was going on.

As the tea took on its characteristic light green color, and the leaves and grains of roasted brown rice became soft and then plump in the strainer, Nacho made small figure eights around her calves. She reached down and scratched him behind the ears, and he flopped quickly on his back.

"You little glutton," she murmured as she bent down and obliged with scratches on the stomach. "Are you not getting enough attention? What's up with your mom, huh?"

"What do mean, what's up?"

Startled, Min stood up. Livvy had come in as she toweled her hair but had stopped in the middle of the kitchen. Nacho ran toward the bedroom. Despite having just got up, Livvy looked tired but, more than that, she actually looked irritated. Min couldn't remember ever seeing Livvy mad.

"SK's canceled all appointments for today," she said.

"Oh," said Livvy, relaxing.

Maybe it hadn't been anger. The expression had vanished so quickly Min couldn't be sure. Now Livvy seemed puzzled. Then, as though she understood, she slowly nodded once and looked at the floor. Her hands moved mechanically with the towel.

"What's going on?" asked Min.

Livvy looked up at her as though she'd forgotten she was there. For a second or two, she seemed as though she might be about to cry.

"Livvy, what's happened?"

Livvy took a deep breath and sighed, but just as she was about to say something, the intercom buzzed.

"Must be SK," said Min, going to the intercom.

She pressed the talk button. "Good morning, SK," she chirped.

Although she expected an answer from the doorman, she knew SK would hear her. Maybe now, she'd get some answers.

"Ms. Ahn," said the doorman. "I have someone here named Ursula to see Ms. Lawson."

"Oh!" said Min, confused.

Though she had never met Ursula, she knew her by name. Shamans everywhere had heard the names of the women who had formed the first goggle network with Livvy.

She turned to look at Livvy, who seemed just as surprised.

"Let her in?" Min whispered, even though the intercom button was off.

"Of course, of course," said Livvy, nodding.

"Okay, I'm buzzing you in," said Min, as she pressed the intercom button.

What a strange day this was turning out to be.

CHAPTER SEVENTEEN

"URSULA," SAID LIVVY as she gave her a small hug. "It's so good to see you."

They hadn't seen each other since the last time they'd been networked together.

Given her slightly regal nature, Ursula returned the hug with more conviction than Livvy had expected. It really did feel good to see Ursula.

"It is good for Ursula to see you too," she said.

Her dark skin glowed with life; her bright pink head wrap matched her bright pink lipstick. A large cabochon of fire opal hung on a thick braided gold chain in the plunge of her neckline. She carried a large velvet satchel over her shoulder that looked like it had something heavy in it.

Min cleared her throat.

"Ursula," said Livvy quickly. "This is Soo Min, my assistant."

Livvy glanced at Min who was staring a bit wide-eyed at their exotic guest. "Soo Min, this is Ursula. I think you've heard of her."

They inclined their heads toward one another.

"Of course," said Min, smiling. "Who hasn't?"

Ursula smiled pleasantly in return but didn't say anything.

"Please, come in and sit down," Livvy said in the lull.

"I was just about to pour some tea," said Min.

Livvy led Ursula into the large living room. Instead of sitting down, Ursula went over to the sliding glass door and its view of the rooftop garden and the clouds covering Century City.

"Shamanism has been good for you," she said.

Livvy couldn't help but remember the first time she'd met Ursula in Watts. She had been the first shaman that Livvy and SK had sought out for help in the battle against Tiamat. Like the rest of the shamans, though, she had initially turned her down.

"It is only right," said Ursula, nodding and turning toward her. "Ursula is pleased for you."

Min set down two cups of tea on the coffee table.

"Thank you, Min," said Livvy.

Min snuck a glance at Ursula and then headed back to the kitchen. They had both sensed she had something on her mind.

Ursula moved over to the chair opposite Livvy and sat down. As she did, she peered into the cup of green liquid and raised her eyebrows.

"Genmai-cha," said Livvy. "A mix of green tea and roasted rice."

"No doubt it is…refreshing," said Ursula, not touching it.

Livvy smiled. In many ways, Ursula hadn't changed which was nice.

Finally, she reached into her velvet satchel and removed a glass jar. She glanced at the label and then held it out to Livvy.

Livvy put down her tea and took it. "What's this?" she asked. "Ursula's Remedies and Herbs," she read. "Holistic, organic, and guaranteed."

She looked through the dark green glass and saw large tablets inside that chinked softly. She looked up at Ursula. "Are these for me?"

"Yes and no," replied Ursula smoothly.

Livvy set the bottle in her lap and waited.

"Ursula would like," she said, then hesitated. "Your endorsement."

Livvy blinked at her. "I don't understand."

Ursula nodded as though she'd expected that. "Ursula would like the lightning shaman's name on her products," she said simply. "Endorsed by the lightning shaman."

Livvy looked down at the bottle. She knew that many traditional shamans employed herbal remedies. In various cultures throughout the world, they were doctors in the physical sense as well as in the spiritual, plus counselor, therapist, and psychiatrist. Livvy had never used herbs for her clients–not that she objected to it. In fact, her few years of medical school had taught her that some plant-based remedies were just as effective as some pharmaceuticals. The only problem was herbal remedies could carry side effects and potentially do as much harm as good if not well understood.

"Not all shamans have benefited from Los Angeles becoming a new mecca for shamanism," Ursula said. "For some, it has brought competition. Much competition for certain of us who practice the ways of vodun."

Livvy peered at her quizzically.

"The Haitian refugees," said Ursula.

"Oh," said Livvy, frowning. "I had no idea."

Ursula pointedly regarded the surroundings. "Ursula has no doubt."

Wait a minute. Livvy sat up straighter. *Is she saying it's because of me?* She looked at the bottle in her hands although she didn't see it. *Is it because of me?*

The last year had seemed like being in the center of a whirlwind. Livvy had never paused to consider what was happening beyond the bubble of activity around her. She looked up at Ursula who was sitting rigid, perched on the front of the chair, waiting. It had cost Ursula more than a bottle of pills to come here and ask for help. Once upon a time, the situation had been reversed.

Livvy looked back down at the pills again. She had no clue about herbs. Traditional shamans sometimes carried the knowledge of thousands of different plants and how they could be used. The natural environment could be a veritable storage locker of treatments but it was a part of shamanism in which Livvy had never participated.

It made her uncomfortable to put her name on something she didn't understand but this was Ursula. She owed Ursula. She trusted her. More than that, though, she wanted to help.

"Ursula understands if you—"

"Yes," Livvy said quickly. "I mean, sure, I can do that. I'd be glad to put my name on it."

She watched as Ursula actually closed her eyes and breathed a sigh of relief.

Gods. Things must be tough.

Livvy started to hand the jar back.

"No," said Ursula, smiling. "Keep it. A gift."

"Thank you," said Livvy, trying to sound happy, though she had no idea what she might use them for.

Ursula smiled in return and glanced down at the tea. She picked up the cup, inhaled some of the aroma, and took a sip. She didn't make a face although Livvy had the distinct impression she would have.

Ursula set the cup back down. "Refreshing," she said.

CHAPTER EIGHTEEN

UNLIKE THE BARE studio across the alley that served as headquarters, Dominique's personal studio was obviously occupied by an artist, although it wasn't her. She silently closed the door behind her. The smells of linseed oil, turpentine, and paint were thick. Light poured in through the tall, frosted windows and washed over the canvases that were everywhere.

They hung on the walls, stood on easels, and were stacked on the floor, ten deep in places. They were every size, from tiny to gigantic, all of them painted to the very edges with vibrant and bold colors. Although none of them were the same, they all had a common subject: the symbols of the transition to the Multiverse.

Dominique saw Nicole sitting on the couch, a small canvas on her lap. Except for her much shorter hair, it was like looking in a mirror. They were twins. Dominique came over and sat down on the arm of the couch.

"Let me guess," she said.

Nicole didn't say anything; didn't even pay attention. They were twins in outward appearance only. Nicole had never spoken a word in her life, nor was she a shaman.

Dominique looked down at the canvas. A bright orange spiral floated against the deep black of the background. Nicole's hand moved quickly with the brush, between the palette in one hand and the canvas in her lap, back and forth. It was a wonder she didn't splash paint everywhere, but she didn't. There was never any paint on her fingers or clothes, nor any on the floor or furniture. It was yet another thing Dominique didn't understand about her sister or the artwork.

From far away the paintings looked as though they'd been created with brush strokes. Up close it was clear that she was painting small dots–many, many thousands of small dots. Back and forth her brush went, from the palette to the canvas, over and over.

"You should see the real thing," Dominique whispered, momentarily mesmerized as she looked over Nicole's shoulder. "You'd be amazed at the goggles."

Nicole froze.

Dammit, thought Dominique, and she froze as well. That had been careless.

After several long moments, Nicole started to paint again, more slowly now, hunching over the image as though she didn't want anyone to see.

Dominique exhaled. Sometimes just the mention of the goggles was enough to send her over the edge, other times she didn't notice.

That had been a close one.

"Have you eaten today?" Dominique got up from the couch. "Let's see."

In the kitchen, the beans and rice dish that was Nicole's favorite was only half-eaten.

"You need to do better than this, Nicole," Dominique called to her across the room. "Make sure you finish this."

Dominique glanced at the counter and saw tubes of paint, plump and full, and she suddenly visualized a different kitchen, in a different country. She'd come home to find Nicole eating paint.

"Home" was putting it too kindly. They'd been on their own for a year, still in their early teens. Like the other residents of the tin city, they had a stifling little room with a dirt floor and a corrugated roof. As usual, Dominique had been out all day.

It hadn't taken her long to realize there was nothing to be stolen from the neighbors. It hadn't taken much longer to realize where food and money could be had. The only people who were well-fed and well-clothed were the foreign military. At that point, though, she had still been scrounging in their trash, lurking at the periphery. It took every waking hour to find what they needed. Even so, she didn't eat until she was with Nicole. Otherwise, it was too easy to devour it all.

When she'd arrived home, it was dark. She lit the small candle that was their only source of light and found Nicole with the tube to her mouth, squeezing it, and swallowing. She grabbed her by the hair, hauled her out to one of the open sewers and forced her to vomit.

Dominique blinked at the kitchen counter, suddenly furious. She grabbed the paint tubes. "Never in the kitchen!" she screamed.

She stomped around the end of the counter, over to a long table under the windows, and slammed them down. "How many times do I have to tell you?"

Again, Nicole hunkered low over her canvas but kept painting.

Dominique stood there clenching her fists. After a minute, she took a deep breath and opened her hands. She ran them through her hair and adjusted her coat.

Her eye fell on the stack of new white canvases near the broom closet. It was dwindling. The art supplies were expensive, but Dominique never failed to acquire them. It was her sister's only form of expression. In fact, other than sleep, it was the only thing she did. The consequences of *not* painting were severe. Nicole would either scream and thrash, hitting herself in the head, or sit in a near catatonic stupor. Dominique made sure the supplies never ran out.

Although the paintings would probably sell well, Dominique never tried to do that anymore. It hadn't gone well the first time she tried to remove one from their tiny hovel in Miami. Nicole had immediately begun to shriek.

Instead, Dominique took any shamanism job she could get, good or bad, and she'd learned to deal drugs. The money in drugs was excellent. For a while, she hadn't even practiced shamanism. Now in Los Angeles, with the advent of the lightning shaman, shamanism could pay well too, *if* you were at the top.

Dominique went back over to Nicole and stood watching her paint for a few minutes.

"Soon," she said quietly. "Soon, we won't have any worries. Liver the Lightning Shaman will be a thing of the past. You'll see. Soon, everyone will see."

CHAPTER NINETEEN

"OH YES," SAID Mamacita. "I know that one."

SK had known that if anybody knew who the dark-haired shaman in black was, it would be Mamacita. He'd come to the shop first thing, knowing it'd be open. What he didn't expect was people shopping already. He and Mamacita had gone in the back to her private office. She'd told the shoppers to ring the bell on the counter when they were ready.

She and SK sat in a small room that had a pale green cast to it from the inverted prism in the high ceiling. It caught the exterior light on the roof with its top surface and transmitted it inside, through something that resembled a pyramid. It helped to lend her office the feeling of an arboretum, though it was hardly necessary since small and large plants were everywhere. The smell of moist earth and plant life permeated the air.

Two ancient leather chairs and matching ottomans were the main pieces of furniture. Small tables and shelves held plants that weren't on the floor. For an office, it lacked any of the usual items, like a desk or filing cabinet. SK sometimes wondered if someone else handled the money side of things. As he had noted on previous visits, it was also devoid of any shaman paraphernalia whatsoever.

He had taken his usual seat on one of the ottomans, elbows on his knees, his fingers intertwined.

"Dominique," said Mamacita, peering at him over her glasses. She leaned back in one of the chairs, her hands folded over her bulging middle.

"Dominique," he repeated, thinking. "Never heard the name."

"Mmm hmm. I'm not surprised," said Mamacita, nodding. "There are a whole raft of new faces lately, some not too friendly, if you get my drift."

"I do," he said, nodding.

"Can you tell me why you're looking for this one?"

SK trusted Mamacita without reservation. He related Livvy's story, hitting the high points.

"Well I'll be damned," said Mamacita, pulling off her glasses. "They're obviously networking goggles but how are they managing to find her? That's a nice trick."

"It is a nice trick and I have no clue how it's being done."

"Well, I'm sure you know that if I knew where Dominique and her friends could be found, I'd surely tell you."

"I appreciate that, Mamacita. At least it's a start."

The faint tinkling bell at the door let them know a new customer had arrived or one had left. No one had yet rung the bell at the desk.

"Speaking of our girl," said Mamacita, slowly. "What's she up to?"

SK sat up straight. He thought of last night's date even though he knew Mamacita couldn't possibly know about that.

"What's she up to?" he echoed, not sure what she was getting at.

"Something doesn't seem quite right with her," said Mamacita, folding her hands over her tummy again and tapping her thumbs together. "I can't put my finger on it but something bothers me. Gives me a little nudge, you know?"

"Anything specific you can point to?" he asked, worried.

"Mmm, nothing specific, no," she said, shaking her head. Then she thought of something. "Well, here's her purchase tab, for example."

From memory, Mamacita rattled off a complete list of everything Livvy had bought–dates, items, and prices–for the last three months.

SK stared at her, astonished. "You memorized it?" he asked.

"Oh, no," she said and chortled a bit. "No, I don't *memorize* anything. I just remember it." She tapped the side of her head and winked.

"You just remember it," he said. "All of it. No big deal."

She nodded. "No big deal," she repeated.

SK shook his head and smiled. "You never cease to amaze, Mamacita."

"True," she said with a little grin.

"Would you mind repeating it?"

She did. A few items caught his attention

"A soul catcher?" he asked.

He knew that some traditional shamans would sometimes use this hollow bone tool to suck the evil spirit from a patient in the real world. In the Multiverse, it might be used to find a client's wandering spirit and bring it back. Livvy had no need of either, nor had he ever seen her with one.

"What could she possibly want with a soul catcher?"

"Well, I'm asking myself the same thing," said Mamacita. "And all the books. That's not all of them, mind you, only the last three months. She must have a library by now."

"Yes, she must," SK muttered.

He hadn't seen any books at her place. Why would she hide books?

"And, well…"

As Mamacita paused, SK realized he was hanging on her words. "Well what?" he asked, his voice tense.

"I don't rightly know," said Mamacita. "She seems different somehow."

SK took in a deep breath. Yes, she seemed different all right but, then again, she would to him. He cleared his throat. "Different how?" he asked.

Mamacita shook her head and frowned. "I can't hardly say. It's a feeling that's crept up on me, bit by bit. She doesn't talk to me like she used to. She doesn't smile as much either."

Mamacita pushed her hands into her lap. "Oh, listen to me," she said. "I sound like a real mother. Maybe our girl's just growing up. A lot of things have changed."

SK nodded. "A lot of things have changed," he agreed.

The bell at the counter dinged but Mamacita didn't move. Instead, she leaned forward, put her hand on his, and fixed him with a glare. "You find that dark one," she said. "And when you do, I want to know."

CHAPTER TWENTY

"YOU ENDORSED HERBS?" asked Min. She held the bottle up, a puzzled look on her face.

Ursula had chatted a little for the sake of politeness but hadn't stayed long. *Just as well.* Though it was good to see Ursula, what Livvy really wanted to do was get back to the Multiverse and see her mom.

Livvy took the two cups of tea into the kitchen. Min followed her with the bottle.

"Do you even know what's in them?"

Even though she must have slept all night, Livvy was feeling tired. The nightmare, the chills, whatever it was, she was tired.

Min unscrewed the top of the bottle.

"Min, just leave it," said Livvy, over her shoulder.

"I just want to take a peek," she said.

Livvy dumped the leftover tea in the sink, set the cups down, and opened the dishwasher.

"Gods, you'd have to be a horse to swallow one of these," said Min. "Or are you supposed to crush them?"

Livvy turned around and Min showed one to her. "Did they come with instructions?"

"Min," said Livvy, the tiredness creeping into her voice. "I don't know." Livvy rubbed her stinging eyes.

"Don't you think we'd better find out before she puts 'lightning shaman' all over everything?"

Livvy turned and picked up one of the teacups. "Min, it'll be fine. I'm sure they're fine."

"You're kidding," said Min.

"No, I'm–"

The teacup slipped out of Livvy's hand, fell into the sink and shattered, sending small shards flying. "*Dammit.*"

"Here," said Min. She put the bottle down and stepped forward. "Let me."

"Min," said Livvy, louder than she'd intended. "Just…just leave it alone."

Min stared at her for a few moments, looking like she was going to say something, but didn't.

"Look, I'm just tired," said Livvy, trying to take the edge off her tone. "I think I'm just going to lie down for a while. Okay?"

Again, Min hesitated then picked up the bottle. "Sure, Livvy," she said, putting the cap back on. "You're tired."

Livvy left the broken cup in the sink and headed toward the swinging doors. "I don't think there's any point in you staying," she said and left the kitchen. Min followed her.

Livvy went down the hallway and headed for the master bedroom. At the door, she turned to see Min looking after her, hovering, not sure what to do.

"Could you lock the door on your way out?" Livvy asked.

"Sure," said Min quietly. "I'll lock the door on the way out."

"Thanks," said Livvy.

She quickly stepped into the bedroom and shut the door behind her, leaning back against it. It hadn't been a lie. She did feel tired and a little sore and achy now that the effect from the shower had faded. She heard the front door open and close as she looked over at the goggles on her nightstand.

• • • • •

"Mom, what's wrong?"

Livvy's mom said something that she didn't quite catch.

"What?" Livvy said.

"I'm fading," her mom yelled, though to Livvy it wasn't all that loud.

Livvy knew something was wrong the minute she'd seen her worried face. Now that she was standing next to her, she could see what she was talking about. There was a sort of fuzziness, a dimming at the edges that was hard to see, but something was definitely happening.

"Maybe the summoning isn't meant to last forever," her mom

yelled.

Livvy hadn't known what to expect but this wasn't it.

She'd never given a thought to how long a summoning would last. As far as she knew, very few shamans had ever tried such a thing. In fact, she had never read the definitive case study that clearly stated a shaman had succeeded.

Now it seemed like a summoning, even if it did work, wasn't going to be permanent. Maybe it made sense. The summoning was already way beyond what was normal. Perhaps the impermanence of it was built into the mechanics of the Multiverse.

Well, that wasn't acceptable.

Livvy put her hands on her hips as they stood looking at one another.

"I could try the summoning again," suggested Livvy. The long protracted lightning strike had been difficult but she could do it again.

"What?" her mom yelled. "I can't hear you."

"I could try the summoning again," Livvy yelled.

Gods, why couldn't anything be easy? She'd done this to be with her mother. Now, she'd just be trying to make sure the summoning wasn't reversed.

Her mom shook her head and looked into her eyes. "Let me go," she slowly mouthed.

"No, Mom!" Livvy yelled. "I'll figure something out."

She'd found answers in the books and articles before. Maybe she'd missed something. She'd pore over every little detail again.

"Just try to hold on, Mom," Livvy yelled. "Please!"

Livvy watched as her mom's shoulders lifted ever so slightly, and she seemed to sigh. Then she nodded her head and smiled a little.

"I'll be back as soon as I can," Livvy yelled. "Just hold on!"

CHAPTER TWENTY-ONE

SK HAD CALLED three times before Livvy picked up.

Was she trying to avoid his calls? He wouldn't be surprised after the way he'd acted last night. In fact, he had not intended to call her today in order to let things settle down after the disaster dinner, but a former client of Carmen's was in desperate straights. After Min had finished the cancellation calls, she had phoned to let SK know the circumstances.

A year ago, Livvy had insisted she could make time for both Sunny and Carmen's patients. Despite having her own clientele, plus all the new people, SK knew better than to try and stop her. He knew she felt responsible for their clients because she still blamed herself for the deaths of the shamans who had cared for them.

"Hi, SK," he heard her say. She sounded a little groggy, like he'd woken her.

"Hi, Liv," he said simply.

There was silence.

He decided to continue. "I'm calling about one of Carmen's people," he said. "He's taken a turn for the worse."

"Okay," she said, waiting.

"Look," he said. "I haven't tracked down Dominique yet—"

"Is that her name? Dominique?"

"Yes, that's her name but I don't know where she is."

"It'll be fine," Livvy said. "I can handle this Dominique."

"Yes, I know you can because you'll have Min to help you."

There was silence on the other end.

"Liv?"

"I don't need Min's help on this, SK."

"I think you do," he said. "It'd be a network of the two of you."

Again, there was silence. This time he waited her out.

"SK, it's not necessary. It's really not."

"Liv, you're the one who asked me to find out about this other shaman and I think you're right. I think she's a problem and I'm not going to let you go to the Multiverse if there's a risk. Not even for one of Carmen's people."

"Min's not ready," she tried.

In fact, Min *was* ready. He knew so. More than that, he knew Livvy knew. Why was she fighting him on this?

He decided to ask her. "Why is this so hard?"

"It's not hard," she said quickly, then paused. "Okay, can we have Min standing by but not networked?"

She was grasping now. Why was she so desperate to leave Min out?

"Fine," he said, feeling a little angry now. "I'll call her. We'll meet at your place."

"Fine," she said, also sounding a little angry, and then the line went dead.

He looked at the phone, surprised. Had that been their first fight?

CHAPTER TWENTY-TWO

"BASED ON MY interview," said Min, "soul fragmentation."

"Self-inflicted?" asked Livvy.

"As far as I can tell."

Livvy nodded.

The three of them sat in the sedan on the curb. They had left the photographers behind at Livvy's condo. Nobody waited for them here. Unless the client's family was holding press conferences where the lightning shaman was mentioned, her schedule wasn't public knowledge. If any media had followed them, they had probably stopped when Min had taken the exit for Pacoima.

The ride over had been tense. SK must have said something to Min because she had looked between Livvy and SK at least a dozen times in the rearview mirror. For his part, SK had said nothing. He didn't fiddle with his phone either. He just looked out the window.

"Are we ready?" asked Livvy.

"All ready here," said Min.

SK opened the car door and got out.

I guess that's a yes.

She sighed and got out of the car. She knew that she and SK needed to talk but now was not the time. As usual, the needs of the client took priority.

Frankly, she was glad for it. Glad to be working again and glad to be helping somebody.

The front door to the tiny home was already open. A short, slim woman in her mid-forties greeted them in Spanish. "Gracias," she exclaimed. "Thank you so much for coming."

Although she tried to smile, her bruised and cracked lower lip made it horrifically lopsided. Livvy immediately reached out her hand. As the woman took it in both of hers, she watched the spark.

Livvy gently reached to the side of her face with her other hand.

"Did he do this?" Livvy asked in Spanish.

"He isn't himself," pleaded the woman. "He hasn't slept for three days." Then she suddenly burst into tears and hugged Livvy, burying her face in Livvy's coat.

"It's okay, Rita," said Livvy. "He's going to be okay."

Rita let go of Livvy and backed away from the front door, letting the three of them enter. The front room was immaculate. Heirloom pieces of furniture, arranged so as not to seem crowded, gave the room the feeling of another era. Juan's brother, seated on the rose-colored sofa, stood awkwardly but nobody else was there. No crowds, no onlookers, no family members. The number of people who were willing to be around Juan had dwindled over time.

A scream came from behind the closed bedroom door in the short hallway. "Stop!" they heard Juan yell. "Stop! I won't do it."

Rita suddenly turned a frightened look to Livvy. As she reached out her hand–then quickly drew it back when she realized what she'd done–Livvy realized that Rita wasn't frightened of Juan. She was afraid Livvy would leave.

"Please," she said. "He needs you."

"That's why we're here," Livvy said. "We're not leaving."

"He was like this all night too," said the brother.

Livvy nodded to him. "Wait here with Rita," she said.

"Leave me alone!" Juan screamed. Something crashed against the door.

Min jumped.

"Are you sure?" the brother asked.

"I'm sure," said Livvy.

"Rita," said SK. "Why don't you let Min take a look at your lip for you."

Rita nodded as Min gently steered her toward the kitchen.

Livvy approached the bedroom door and knocked lightly.

"Juan, it's Livvy," she said. "I'm coming in."

Livvy felt a slight pressure on her lower back and turned her head. SK was letting her know he was there. Their eyes met and Livvy breathed a sigh of relief despite the situation. He was the intercessor and he was with her. She nodded, turned back to the door and opened it.

• • • • •

Juan had jammed himself into the far corner of the bedroom. He wait on the floor next to a gleaming high top dresser, his knees drawn up to his chest. Like Rita, he was in his mid-forties and slim. He worked odd jobs, handyman, construction, in various parts of the San Fernando Valley while Rita worked as a nanny. She took long bus rides to the neighborhoods where nannies worked.

"Hi, Juan," Livvy said, as she sat cross-legged on the carpeted floor in front of him.

SK closed the door and stood in front of it. He set the mat and shoulder bag at his feet.

"They keep telling me to hurt people!" Juan screamed as he pressed his fists to his ears.

Juan had heard voices since his late teens. Sometimes they told him he was in danger, or his mother and father were poisoning his food, or his brother was going to knife him in his sleep. When the voices were particularly loud, he would hide in his room for days. Over the years, Carmen had managed to keep him together, at least enough that he could function, but it was becoming more and more difficult.

"I know," said Livvy, her voice low and non-threatening. "I'm here to help."

He turned frantic eyes on her and then SK.

"You remember, don't you Juan?" she said. "We're here to help."

The babbling erupted. "Remember! Time! Here, there, the hand, the time, remember."

This 'word salad' had gotten worse over the years. It was as though Juan was growing tired–tired of fighting the voices in his head, tired of having to keep a tight hold on himself in order to get through the day. Just tired.

He banged his forehead on his knees.

"Juan," said Livvy.

According to Rita, Carmen had thought Juan was the victim of someone's ill will. It would have been easy to make that mistake. Livvy had worked on that assumption the other time she had seen Juan. She had searched the Multiverse to find who or what might have targeted him. Although she hadn't found anything, the trip to the Multiverse seemed to have done him some good. That was months ago. Now he was banging his head.

When Rita had begged not to have her appointment canceled, Min had gotten a thorough and detailed patient history from her. Juan's problem didn't appear to be anyone's doing except Juan's. It was a classic case of soul fragmentation. Livvy hadn't seen any evidence of the fracturing in her initial visit, but it made sense.

"Juan," said Livvy, her voice calm and level. "I'm going to touch you."

He kept banging his head.

Livvy came forward, up on her knees, and slowly stretched out a hand. "Juan," she said.

Her fingers touched his hair with a small spark and he stopped moving, leaving his head on his knees. "There," she said. "That's better."

Without warning, he raised his head and grabbed her wrist with one hand, the other arm still wrapped around his knees.

"They say to hurt you," he ground out through his clenched teeth.

Livvy heard SK move behind her.

"It's okay," she said quickly, as much to SK as Juan.

He was grabbing her wrist so hard his fingernails had broken the skin.

"It's okay, Juan," she said. "I know you don't want to do that."

In response, he squeezed harder. Livvy ignored the pain, looked into his eyes, and smiled softly. His eyes went wide as he searched her face.

"No!" he screamed. "I don't want to hurt anybody." He flung her wrist aside and put his head back down on his knees.

"Good," she said, putting her hand back on his head, gently stroking his hair. "I know you don't want to hurt anybody." She moved her fingers further into his hair, massaging.

"We're going to set up some relaxing candles," she said quietly, staying in contact with him. "And the incense will help us be calm."

She heard SK open her bag.

"I don't want to hurt anybody," he whimpered. "They tell me to do it."

"I know," she whispered, matching his tone.

She moved closer to him and slid her fingers down the back of his neck, massaging, feeling the tension there release. She heard the sound of SK's lighter, then the sound of the curtains being drawn as the room darkened.

"It's the voices," he whispered, barely audible.

"I know," she said lowly. "We're going to stop the voices."

He gave a tiny nod.

"That's good," she whispered as she began massaging his shoulders. "That's good. I know you're tired." He started to slump a little. "Yes, you're tired. Very sleepy."

He slumped to the side and his arms slid down his shins. Livvy could see his face and his eyes were closed.

"It's okay to lie down," she whispered as he leaned toward the floor. "I've got you, Juan."

She moved sideways with him as he nearly fell over. She cradled his head in her hands and gently laid it on the floor.

"It's okay to sleep."

She smoothed his hair as he lie still, curled on his side, his mouth slack.

"Sleep, Juan. I'll see you on the flip side."

When she turned back to SK, her mat was already laid out, parallel to the iron frame of the antique bed. Three purple candles were lit and glowing, each on a small metal dish. A thin stick of incense leaned out over the long wooden tray meant to catch the ash, and a small wisp of smoke rose steadily from it. Livvy quickly crawled over and lay down. The goggles were plugged into the network box on the other side of the mat next to SK. He held them out to her as she leaned back.

"Back in a bit," she said, taking them.

"I'll be here," he said.

· · · · ·

In the Middleworld, the clouds above streamed along the dirt path toward the black lake, Livvy immediately headed in that direction. She began at what seemed to her an easy trot but the forest on either side of the path zoomed past, nearly a blur.

A small figure on the beach quickly grew, and in only moments she was standing with Juan. The wind she had created with her high-speed approach ruffled his shirt, and he turned around just as she was coming to a stop. He jumped back.

"Livvy!" he exclaimed. "Where did you come from?"

"From the real world, just like you," she replied.

"Oh," he said, as if that explained everything. "How do you move so fast?"

Livvy gave a little shrug, not really sure herself.

"It's a shaman thing."

He nodded and seemed about to ask another question when Livvy touched his arm.

"It's time to find your other selves."

He switched gears. "Oh, I've already started."

"You…what? You've already started?"

"Yes."

He bobbed his head quickly and pointed across a small looping inlet of the black lake. "But that guy over there won't let me come near."

Livvy followed his arm and sighted down it. There, at the edge of the water, stood another Juan. He raised his hand about waist high and waved.

"I tried to walk around the edge," said the Juan next to her. "But he keeps circling. I swear I've been around this lake fifty times."

Well, he won't be able to circle away from me.

"Give me your hand," she said.

No sooner had he placed his hand in hers then she was running at top speed. In what seemed like an instant, they were standing with the other Juan, who jumped back, his identical shirt ruffling in the wind.

"Hi, Juan," said Livvy and the first Juan in unison.

The second Juan gaped at them both and started to back away.

"No you don't," said Livvy.

She easily took him by the upper arm. If she'd wanted, she could have hefted him overhead. It was enough, though, just to keep him from leaving.

"Why don't you let me come close?" asked the first Juan of the second.

"Why should I?" said the second Juan, pouting.

"Because I'm you!" said the first Juan.

"How was I supposed to know that?" asked the second Juan. "You come running after me all the time!"

Soul fragmentation. Something in the real world had happened to

Juan, maybe when he first started showing signs of his condition in his youth. It might have been terrible, or it might have been something that only seemed terrible. It didn't particularly matter. The real Juan had splintered his spirit, cleaved it off to protect himself, to distance himself from something. Although his crisis may have passed years ago, his soul had remained fractured and, unless somebody did something, it probably always would.

"Okay, you two, enough," said Livvy, shaking them a bit.

A clap of thunder pealed across the lake and echoed from the mountains. Both Juans ducked their heads. The flashes of lightning within the clouds were reflected in the mirror surface of the lake.

"Great," said Livvy.

According to her spirit helper, there was at least one more Juan and he was in the Underworld.

"Let's go," she said as she strode toward the water.

"Where are we going?" they asked in unison.

"To get in touch with yourself."

She splashed in, dragging them with her. She drew them close to her but needn't have as they started to hug her from both sides. Thankfully, before she tripped, they had reached the swirling black waves and submerged.

As a unit, they flew from the fountain into the Underworld. Livvy landed on her feet and gripped them tightly until they could stand on their own.

"Wow," they said together.

Livvy let them go as they turned to watch the receding inverted funnel of water.

Where's Mom? Livvy searched in every direction, nearly spinning in place. *Oh gods. Has she disappeared?*

"What are you looking for?" asked one of the Juans from behind.

"Nothing."

"It doesn't look like nothing," said the other.

She turned back to them. Even though she knew Juan wouldn't remember this, she still felt compelled to lie. "I'm looking for *you.*"

Spurred to action, they began searching in every direction as she had done, which she knew was useless.

Focus. Get this done first, then look for her.

She quickly checked the direction of the clouds. "Okay Juans,"

Livvy said, as she took their arms again. "This way." Unable to keep up with her, Livvy lifted them off the ground as she ran.

The clouds above switched direction several times, navigating her to the third Juan's location. The skyscrapers of the plaza quickly gave way to shorter business buildings then utility companies, warehouses, and small factories. They were among the oldest buildings in the Underworld—brick buildings with broken windows, most one story tall. Livvy had never been in this section of the Underworld, nor did she care for it. The grime and cracks in the facades made it seem abandoned, a reminder that the living had no place here.

In seconds, they stood in front of one of the crummier places, its painted wooden sign hanging at an angle above the weathered double doors. "Juan's Boxing" the sign read. The doors creaked inward as the wind of Livvy's arrival blew past. The clouds above had come to a freeze-frame standstill.

"Boxing," said the Juans.

Self-defense, thought Livvy.

It made sense, unfortunately. This was where they were going to find the violent Juan, the one who wanted to hurt people. Suddenly, in the silence, a bell that marked the beginning of a round in a boxing match rang out from the interior.

"I think that's our cue," said Livvy, and she pushed them through the door.

● ● ● ● ●

I ought to call in Min right now. Have her plug in and make sure everything is all right in the Multiverse.

Then SK looked down at Livvy, lying on her mat.

I ought to but I said I wouldn't.

SK sat down on the floor next to her. He had checked both her and Juan and then gone around the room and unplugged everything from the wall sockets. He knew Min was outside keeping the family company. He'd told her when he called to bring her goggles and be ready for a Multiverse journey. She hadn't seemed bothered in the least about Dominique.

"I'll get to work with Livvy!" she had said, excited.

"More than likely not," he said, "but I want to be prepared."

He looked down at the network box with Livvy's goggles connected. He and Livvy had agreed that she would start out alone and Min would wait in the wings. It'd be up to him to make a judgment call based solely on what he could observe in the real world: respiration, heart rate, and any other signs of stress.

He watched Juan's even breathing; his eyes were closed as he lay on his side, as if he were simply taking a nap.

There was no reason to send Min into the Multiverse now—no reason he could put his finger on. Only a feeling of unease.

He shifted his legs a little.

He was worried about Dominique, of course, but the real worry came from Livvy. Why the resistance to Min? Why the secret books? Did they have something to do with Dominique?

Livvy's diaphragm rose and fell easily, and the pulse at her jugular was strong and steady. He looked down her length and stopped at her wrist. Even in the dark, candlelit room, he could make out the bloody fingernail marks that Juan had left.

"Oh Liv," he murmured.

He looked back at her face, calm and still.

They needed to talk but, despite being up most of the night, he still had no idea what he would say—what he *could* say. For now, it was sit and watch.

There weren't any sparks in the outlets and he knew that, for soul fragmentation, the wait might be longer. He settled in and made himself as comfortable as possible, but he couldn't help but look at the network box and then the door.

$$\bullet \bullet \bullet \bullet \bullet$$

The inside of the old building was like a giant cave. It was like every boxing ring and gym Livvy had ever seen in a movie: punching bags, free weights, and rubber mats scattered about, plus jump ropes and boxing gloves hung on the walls. The far edges of the room were dimly lit and nearly black. The only light, suspended from a single kinked electrical cord, projected a glaring circle on the boxing ring. The white and empty canvas seemed to glow in the brightness.

"I'm not going to fight," said the first Juan as Livvy dragged both Juans forward.

"Maybe we don't have to," said the second Juan.

Two stools sat in opposite corners of the ring, but they were empty. The third Juan was nowhere to be seen.

"Come on," pleaded the second Juan. "Let's go."

"Not until we've got all of you," Livvy replied, still gripping both of them.

At the edge of the ring, the overhead light spilled onto the clock and bell they had heard from outside. Livvy surveyed the room again but they seemed to be alone.

"Juan," she called. "Show yourself. I know you're here."

She waited as the two Juans next to her turned their heads in every direction.

"Juan," Livvy called. "I know you're here and I'm not leaving without you."

"We will see about that," said a deep voice from the dimness.

Livvy and the two Juans turned toward the sound as a large man emerged from behind one of the boxing bags. He dragged the third Juan by the arm, who was dressed exactly like the first two and wore a frantic look on his face, like a trapped animal.

The large man was dressed like a boxer: shiny black shorts and hightop leather shoes. He was bare chested and bronze skinned, with a thick torso, and sinewy muscles that seemed sculpted under the harsh light. His long, black hair was held in a ponytail with a large jade ring. In his earlobes he wore spools of dark green jade. Livvy watched as he strode forward toward the ring. On his chest he wore a gold pectoral glyph strung between multi-colored beads. He pulled the third Juan up a small wooden stairway and thrust him through the ropes into the ring. Then he ducked through himself, a hand to the amulet to keep it from being caught.

Juan was indeed suffering from soul fragmentation, but Carmen had been right too–Juan was under attack from a hex, one created by this Maya ancestor spirit. Some shaman had contacted him for help, help of the bad kind. With this ancestor preventing a reunion, there was no way Juan would recover. Livvy could see where this was going.

"Stay here," she said to the first two Juans, releasing them.

"No problem," they said, crouching near the opposite corner.

Livvy climbed the three steps nearest her and entered the ring.

The Maya shoved the third Juan forward.

"Fight!" he commanded.

The third Juan stood there, frozen, staring at Livvy and the two other Juans.

"I said fight!" the Maya screamed.

The third Juan jumped forward, the canvas floor reverberating like a drum, as he raised his hands in fists.

Livvy stepped toward the center of the ring, never losing eye contact with the third Juan. "No, Juan," she said quietly. "You don't have to fight."

"Fight!" bellowed the Maya.

"I have to fight," screamed the third Juan, his eyes wild with terror. "I have to!"

"No," said Livvy, shaking her head as she took another step toward him. "No, you don't. In fact, you can't. This isn't between you and me."

"It's not?" he asked, confused.

"No," she said coming closer. "It was between you and your other selves," she motioned her head behind her.

The third Juan looked at the first two.

"She's right, you know," said the second Juan.

Livvy came to a stop in the center of the ring, directly in front of the third Juan. Slowly, she reached out her hand and put it on top of his front fist. "You can't fight me," she said. "You'd never win."

She easily pressed his fist downward although he struggled mightily to keep it up. He stared at his fist as though it wasn't his to control. She tightened her grip on it, making him wince as he bent his knees to move lower. But rather than force him to the canvas, she moved him to the side and then back behind her.

"Fight, you coward!" bellowed the Maya as he crouched low.

The ropes vibrated in sympathy.

"Wait with the other Juans," said Livvy, not turning to look as she released him.

She heard and felt his steps retreat on the canvas.

"He will fight," said the Maya as he took a step forward. "He will have no choice when you are dead."

Livvy tensed and matched his stance. Inside the building, calling down lightning would not be a great option. The lightning would come because it had to, but it would have to pass through the roof to do so. The roof would probably catch fire and debris would rain down on them. The Maya began to circle left. Livvy did the same. Instead of lightning, she would have to trust her innate shamanic power and her ever-growing speed. The two together ought to be enough.

He lunged at her, aiming to wrap her up in a bear hug but, as she suspected, she was much too fast for him, as though he were moving in slow motion. She danced away.

"Coward," he growled. "Fight."

He bared his teeth and Livvy saw they had been inlaid with jade and filed to points.

"I will kill you!" he yelled. "And then the gods will feast on your heart!"

Again he lunged at her but this time he anticipated her escape. As Livvy skipped to the side, his outstretched hand caught her jacket and there was a ripping sound.

That was close.

Livvy backpedaled. The ring wasn't as big as it seemed and the Maya had a very long reach. Whatever she did, she could not allow him to lay a hand on her. That could be trouble. She ought to have the strength to overpower him, but she didn't particularly want to find out. All she really needed to do was incapacitate him.

He began to run backwards, speedily shuffling his feet until his back met the ropes. He stretched them outward and paused, and then he caromed off to Livvy's right. She moved left as he gained speed, bouncing off the ropes again, without pausing. Together their feet were drumming out a constant pounding. Livvy sped across the ring to see him pass in back of her. He rebounded yet again, gaining momentum.

She waited to see if he'd go left or right, but he came directly at her instead. Although she had thought to continue moving with her momentum, now she reversed direction. In that small fraction of a second, he reached behind his back and something flashed is his right hand, something dark and glittering.

The Juans all screamed together, "Look out!"

Livvy spun away at the last second. She continued left but felt something bite into the front of her right shoulder. The Maya was continuing to bounce off the ropes and, rather than look down at her shoulder, Livvy watched his hand. He was holding a large obsidian knife, hafted with a leather strip to a large bone handle. He switched hands and was running now.

Enough of this.

"Get down!" she yelled at the Juans and reached a hand toward the sky.

"Wind," she yelled.

Every window shattered instantly and the front door blew off its hinges as a hurricane level wind surged into the building. In her peripheral vision, she saw one of the Juans trying to climb into the ring as the others tried to stop him. He was panicking.

"No," she yelled to him.

She kept her left arm up as the wind continued to scream past. Juan would be blown along with it if he didn't stay below the ring.

"Stay back," she yelled, motioning with her other hand.

Without warning, she felt a thud in the front of her right shoulder and turned back in time to see the Maya flying past her, carried by the wind.

As she kept her left hand raised, Livvy staggered back and looked down. The bone handle protruded from her coat where the knife was buried to the hilt. A dark red stain began to spread.

• • • • •

In the real world, Livvy's breathing was quicker and heavier. Beads of sweat had appeared on her forehead.

SK tensed.

He looked at Juan, who hadn't stirred and, if anything, seemed more restful. He looked back at Livvy and then the wall sockets. They were completely dark.

Where's the lightning? What's going on?

• • • • •

"Wind," Livvy said again, between clenched teeth.

The folding chairs around the ring flew through the air and crashed into the opposite wall. The Maya was pinned against the ropes across from her, his pectoral amulet gone. He shielded his face from flying debris and the pressure of the still growing gale. The ropes looked stretched to the breaking point.

Livvy struggled to stay upright against the wind at her back, her hair and clothes whipped forward. With her free hand she reached up and clasped the bone handle of the obsidian knife, now slick with her own blood. She gave it a quick jerk and screamed but pulled the blade clear. She held it in front of her and then tossed it away.

Instead of landing on the canvas, the knife instantly weathervaned in the air stream and shot forward. It flew through the air as though guided by a wire and struck the Maya in the center of his chest. To Livvy's horror, it didn't stop there. It burrowed in and disappeared entirely. No blood flowed from the wound. Livvy soon realized a stream of red was blowing out the Maya's back and spraying onto the far wall. Suddenly, the knife impaled itself in the center of the red splatter along with a human heart.

She lowered her arm and the wind immediately died. Without its pressure, she stumbled backward and leaned heavily into the ropes. Everything the wind had pinned to the far wall fell to the floor in clangs and clatters.

The Maya, without the wind to prop him up, pitched forward and landed on his knees. He stared down at his chest and then up at Livvy as though he were going to ask a question. Instead, his mouth froze and he fell forward with a booming thud on the canvas.

There were several moments of silence and then the end-of-round bell dinged once.

Livvy looked down and saw the three Juans there, grinning up at her, one of them with his hand on the lever.

"Outside," she breathed, holding her throbbing shoulder.

They waited for her at the bottom of the short steps and followed her outside to the street.

Livvy immediately checked the clouds above. They were still frozen. There were no more Juans to be found. *Good*, she thought, looking down at the spreading bloodstain on the front of her coat. It hadn't been the best Multiverse journey.

"Are you going to be all right?" asked one of the Juans.

"That looks pretty serious," said another.

In the real world, it'd be deadly, she thought. *In the Multiverse, it just hurt. A lot.*

"I'm going to be fine," she reassured them. "But the sooner we can get this done the better."

They all nodded in unison.

"Okay you three," she said. "Stand together."

They bunched together in front of her.

"Turn and face each other."

They obeyed as the one in front did an about face and the other two angled toward the center.

From deep within the clouds that had begun to churn, thunder pealed. The trio looked up.

"I want you to stay absolutely still," she said, causing them all to look back down at each other. "No matter what you see, feel, or hear, it's very important that you not move. Have you got it?"

They nodded in unison, accidentally butting their heads.

"Okay," she said. "Let's do this."

She raised her right arm to the sky, checked the Juans one last time, and looked upward. "Lightning," she said.

The blazing bolt of electricity burst from the middle of the swirling mass above and landed directly on her hand. As usual, the energy of it flooded through her, down her body and into the ground. She began to reach up her other hand toward the trio and moved forward. As though she were engaged in a stately minuet, she raised her one arm and simultaneously lowered the other, curving them both into wide semi-circles.

The lighting arced in a circular loop from one hand to the other, encompassing the Juans. The light from it lit their faces, and the static discharge blew around them like a dust devil.

Slowly and deliberately, Livvy inched closer to them and drew the circle of light tighter. The Juans shuffled their feet forward, pressing against each other. Almost close enough to hug them, Livvy drew them into an ever smaller circle. The ring of lightning was building to an incandescent white that made them shut their eyes.

Then, they started to blend.

Bathed in the brilliant glow of the surrounding energy, the arms at their sides started to blur, melding into single thick arms between them.

Livvy tightened the circle.

The arms disappeared, absorbed into their ribs as the bodies compressed. Their legs began to combine as the arms had done. A thick single torso emerged in the center. Finally, the three heads met in the middle, faces pointed inward.

Livvy drew her arms in tighter around the misshapen figure and felt the resistance of the energy. With steadily increasing pressure, she made the brightening circle smaller, pulled the body closer, and was almost able to grasp her hands together. Finally, the three heads collapsed into one with a popping sound. She wrapped Juan up in a crushing hug and felt his body squirm in its last fit of transformation. Then he became still.

The lightning ended with a final burst and vanished. She was looking at just the one Juan. Livvy carefully let him go and backed away.

He blinked several times and looked down at his body. "Is it… me?" he asked.

Livvy smiled. "Yes, it's you, Juan. How do you feel?"

"Good," he said. Then he nodded and grinned. "Yes, real good." He inhaled deeply. "Like my old self."

Livvy smiled at him. "Good. Then, it's time to go."

"So soon?" came a woman's voice from behind her.

Livvy turned around, fairly certain of who would be there. What she saw when she turned around, though, made her move Juan behind her. There were more shamans this time.

"Dominique," Livvy said, not letting go of Juan.

Dominique seemed surprised. "I'm flattered that the Lightning Shaman would know my name."

Several spirit helpers had already arrived for the assembled group: a Galapagos turtle stood in their midst, a vulture perched nearby on one of the buildings, and a lynx curled around the legs of one of the women. She didn't recognize any of the new ones. The two from the previous time weren't with her.

A hawk of some kind swooped down to land on the gloved forearm of one of the shamans. As before, Dominique stood in the back, no spirit helper apparent.

Livvy quickly ran over her options. The one with wind wasn't here so she could try that. She could also call down lightning and get it over with. Or she could just get her client out of here and be done. With blood trickling down her arm and knowing Min was standing by, time was running out.

She opted for being done.

Without a word, still gripping Juan, she spun them both around and ran. The shamans, the street, and the old section of downtown rapidly disappeared behind her. Livvy had no idea what they had planned but she wasn't waiting to find out. The skyscrapers blurred to the left and right and in only moments she was at the fountain.

Unfortunately, now that she was here, she could see what they had planned. The two shamans who had been with Dominique the first time were waiting.

• • • • •

SK paced from Livvy to the door and then back again. The electricity had already surged, the rivulets of blue energy had snaked their way out of the sockets, and SK had watched to make sure neither Juan nor Livvy would be electrocuted.

Then it had stopped.

Livvy's breathing had returned to normal and that should have been the end of it.

But it wasn't.

The incense had gone out and the candles were getting low.

He crouched down next to the network box. He glanced at the wall sockets.

"What's going on, Liv?" he said, watching her.

He waited, as though for an answer.

Enough of that.

He stood up and went to the door, quietly turning the knob. Min got up from the couch where she'd been sitting with Rita.

"Bring your goggles," he whispered.

• • • • •

"Your squad is not enough," said the heavy one who could produce quakes. She and the spiky redhead stood between Livvy and the fountain.

The quake shaman jutted her chin out behind Livvy and to the left. At first, Livvy thought she might think Juan was a shaman, but when she glanced behind her, she saw her mom.

Although she had wanted to scream the word "mom," she managed to stop herself in time. No wonder she hadn't seen her earlier. She was partially transparent now.

Oh Mom!

She was trying to say something to Livvy and pointing at the other shamans.

Livvy held out a hand to her in an emphatic stop gesture and, thankfully, her mom stopped.

The hawk and the vulture soared over them and perched nearby. The other shamans wouldn't be far behind. The ones here already knew they couldn't stop her but they were blocking her only means of leaving the Underworld. They didn't have to stop her, just delay her. She turned quickly to her mother and took Juan by the waist.

Livvy pointed directly at her mother's chest and mouthed "You." Then she pointed at a nearby building. "Go." Her mom looked at her and then the building, frowned, and shook her head no. Livvy quickly repeated the gestures.

"You. Go. Now."

They locked gazes.

"Please," Livvy implored silently.

Her mom glanced at the shamans behind Livvy and the growing number of spirit helpers. Finally, she nodded. Livvy watched her for a couple of moments as she ran toward the building.

Without warning or turning around, Livvy reached a hand to the sky. "Lightning," she said.

A crashing thunder peal rattled the plaza. Windows reflected light in jittery waves and birds took flight. The lightning erupted on top of her hand. The other arm still gripped Juan. Livvy looked down at him.

He was grinning wildly, elated at the feeling of energy that surged through them both. She put her mouth next to his ear. "When I say now, extend your arms."

She didn't wait for his response but whirled them both around and yelled, "Now!"

As instructed, he pointed both his arms in front of him as Livvy charged forward. Holding him around the middle, she aimed him like he was a cannon.

Lightning leapt from his hands and struck at two points along the ground as they headed directly for the water. As they moved forward, two lines of small craters were burned into the pavement like two paths of giant, black, smoking steppingstones. They led toward the locations of the two shamans.

With only seconds to spare, each of them leapt aside to avoid being incinerated.

The redhead scrambled to her feet. "Wind," she screamed but it was too late.

With one, long and soaring leap, Livvy and Juan landed in the fountain.

• • • • •

As soon as she surfaced, Livvy realized she wasn't alone in the black lake. Hands reached out to help her. It was Min.

They both dragged Juan to the shore where he collapsed to his knees. Livvy was breathing hard and bent over to catch her breath.

"SK sent me," said Min. "I was just about to submerge."

Livvy could only nod.

She'd been right. Time had almost run out. Another minute and Min would have been in the Underworld, seen the other shamans, and worse, seen her mother.

Livvy stood up and looked down at Juan, who seemed completely drained, not even noticing Min.

"Livvy, what happened to your shoulder?" Min asked, alarmed.

"Ancestor spirit," Livvy finally managed, then she looked down at it.

The pain there had turned into a dull thrumming but even through the wet clothes, the stain was still spreading.

"I think we'd better get out of here," Min said, helping Juan to his feet.

"Sounds good to me," Livvy agreed.

• • • • •

Livvy started to reach up to remove her goggles, but the pain in her shoulder stopped her. She sucked in a quick breath.

"Liv, what is it?" she heard SK ask.

"My shoulder," she exhaled. "Can you get the goggles?"

She felt his fingers around the padded edges of the goggles and saw the light of the room once he lifted them away. She blinked at the ceiling and saw SK's concerned face. She tried to sit up.

"Just stay there for a second," said SK, and she felt his hand on her arm.

She lay back down with a thud.

"Did she say her shoulder?" Livvy heard Min ask.

"Yes," said SK. "What happened?"

"Here, let me take a look," said Min and her face appeared. "I'm going to move your coat aside. Let me know if it hurts."

Gently, Min lifted the lapel of her silver coat and looked underneath.

"Oh gods, Livvy, you're bleeding," she said.

"*Bleeding?*" SK said, moving closer, his voice tense. "How much? How is that possible? What happened over there?"

"I don't think it's much," said Min. "Most of it's dry, actually."

"Ancestor spirit," said Livvy. "It turns out Carmen was right. Soul fragmentation too. Anyway, he managed to plant an obsidian knife in my shoulder."

Livvy looked down at the area as Min lifted the edge of her V-neckline and pulled gently back. While not nearly the size of the wound in the Multiverse, there was still a one-inch gash where the knife had been. It had already started to clot, but her shirt had a fist-sized red blotch on it.

"It's okay," said Livvy. "The pain is already subsiding."

"Like hell, it's okay," said SK.

Then the headache started.

"Tissue?" Livvy whispered, knowing what would be next. Min fetched it from her bag and Livvy quickly put it to her nose.

Then she heard Juan stir behind Min. "What's going on?" he said, his voice thick and groggy.

"Help me up," Livvy whispered, wiping at her nose.

She sat up on her mat, flanked by the two of them, one on each arm as support. Juan was sitting up as well. He glanced around the room at the three faces.

"I don't understand," he said.

"How do you feel?" Livvy asked, ignoring the headache, though she had to sniff.

"I feel fine," he said, without thinking. He paused. "No, actually," he said, slowly. "I feel better than fine. I feel great!"

It must be the lingering aftereffect of the lightning she had channeled through him, she thought. No doubt he felt good.

"Am I cured?" he asked, looking at each one in turn.

"Any voices?" asked Livvy.

He listened and looked at the ceiling then bowed his head as though he were trying to hear something faint.

Livvy and Min exchanged looks.

Finally, Juan raised his head.

"Nothing," he said, grinning. "Not a thing."

Livvy nodded and smiled. "Then you're cured," she said.

"Then it's time for us to go," said SK.

CHAPTER TWENTY-THREE

"WHAT KIND OF crew was that?" Pipsqueak asked as Dominique took off her goggles.

Dominique ignored her. Since her question had lacked the 'ma'am' at the end, she knew Pipsqueak wasn't addressing her. She hardly heard her anyway as she seethed over the missed opportunity—even with the tactical advantage. Maybe new shamans were in order. These ones obviously weren't up to the task.

From where she was sitting, with her mat at the front and at a right angle to the rest, Dominique looked sideways at her squad. Pipsqueak was a decent shaman but mostly around for her electronic skills. She got to her feet.

"No worries though," Pipsqueak said to Tambourine. "She ran. Kind of weird how we could see through her." She picked up her water bottle and took a drink.

"Repeat that," Dominique demanded.

Most of the other shamans in the room would have stammered but Pipsqueak had been with her long enough. In a monotone that nearly sounded like a robot, she repeated herself. "No worries though. She ran. Kind of weird how we could see through her."

"See through who?"

"There was a woman with her," Pipsqueak said. "I thought it was another shaman. We both did."

Dominique glanced at Tambourine, who was nodding, then focused back on Pipsqueak.

"Who was she?"

"I don't know. The lightning shaman said something to her, or did sign language with her or something, and she ran off."

Dominique stared hard at Pipsqueak. "You're sure."

"Yes, ma'am."

Dominique looked over to Tambourine, who was still nodding.

The full water bottle in Dominique's hand crackled and it started to leak from the cap.

As Pipsqueak fetched paper towels, Dominique watched the drops without seeing them and nodded silently to herself.

There was more to Liver than she had imagined.

CHAPTER TWENTY-FOUR

SK WAITED, ARMS crossed, his foot tapping out an impatient staccato. He stood with Nacho in front of the sliding glass door that led to the rooftop garden.

Min had insisted on putting a bandage over the nearly healed wound on the front of Livvy's shoulder. As inexplicably as the gash had appeared, it was now almost gone.

First, the unwelcome visits from Dominique, thought SK, *now something in the real world that should have stayed in the Multiverse.*

Something was changing.

Although Min had only just arrived in the Middleworld when Livvy had emerged with Juan from the black lake, she hadn't reported seeing any other shamans or anything unusual. That, at least, was good. Min had asked about the upcoming appointment with Claire and whether it would be canceled.

That was going to be a problem.

"Let's wait on that," he said. "Why don't you go home, get some rest."

Worried about Livvy, Min had wanted to stay, but SK simply said he needed to talk to Livvy, alone.

"I understand," Min said.

SK was pretty sure that she didn't.

Livvy was tugging down the sleeves of the blouse she'd just put on when she came back into the living room.

"Where's Min?" she asked.

"She's gone home," SK said. "I'll give her a call later."

"Oh," said Livvy, sounding surprised.

"We need to talk," he said.

She lowered her gaze to the floor. "Oh," she whispered.

Livvy had stopped at the edge of the living room, as though she were afraid to enter. When in doubt, she bit her lower lip. Sometimes when she did that, she was worried about something serious, a client usually. Sometimes, she was just trying to pick the type of tea she'd order. SK had never mentioned it to her, afraid that she might stop. It let him know when she was unsure. It was also kind of charming. She was biting her lower lip now.

"It's all right," he said, even though he knew it wasn't. "Why don't you sit down."

"I can do that," she said but didn't look up.

She stepped past the two chairs and coffee table and curled up on the far end of the couch. She drew a pillow in front of her and finally turned her eyes to him, on nearly the same level. Nacho jumped on the couch next to her and Livvy absently stroked his back.

Although the sky was overcast, the sun had found a small gap at the horizon as it was setting. Behind SK, a warm red glow flooded through the glass doors. As Livvy waited for him to say something, he found himself mesmerized, as though it had been ages since he'd seen her in sunlight. Her hair took on a faint orange tint and the green of her eyes brightened. She looked directly into the sunset for a moment, intensifying the effect, and then back to SK.

He remembered her in the restaurant. It was so easy to stop thinking of her as a shaman. All these months trying to deny how attractive she was—it suddenly seemed like a weight he'd been carrying. He had set it down, briefly, but it was time to pick it up again. He put his hands in his pockets and began casually.

"Min says she met you in the Middleworld," he said.

Livvy nodded. "I was just bringing Juan out of the black lake," she confirmed.

"You say there was an ancestor spirit involved."

"Yeah, Min was right about soul fragmentation—there were three Juans—but it turns out Carmen was right about the ancestor spirit after all."

Livvy recounted the story of the Maya warrior and the obsidian blade. SK listened and watched as she relaxed, looking more comfortable than he'd seen her all day. She rubbed the front of her shoulder when she described the fight.

"I have no idea why it should have manifested in the real world," she said. "I didn't think that was possible."

"It shouldn't be," he said. "How's your shoulder?"

"You know, I hardly feel it anymore."

"How's your wrist?"

Livvy ran her fingers over the bruises there. "Oh it's fine," she said, not looking at it. "He didn't want to hurt me."

"And what about Dominique?"

The sudden turn in conversation had surprised her, as intended. Her face changed immediately, her expression guarded. "What about her?" she asked.

"Did she appear in the Underworld?"

"No," Livvy said quickly. "I didn't see her."

She was lying. SK was certain of it. He crossed his arms over his chest and looked at the floor. Why would she lie about it? She had been the one to ask for his help. Why keep it from him now?

He looked up at her. Maybe there was another way to get at the truth.

"Why the resistance to Min?"

Again, she seemed surprised. "I'm not resisting Min," she countered. "Min was there."

"She was there because I decided to add her, but she should have been there from the start."

"She would have confused things," said Livvy. "Gotten in the way."

They locked eyes for a moment.

"Liv," he said simply, but the one word said a lot.

She had been the one to network goggles for the first time. Livvy knew better than anybody how shamans could help one another in the Multiverse.

"I work better alone," she said, looking away.

So transparent. Does keeping Min at a distance have something to do with Dominique?

He wasn't getting anywhere with either line of questions.

He paused and took a deep breath, taking care to soften his voice. "About the other night," he said, as he stared hard at his shoes.

He wanted to strike the right tone, something completely neutral, right down the middle. They both needed to regain their balance and maybe some distance too. Finally, he looked up at her.

The last rays of the setting sun were glinting, positively dancing, in her eyes. Startled, he saw they were filling with tears. She clutched the pillow in front of her like it was a life preserver and he felt his chest tighten. Whatever words he had been about to say caught in his throat.

"SK, I'm sorry," she said, her voice trembling and low. "I am so, so sorry."

As neutral as he had hoped to be, she was the complete opposite. She was more than sorry. Never able to hide what she was feeling, raw emotion filled her voice. "Sorry" didn't even come close to what it expressed.

Suddenly, SK found himself standing at the end of the couch, directly in front of her.

How had that happened?

He reached a hand out to her arm and a bright blue spark popped. Without hesitation, he reached up and touched the soft skin of her cheek. He looked directly into her eyes, the pupils expanded as if with surprise. Her lips parted as if she might say something. Fearing that she might, he closed the distance. His hand slipped behind her ear and then her neck. He drew her gently forward as he leaned in. For a moment, he paused, as he realized what he was doing.

Then, his lips were on hers–the sensation, magnetic. Her lips were soft and warm and for an instant he thought he smelled… rain. She responded to him in slow motion, as though she too had just realized what was happening. She kissed him back lightly, but a rush of emotions jolted through him.

He knew Livvy, sometimes better than she knew herself, but this–this other side to her–he had not suspected. He closed his eyes and imagined the moment never ending, inhaled the fragrance of rain, and felt the silky smoothness of her lips.

Finally, with more effort than should have been necessary, he slowly drew back and felt the last lingering brush of her lips against his. He opened his eyes.

Her eyes were still closed and he watched in fascination as a small furrow appeared between her eyebrows. He gently smoothed it with a finger before letting her go and she eventually opened her eyes. For several long moments, they stayed like that, just looking at one another. He saw a hint of confusion in her face and realized he probably looked the same.

He certainly felt confused. Surely kissing her had not been what he'd intended.

Had it?

A smile gradually formed on her lips, matched by his own. He slowly backed up. Rather than risk a word that might ruin this moment, this phenomenal feeling, he simply walked to the front door and left.

CHAPTER TWENTY-FIVE

LUCKILY, THIS WOMAN had never seen Dominique or the shaman that she'd brought with her this time. As she'd expected, the woman was loitering in the plaza–waiting for Liver to return. Only Pipsqueak and Tambourine had seen her or been seen.

Even so, the woman immediately started to back away.

Dominique quickly held up the necklace, a silver chain with an amethyst crystal pendant. Then showed her what she held in the other hand by opening her fingers to reveal three, small, irregularly shaped balls resting in her palm. She offered them to the woman.

When the woman stopped and looked at them, Dominique offered them again, raising them a little higher. "For you," she mouthed.

She turned to the other shaman. "Get the torch ready."

Although the fading woman hadn't come forward, she had stopped backing away and was watching them. Dominique had guessed that one amethyst pendant would look like any other.

The other shaman took the tall torch, which was already burning, raised it up as high as she could, and then impaled the bottom into the ground. She tentatively released it, making sure it didn't topple, and then turned her weaselly face up to Dominique and backed away.

Dominique turned toward the fading woman, flashed her practiced smile, and beckoned her forward, still holding out the three balls. "For you," she mouthed again. "Come."

The woman hesitated, looked at the crystal Dominique held, and took a few steps forward.

"Yes," Dominique said and beckoned her closer.

Only a few paces away, Dominique held up her hand to stop, which the woman did. She was starting to take orders well.

The first ball was white or, to be more precise, the color of bleached bone, since that's precisely what it was. In the real world, she had crushed the chicken bones in a mortar and then used drippings from the roasting pan as a binder, rolling the mush into a ball. She deftly popped it into the torch where it sparkled briefly, causing the flame to rise higher and smoke to pour from it. Dominique fanned it lightly and the smoke drifted in languid, curved tendrils toward the faded woman. They gently washed over her as she closed her eyes.

The second ball was black, the charred remains of a cremation that Dominique had bought from a funeral home employee for the price of a few packets of crack. It went into the torch with a slight pop and sizzle that brightened the flame and sent a wave of dense smoke over to the woman. As Dominique watched, the woman's entire body slowly took on a darker hue, as though she were absorbing the particles. She was no longer transparent.

The third and most important ball was, of course, red. This blood, though it hadn't required trade, had cost Dominique personally. Rather than dwell on it, she immediately put it into the flame and watched as it began its work.

The torch flared high and bright, coloring them all with its intense ruby glow. The heavy smoke drifted directly to the woman's head and cascaded down the rest of her body. Like a silky veil, it slowly fell away, revealing the woman, eyes still closed, as though she were actual flesh.

"Welcome back," said Dominique.

The woman's eyes popped open at the sound of her voice and Dominique stared at them. She'd seen eyes that color of green only once.

"I heard you," exclaimed the woman.

"And I heard you," replied Dominique.

The woman looked down at her hands and the rest of her body. "I can't believe you did that," she said. Even her voice sounded familiar.

"Did Livvy send you?" she asked, looking from Dominique to the other shaman. "Is she all right? Will she be here soon?"

The voice, the face, the movements—she was an older version of Liver. They *had* to be related. An older sister perhaps? No. Her concern for Liver seemed more than that and she was too many years older.

It was her mother.

"No, no, and no," Dominique said, in answer to the questions.

The woman looked confused and then worried. Far-off thunder rang from somewhere beyond the skyscrapers, and Dominique looked that way. Had Liver come back? She hadn't realized how dark the sky had become. It was completely covered in clouds and small flashes of lightning were appearing in the distance.

When she looked back to the woman, she was staring at the sky as well.

Dominique quickly glanced at the weasel-faced shaman, who waited with an eager look on her face. Dominique nodded. Time to be done.

CHAPTER TWENTY-SIX

THE STREAM OF customers was non-stop today. The door had not stopped chiming. There were a couple of young women reading in the book section and another browsing among the clothes. Mamacita casually glanced up to greet the newest arrival. Disbelief was her first reaction but then quick understanding. The lay of Los Angeles had just changed.

The dwarf took a moment to fold up his umbrella and leave it in the bin next to the front door with the others. His small hand lightly brushed a few drops of rain from the top of his shoulders.

"Hello, Mamacita," he said as he approached.

"Mayet," said Mamacita.

"The years do not touch you," he said with a hint of a French accent, smiling. "And it has been…a few, since I last saw you."

Mamacita smiled pleasantly back at him, aware that the customers were now listening and watching.

"Yes, a few," she agreed.

Pete came to the front of his cage to get a closer look.

"Pete?" asked Mayet, surprised.

Pete was short for Repeat and he was only the latest in a line of identical white cockatiels. As they aged and passed on, Mamacita replaced them and gave them the same name.

"So to speak," intoned Mamacita.

"Ah," he said.

Mayet stood a few inches shorter than SK and was older. His balding head was shaved close but his salt-and-pepper goatee was full. He was dressed in a brown business suit and was carrying a compact metal attaché case, as though he'd stepped off a commuter train.

"It seems unseasonably wet outside," he ventured. "I had heard it never rained here."

"Well, the weathermen just never seem to get it right," she said, keeping her tone amiable.

"How like France then," he offered.

He laid his gleaming case on the counter between them, looked her directly in the eye, and waited.

Oh, yes. Los Angeles is changing—and not for the first time.

It had been bound to happen and she always had her part to play.

But so soon?

"May I ask you to leave your cards?" she said.

He slowly inclined his head toward her, a look of satisfaction on his face, his eyes never straying from hers.

Rather than reply, he unlatched the two locks on the case and opened it. From it, he removed a carved wooden business card holder and a short stack of business cards, black with silver lettering—only his name and a phone number, a Los Angeles number. He set the cards in the holder and slid them to the middle of the counter.

Mamacita then slid them next to the cash register, facing out.

Mayet closed his briefcase, removed it, and glanced around. Everyone was looking at him, as expected. He looked back to Mamacita.

"It is good to see you again, Mamacita," he said and smiled.

Although she nodded once and smiled back, she couldn't quite bring herself to say the same thing.

CHAPTER TWENTY-SEVEN

LIVVY LOOKED UP from the latest book as Nacho coiled around her ankles. She had been in the walk-in closet for hours poring over every scrap of information on summoning that might help her to understand what to do for her mother's fading in the Multiverse. The answer, though, was becoming painfully clear.

There was no answer.

The dark arts weren't something you typically read about in books. It'd taken her months just to get this far. She replaced the book on the shelf, sighed and picked up Nacho.

"What am I going to do?" she whispered into the soft fur on the top of his head.

He'd been hovering nearby ever since SK had left.

SK.

Her mind wandered back to him and the kiss for the hundredth time.

Livvy didn't know how long she had remained sitting on the couch after he had left. Too stunned to move, she had barely been aware of him leaving. When she had finally gotten up, she was stiff and it was completely dark outside. She had even teetered at the edge of the couch when she stood up and had to sit back down for a second, more tired than she'd realized.

He had kissed her—the moment that she had envisioned repeatedly, yet now she could barely recall it. Only a vague warm glow remained.

Nacho squirmed in her arms because she'd frozen.

"Sorry, Nacho," she said and let him jump down.

She closed the built-in linen cabinet at the end of the closet and thought of her mom. Her fingers lingered on the knobs as the sinking feeling in her stomach finally reached bottom.

"Mom," she whispered.

According to the few instances where summonings had been described to researchers, it was barely considered possible. There was no information at all about the aftermath.

Maybe it'd be possible to summon her again, once she'd gone–but Livvy didn't want her to go. That was the problem. That had been the whole point.

She shook her head and backed away from the cabinet.

It wasn't doing any good to stand here and debate it. Time was running out.

• • • • •

"Livvy!"

Livvy heard her before she saw her.

"I've been waiting for you!"

Livvy barely had time to process what she was seeing before her mom was hugging her. She heard the water of the fountain splashing down behind her as she felt her mom's familiar embrace.

"Mom!"

How this could be she didn't know, but at that moment she didn't care. She held her mom tight and closed her eyes. "Mom," she said into her hair.

A rumble overhead broke the quiet of the moment and Livvy opened her eyes. She had meant to stand back and start peppering her mom with questions when a strange movement in her peripheral vision caught her eye. She glanced over, still holding her mom. It was just an ancestor spirit.

She was about to look away when she realized something was wrong. The ancestor spirit, a middle-aged Asian woman in a saffron wraparound robe was staring at them and heading in their direction. In all her time in the Multiverse, Livvy had never had an ancestor spirit approach her.

Not every dead predecessor became an ancestor spirit. Only the most venerated and powerful of elders managed to take up a permanent residence in the Underworld–a vanishingly small percentage. They came from all time periods and places and Livvy had often marveled at their appearances. But since they weren't her ancestors and went about their own business, they typically passed her by without so much as a glance. In fact, she often felt as though she didn't really exist for them.

"Livvy," her mom said. "Is this a friend of yours?"

Livvy had been about to reply and say that this was an ancestor spirit except her mom hadn't turned around. Livvy let her mom go and spun to look in the opposite direction. Another ancestor spirit was approaching–a tall, bearded, blond gentleman in a black suit. In fact, as Livvy and her mother turned, ancestor spirits were emerging from every street and alley surrounding the plaza. Unhurried and almost stately in their march, they came nearer.

"I don't understand," her mom said.

"Me either, Mom. Stay close."

She had hardly needed to tell her since her mom was already clinging to her arm.

Livvy had never imagined so many ancestor spirits existed. The plaza was filling with them. The crowd was becoming so dense that Livvy couldn't see through it. Without bumping each other and without a sound, they steadily approached, their eyes fixed on… her. It wasn't her and her mom, Livvy realized, now that she could really see their eyes. It was only her.

"Okay, Mom," Livvy said lowly. "Let go now and give me a little space."

She felt her mother's grip lessen and then fall away. Livvy stepped away from her. If the ancestor spirits had business with her, then let it be with her. She might also need room to call down lightning.

"What do you want?" Livvy called out.

Muted thunder rumbled up above but none of the ancestor spirits looked up or made a reply. Instead, they continued to stare at her and approach.

"Just tell me what you want," Livvy tried again.

They were completely surrounded. The ever constricting circle of faces moved closer.

"Livvy, what's going on?" her mom asked, panic in her voice now.

"I don't know, Mom," Livvy said without looking at her. "Just stay back."

Livvy raised her hand to the clouds where muted bursts of light flashed as though from a giant softbox. Unfortunately, the ancestor spirits took no notice.

"I'm warning you," Livvy yelled, though she had no intention of giving them more time.

"Lightning," she said.

And waited.

Nothing happened.

She jerked her face upward and stared at the sky. The mass of clouds was thick and churning, as usual, with lightning arcing within but—was it a trick of the light? Livvy squinted. Was the darkest part of the mass separating, like an enormous dividing cell? No. The clouds flowed one way and then another. It was just the chaotic and random movement of the stationary storm.

What in the Multiverse?

Lightning had *never* failed her.

"Livvy?" her mom said, her voice trembling.

Livvy whirled toward her but couldn't see her in the crowd. "*Mom?* Mom, where are you?"

A hand was waving over the tops of heads, about five people back but moving further away. The crowd was flowing around her, centering on Livvy. The crush of the growing number of bodies between her and her mom was forcing them apart. The only unoccupied part of the plaza was directly behind her, in front of the fountain.

"Mom, are you okay?" she yelled, beginning to back up.

"I'm fine but I can't see you. Are you all right?"

"Yeah," Livvy answered, though she was far from sure.

What had happened to the lightning?

She couldn't help but look to the sky as she backpedaled. The energy of the lightning within the clouds could hardly be contained. Why didn't it come down?

When she looked back to the crowd, it was nearly on top of her. The faces in it were like a sea of varied colors. Some wore hats, some jewelry, some had beards, others makeup. They were silent faces but stern and all eyes were on her. They were close enough to touch and still pressing forward.

She raised her arm again, higher this time.

"Lightning," she said.

Suddenly, she felt the lip of the fountain crash into the back of her knees. She hadn't realized how fast she'd been moving.

Completely out of control, she fell backward with a giant splash. As the water rushed over her and drew her down, Livvy knew she only had moments but it was enough to see a bright flash that quickly winked out.

CHAPTER TWENTY-EIGHT

"HOW MUCH LONGER, Pipsqueak?" Dominique demanded.

"I'll be done today, ma'am," she replied, not bothering to look up from the soldering. "If the parts get here soon."

Dominique turned her glare on the door.

Where was that Tambourine? She'd sent her to Mamacita's an hour ago.

The network configuration had grown to four homemade network boxes. Wires hung out everywhere, connected to each other, connected to the goggles, connected to the box.

Dominique had the shamans write their names on their goggles so they wouldn't get confused. It'd be easy in a rat's nest like this. She looked away. She didn't like mess.

On the floor, lined up in neat rows and columns, there were twelve mats, though only ten were occupied by shamans. Dominique strode slowly past them, her rubber boots softly thudding. Several shamans seemed as though they were sleeping but some were probably high. Only one wore goggles.

Dominique looked back at Pipsqueak. If she finished today, she'd want her squad ready for battle tomorrow. Now was the time to let them use the drugs she'd doled out. For the attack, she'd need them sharp.

There was a knock at the door. It was Tambourine.

"What took you so long?" Dominique barked.

It was a tone that generally had people melting down in seconds but Tambourine simply reached into the plastic bag and brought out a business card. She handed it to Dominique. Then she dug out the crystal pyramid and set it on the table and handed the rest of the contents to Pipsqueak.

The card was black with silver lettering. "Mayet," Dominique read aloud.

Tambourine waited.

"So?" Dominique demanded.

She flipped the card over but it was blank on the reverse. She looked back at Tambourine.

The woman actually smiled, though it was uneasy.

"There is a new dwarf in town."

CHAPTER TWENTY-NINE

ALTHOUGH LIVVY HAD moved, Min had decided to stay in Korea Town, though she had upgraded to a luxury apartment on Wilshire. It was sparsely and tastefully decorated with black lacquer tables and chairs with deep green cushions. A large three-panel folding screen hung on the wall above the couch, a delicate painting of black and white herons taking flight against a gold backdrop.

"Thanks for seeing me quickly," said SK, as he took a seat.

"Of course, of course," she said, following him into the living room.

The low table was already covered with small bowls of various types of snacks: fish cakes on skewers, kimchee, deep-fried sweet sticky rice balls. Normally, he would have already been helping himself to the food but today he was distracted. Min poured two small cups of ginseng tea and sat down.

"It's about tomorrow," he said.

Min sat with her hands folded in her lap, her knees together, and nodded.

"You'll be networked with Livvy for the job," he continued.

Min's eyebrows went up.

"I'll smooth it over with the client," he said.

He already knew how it would look. The client had made this appointment with the all-powerful Lightning Shaman. Why would she need help?

"You'll be her apprentice," SK said.

Min gave a little smile and nodded. Both she and SK knew she was far beyond the apprentice stage. Her own talent was so completely overshadowed by Livvy's, though, that few people knew she still practiced shamanism.

SK nodded, relieved. "Thanks, Min. I appreciate this."

SK had thought about trying to get Livvy's old crew together, at least the ones who were still in L.A., but he also knew the client would probably say no. To say that she wanted privacy when it came to her medical issues was an understatement. It was already going to take some quick talking to get Min admitted.

Nor would he be talking to the client too soon. The less advance notice of the change, the less chance the media would find out. It was already going to be a frenzy. Outside the world of shamanism little was known about networking goggles but there were rumors—and all of them swirled around Livvy.

SK reached for a skewer. "I'm still trying to find Dominique and these other shamans that travel with her," he said before taking a bite.

Min picked up her tea and took a sip. "I don't think Livvy was too pleased to see me in the Middleworld," she said.

SK slowly nodded his head. "I know," he said. "But I'm not listening to any excuses this time. Whatever the objections might be, you're going."

"Got it."

SK picked up a small plate and a pair of chopsticks. "What I don't understand is the reason for the resistance," he said, placing a couple of rice balls and a big pile of kimchee on his plate.

Min shrugged and shook her head. "Me either," she said, "but I just have this feeling she's…" SK looked at her, his mouth full. "Well, that she's hiding something."

He nodded as he picked up his cup.

"I don't know why I think that," Min said. "And maybe I'm wrong."

SK washed the food down with some tea. "I don't think you're wrong," he said. "She was the one who told me about Dominique in the first place, so I have no idea what it might be." He paused as he picked up another skewer. "Do you?"

Min shook her head. "Afraid not."

He ate in silence for a minute as Min sipped her tea. When he finished, he put his plate back on the table.

"Min," he said.

She looked at him.

"I don't take sides when it comes to shamans. I can't."

She nodded.

He thought suddenly of the kiss and his words sounded hollow.

"At least I shouldn't," he continued. "But you can and you should. That's what I need you to do."

"Be on her side," she said, nodding energetically.

"But I don't want either of you getting hurt," he said.

He still didn't know how Dominique was managing to find Livvy in the Multiverse and he didn't understand how a Multiverse wound could manifest itself in the real world.

"If anything happens tomorrow, I want you both out of there," he said firmly. "Understood?"

Min grimaced slightly.

"I know," he said. "She's the lightning shaman and she's not likely to do anything she doesn't want to do but I know you can do this."

Her smile returned at that. "You know I'd do anything for Livvy," she said, nodding her head with finality. "You can count on me."

"Thanks, Min. I knew I could."

I just hope it's enough.

CHAPTER THIRTY

"BONSOIR," SAID MAYET, as he rose to his feet.

Despite herself, Dominique couldn't help but feel excited. From time to time, she had worked with shaman intercessors but never a dwarf, never a water baby. What intercessor could be more perfect for her gift? She had long imagined such a pairing.

Focus, she thought. *This is your chance.*

Dominique offered her hand, palm down. Mayet immediately bowed over it, supported it with his own, and lightly kissed it.

She had assumed that he spoke French—not much of an assumption, judging from his name. He had made it clear he was comfortable with either French or English. She said she missed French and liked to speak it when she could, which was a lie. She hoped it might provide a quick bond that could be useful.

"Enchanté, Dominique," he said, straightening.

"Enchantée," she replied, remembering to smile, and took a seat.

She had selected a small café and he was early. As usual, she was precisely on time.

He signaled the waitress as Dominique took her seat. They both ordered Cafe Au Lait in English before returning to French.

"I understand you have just arrived," said Dominique, pitching her voice into a sultry tone that came easily when she wasn't issuing orders.

"That is correct," said Mayet. "I am familiar with the area, of course, from previous travels, although not particularly as a shaman intercessor. I have always liked Los Angeles and come here as often as I can."

"Well, in terms of shamanism, I would say you have arrived just in time."

"Is that so?" he inquired politely, as though her answer didn't matter.

He must want to know what is going on with SK, she thought.

"There are many shamans here who could use your services," she said, nodding. "Oh, yes. Many."

The waitress returned with their coffees. Dominique paused until she left.

"There are many clients and there are many shamans," she said and shrugged. "But not enough intercessors for all the work there is to be done."

"I see."

She knew she was only confirming what he already assumed. Otherwise, he wouldn't have come to L.A. With few or no clients, this would be her best opportunity to approach him and the timing couldn't be better.

"For example, I myself could use the services of an intercessor."

"Oh, yes?" he said, still acting as if it made no difference.

"Yes," she said simply.

"I see," he said. He thought for a few moments. "Of course, I would like to see your work before recommending you to clients."

"But of course. That goes without saying, I'm sure," she said, smiling–but not too much. "In fact, I have a client tomorrow. If you like, I'm sure they wouldn't mind an observer. In fact, I'm sure they'd be grateful." She batted her eyes. "As would I."

"Mmm," he said, mulling it over. "Yes," he said finally. "Yes, that would be good."

"Excellent," she said.

CHAPTER THIRTY-ONE

NO MATTER HOW fast she ran, her mother caught up. Now Livvy's mom had her by the hair.

"Why did you summon me?" her mom screamed.

Livvy had to grab her own hair and pull it out of her mother's grasp. She pushed her mother back, across the sidewalk, toward the nearest building.

It was another nightmare. It had to be. Her mother would never act like this.

"Time is running out," her mother screeched.

Livvy backed up into the street. Unlike the previous nightmare, she and her mother were in the Underworld, moving deeper into the Multiverse. The tall buildings seemed to be closing in, tilting toward them. The sky was pitch black, as though it were night but there was no such thing as night in the Multiverse. The thousands of windows above them glowed with interior light, as if every space were occupied. The whole thing was impossible but Livvy kept backing into the street anyway.

Her mother followed, one plodding step after another. Each of her words fell in time with the steps. "Why did you summon me?"

"Please, Mom," said Livvy, keeping the distance between them. "I needed to see you."

"Then look at me," her mom screamed. "I'm fading!"

It was true. In the dream, she was still fading. It wouldn't be long before she was transparent. And, if she became completely transparent, she would be gone.

Her mother lunged for her. Livvy easily dodged away and they started to circle one another.

"You're the one who summoned me," said her mother.

Livvy didn't say anything.

"This is all your fault."

"That's enough," said Livvy. "This is a dream."

"Are you so sure?" said her mother, continuing to circle. "You've never dreamt of the Underworld have you?"

Of course her dream would say that but it was true.

She had always been prone to dreams and nightmares but the Multiverse—not so much.

Her mother smirked. "No, I didn't think so," she said. "You're crossing over."

"It's only a dream," Livvy insisted.

Her mother laughed, a dry and shrill sound. "You keep telling yourself that," she said. "It doesn't change the fact that this is the Multiverse."

Her mother stopped circling and gestured around them. "Look at it! It's the Multiverse. Nobody just dreams about the Multiverse."

Was that true?

Her mother chuckled. "Oh yes, I'd be worried too."

When Livvy didn't reply her smirk turned into a snarl. "But enough about you," her mother said, starting to advance on her.

"I don't understand what happened," said Livvy, backing up again. "It's not that easy."

"I didn't say it'd be easy," her mother said. "But is *this* what you want?"

Slowly, her mother's face transformed. Her cheeks sucked inward, the skin puckering in long creases. Her green eyes became dim as a filmy gray opaqueness covered them. Patches of her scalp fell away, taking stringy gray hair with them. Her nose shifted and fell, dangling only by a thread of withered skin. Finally, the eyes too sunk inward.

"No!" Livvy screamed.

The nose fell completely away.

"No!" Livvy screamed again. "Stop it!"

"Livvy," came the croaking sound from the opening and closing jaws. "Livvy," it repeated.

"No!" Livvy wailed, trying to back up.

She felt something on her arm.

• • • • •

"Livvy!" said Min.

Livvy's eyes snapped open but the image of the rotting skull wouldn't disappear. It seemed to be hovering over her.

"No!" she screamed again.

"Livvy," said Min. "It's me, Min!"

The skull disappeared and Min's face replaced it. Livvy's eyes darted around the ceiling and the room, looking for the skull.

"You were having a nightmare," said Min, still holding her arm.

Livvy tried to focus on Min's face.

"It was a nightmare," Min tried again

A nightmare? Yes, a nightmare. It had been a nightmare.

Min let go of her arm and sat on the edge of the bed. Livvy sat up with difficulty and realized her t-shirt was soaked with sweat.

"That's two days in a row," Min said quietly.

If only.

She'd been having nightmares for weeks at this point–ever since she'd started the summoning. The only thing that had changed in the last couple of days was the screaming.

"What time is it?" Livvy asked.

"Nearly ten," said Min.

"Ten?"

It felt like she'd only slept for a couple of hours. How could it be ten already?

"We've got to get ready," said Min. "Today is Claire."

CHAPTER THIRTY-TWO

THEY ALL STOOD next to their mats instead of sitting on them. Dominique knew they paid better attention that way. Front and center, she stood next to her mat as well. She faced them, feet shoulder width apart, hands clasped behind her back. There were thirteen shamans total, including Pipsqueak, Tambourine, and herself.

"We will attack in waves. First column," she said, nodding to her left. "Then second column, then third, then fourth." She swept her gaze over them all. "On my command only. Understood?"

They all nodded.

She tilted her chin down and glowered at them.

"Say it," she snarled. "Understood?"

"Yes, Dominique," they said in unison, except for Tambourine, who was a beat behind the rest and looking at the floor.

"Tambourine!"

Her round face jerked upward and her mouth hung open a bit, as if she'd been asleep.

"What did I just say?"

The woman snapped her mouth closed and quickly shook her head, making the gold hoop earrings bob and sway. Dominique felt her anger quickly flare. If not for Tambourine's considerable shamanic power, she'd have rid herself of this one long ago.

"Half rations for you," yelled Dominique.

Tambourine slowly lowered her eyes and glared at the floor in front of her. Dominique knew Tambourine needed the drugs and that half a fix was almost as good as none. Fine. Maybe she'd listen next time.

"Flore," Dominique said, fixing another woman with a stare.

"Yes, Dominique," the woman barked convulsively.

This was the weakest one. The woman could barely make it from the Middleworld to the Underworld and even now got lost in the black lake sometimes and had to turn back. Already forty, there was little chance she'd ever make a truly competent shaman. The only good thing about her was the fact that her name already sounded like a nickname.

"You'll be the client," said Dominique. "No goggles. You'll just lie there."

The woman seemed relieved–a coward as well. "Yes, Dominique," she yelled.

Dominique looked the rest of them over. The timing had been excellent. They were all alert and ready.

She checked her watch. "Fifteen hundred hours," she said. "Until then, rest on your mats, drink plenty of water." She paused. "But no drugs. None whatsoever. When we're done with Liver the Lightning Shaman, there'll be drugs for everyone. Anything you want."

They fidgeted at the thought.

"Understood?"

They answered loudly, in unison. "Yes, Dominique!"

CHAPTER THIRTY-THREE

HURRY UP AND pick something. SK will be here soon.

Even in the closet, Livvy could hear Min in the kitchen humming cheerily and talking to Nacho. It was disconcerting. The nightmare had left her exhausted, as usual, but this time there was also a lingering feeling of anxiety. Why was she finding it so hard to tell the difference between a dream and the Multiverse? Was what her mother had said true? It had been a dream, hadn't it?

More importantly–what had happened to her lightning the last time she had truly been in the Multiverse?

"Livvy," called Min. "Time is getting short."

I know it!

"Okay," she called back.

She probably wouldn't even need lightning today but…her spirit helper. She broke out in a sweat and shivered.

Was her spirit helper still with her?

Outside, as if in answer, thunder erupted so close that she felt it. That was a good sign.

"Livvy," called Min. "We might need extra time in this weather."

"Right," Livvy called back.

As she reached out toward her clothes, a giant spark popped. Another good sign.

Okay. Just calm down. Get to the client, get to the Multiverse. You won't know anything for sure until you're there.

She looked at her clothes. It'd be media madness today, as it always was with big clients. She picked an outfit she knew was camera friendly, took the clothes off their hangers and got dressed.

When Livvy came into the kitchen, Min had just finished pouring some food into Nacho's bowl and was standing up. She was wearing a new robe today, black velvet as was her style but also double-breasted with intricate bone buttons carved with owls. The hem lightly brushed the floor as she twirled once in place.

"What do you think?" she asked, all smiles.

"You look great," said Livvy, a bit surprised.

"Good," she chirped. "Had to look my best today, since we'll be working together and everything."

Livvy's breath caught as she stared at Min. With all that had been going on, she hadn't really thought through what was going to happen today.

"Wait," said Min. "Didn't SK talk to you?"

No. Well, not exactly.

She had said she didn't want Min along but the evening had ended in a kiss and the issue of Min helping in the Multiverse had never been resolved–at least not as far as Livvy was concerned.

"Talk to me about what?"

The toaster on the far counter behind Min popped up two round waffles. Three different bottles of syrup were already standing by. Min turned toward the kitchen.

"Waffles are done," she chirped.

"Min!" yelled Livvy. "Talk to me about *what?*"

Min stopped and turned. Nacho looked up from his bowl. "About working together," she said, frowning. "Are you upset?"

"No, I'm not upset!" Livvy yelled.

Nacho slinked away.

Min looked puzzled, but her face held a little smile. Livvy felt anger mixing with frustration and exhaustion. Anger at not being able to be with her mother. Anger that Min might see her mother in the Multiverse. Anger that SK had apparently already made arrangements with Min but hadn't told her. Anger that, if the lightning didn't work, she really *might* need help.

"Is something funny?" Livvy yelled.

Min flinched and the little smile vanished. "No," she said. "No, it's not."

"I'll talk to SK," Livvy muttered.

"It's already been cleared with the client," Min said.

"*What?*" Livvy screamed.

With the client? Then there's no going back!

She'd have to use Min now. You couldn't offer two shamans and then take one away.

By all the gods, why had they done that?

"It's to protect you," said Min, calmly.

Even her calmness was irritating Livvy now. "I don't need your protection," she yelled and turned away, pacing to the sliding glass doors.

It had begun to rain and the wind was driving into the glass with a spattering sound.

Gods, how was this possibly going to work? She needed to talk with her mother and she didn't need anybody eavesdropping–especially not on what they had to talk about.

"I'll only be there to help if you need it," Min said quietly.

"Your help," Livvy scoffed, turning on her. "It's hard to imagine."

Min stiffened slightly, raised her chin and looked directly at Livvy. Her mouth was drawn in a tight line but she didn't say anything.

"Grow up, Min! Life isn't all giggles and rainbows and kittens."

Min inhaled sharply and blinked–twice at Livvy and twice at the floor. When she looked back up there was a certain hardness to her expression. Livvy braced herself for whatever Min might say but all she did was nod gravely and turn away.

It was not what Livvy had expected.

"Min," she said quickly.

Min stopped but didn't turn around.

"Min, I'm sorry. I didn't mean that."

The door buzzed. It was SK in the lobby.

Min went over to the toaster and pulled out the waffles.

"You forgot your amethyst pendant," she said over her shoulder.

Livvy glanced down. Yes, she had. "I don't need it," she said, hoping Min would turn around. "It'll be fine. If you're ready to go, I'm ready to go."

"Really," said Min. She dropped the waffles in the trash and finally turned around. Her face was set like a stone. "Well, you might want to put on some shoes."

CHAPTER THIRTY-FOUR

FLORE WAS LYING on her mat, eyes closed. Most of the other shamans sat cross-legged on theirs.

"You didn't say there'd be a network," said Mayet, as he set down his briefcase.

Dominique spoke in French. "Oh didn't I?" she said, smoothly. "You know, I think I'm so used to working in the L.A. manner that I don't think of it any more."

She watched as Mayet digested that. She had gambled he wouldn't know how far networking had spread–which wasn't far–or what shamanism in L.A. was like–not like this–since he hadn't had time to connect with many shamans.

She had expected him to ask about the network–or at least about the other shamans–but he didn't. Instead, he sniffed absently and stood a little straighter.

Doesn't want to appear unknowledgeable. Interesting.

"May I take your coat?" asked Pipsqueak.

Mayet continued to stare at the group. Then, as though he had just processed the question, he started to remove his coat. "Yes, thank you," he replied.

Pipsqueak helped him out of it.

"Would you care for some coffee or tea?" asked Dominique.

"No, no, no," said Mayet. "Do what you normally do. I'll be fine."

He approached the network boxes at the front of the squad. Long wires trailed from them, running off the rough wooden table on which they rested, and then down between the long columns of shamans. The wires had been covered with gray duct tape that matched the polished cement floor. The lines of tape were straight, parallel, and cut to precise lengths. When the tape reached a mat, it ended in a perfectly square cut and the wires continued, eventually connecting to each shaman's goggles.

Mayet peered down at the blond-wigged, nail-studded nkondi, strapped to the top of the nearest network box. He cocked his head and frowned.

"A little something from home," Dominique said, keeping her tone conversational. "It helps some of the girls to settle in, to have something familiar nearby."

Mayet nodded and strolled to the other side of the coffee table, obviously intrigued by the setup. Dominique watched him carefully. He evidently wanted to be a part of this as much as she did. Everything was clicking into place. There was no way she could fail.

"And your client," said Mayet, looking at Flore. "She is in need of this," he gestured around, "this network."

"Honestly," said Dominique. "No."

He looked at her, surprised.

"But it is easier and quicker for us, and in the end that is better for the client."

He considered that. "And what is the nature of her ailment?"

"Hexed," Dominique declared. "An ancestor spirit, maybe two."

His eyebrows went up. "Two," he said slowly. "I see." He looked over the columns of shamans. "Two," he muttered, nodding.

Dominique glanced at her watch. "I think it's time we get started," she said.

Almost as one, the shamans began to lie back on their mats.

Pipsqueak jogged over to her mat and lay down.

"Mayet," said Dominique. "I'll be here." She gestured down to her own mat, in front of the coffee table. A small square cushion had been placed beside it.

"Oh," he said stepping over to it. "How thoughtful."

Dominique watched him sit down. He didn't suspect a thing. This was going to be easy.

CHAPTER THIRTY-FIVE

COMPARED TO THE quiet car ride, the sudden media barrage was like a wall of sound and light, even through the tinted windows. Despite the downpour, the media had turned out in numbers. Video lights glared and camera flashes exploded on all sides as Min waited for the wrought iron gate to swing open. Livvy turned her face away from the cameras just as SK was doing the same thing. Their eyes met and she quickly looked down.

The ride to Bel Air had been quick but the strained silence had made it seem grindingly long. SK had begun with the usual good mornings but must have realized something was wrong. Min was serious and quiet and, so, not very Min-like. For her part, Livvy was finding it hard to push down a feeling of lingering dread, especially as they approached the house.

Let go of it, she thought. *It's not the client's fault. Focus on her.*

Min proceeded through the gate and up the curved drive to the main house. Matthew, Claire Stockard's son, was already waiting at the immense front door.

Though legendary, Claire's Hollywood star had faded decades ago, almost as Matthew's had begun to rise. He had begun as an actor but had quickly moved behind the camera and now was one of the most sought-after directors in the industry. It was only through his movies that his mother worked at all.

Min parked and the three of them got out. Even from this distance, they could hear the cameras clicking at the gate. Photographers and cameramen were crowded together under umbrellas, jostling each other to get a clear shot.

As Livvy approached, Matthew reached out his hand. "Welcome back, Olivia."

She reached out her hand and a spark jumped between them as

she grasped his hand. He jumped slightly although he'd been expecting it. He smiled awkwardly.

"I never remember what it's going to be like," he said.

"SK," he said, shaking hands with him.

He was purposely standing to the side of the car so the photographers had a clear view. *Always an eye toward publicity.*

"And a special welcome to Soo Min," he said, shaking hands with her. "SK said you'd be assisting today."

Min only nodded.

"Well," said Matthew, glancing one more time in the direction of the gate. "Shall we go in?"

He ushered them into the grand foyer as a maid closed the door behind them. Their shoes clicked along the marble floors and echoed in the high ceiling. Matthew then led them up the incredibly wide and spiraling staircase. This was a Hollywood mansion from the heyday of Hollywood mansions. An enormous chandelier hung in the center, two stories tall. Small windows that spiraled upward with the staircase shone their light on it. Even the dull gray of the day didn't prevent the faceted crystals from splashing small rainbows along the steps. Despite having seen it before, everyone except Matthew glanced at it as they circled around.

They had been here twice before, both times after Claire had come out of rehab. They all knew that what Claire really needed was a break from her lifestyle, continued counseling, and a personal physician who wasn't so quick to prescribe something, but she had never been one to commit to something. As time had gone on, her addiction seemed to return with more and more vehemence while her ability to control herself between bouts seemed to grow weaker and weaker. Livvy had already had this conversation with her and Matthew, together and separately. Eventually, her habits would kill her. Today's visit would be another band-aid on a situation that needed surgery. She would wake from the Multiverse rejuvenated and whole in spirit but it wouldn't last.

"Mom is already lying down," said Matthew at the top of the stairs. He stopped and lowered his voice. "Actually, she's hardly been out of bed for a few days now."

He sounded worried and it was the reason that canceling this appointment had been out of the question—aside from the media attention Matthew had created. Claire was in trouble.

They continued down the wide hallway, past the antique Louis XIV side tables, gilded mirrors and marble tiled floors.

"Has she had any specific complaints?" asked Livvy.

Matthew shook his head. "No," he said quietly, slowing down. "Just that she's tired."

He stopped in front of the only closed door on this level and reached for the knob. Livvy put a hand on his arm to stop him. A spark popped but she ignored it.

"Has she been eating?" she whispered.

"Less and less each day," he whispered. "Mostly broth."

Livvy nodded. She glanced back at Min and SK as they exchanged looks. Claire was withdrawing from the world. Their visit had come in time but it was worrying.

Livvy looked back to Matthew. "Okay," she said. "Let's go."

The bedroom was so dark it took a moment for their eyes to adjust. On previous visits, the French doors to the balcony at the far end of the room had been open and the sunshine had poured in. Even though it was cloudy today and the doors were closed, the curtains had been drawn.

"She says the light hurts her eyes," Matthew whispered.

Although the room was dim, Livvy knew there must be roses—lots of them. Their scent was everywhere, even a little cloying.

"It's my eyes that hurt," came a brittle voice. "My ears are fine."

"Mom, Olivia's here," said Matthew.

"I know," she replied.

Livvy went directly over to the bed. Another maid was perched next to it in a chair. On the side table was an ornate silver serving tray with a plate covered by a silver dome. The utensils were wrapped in a napkin next to it, unused. Livvy smiled briefly at the maid.

The bed was an enormous four-poster of polished white wood with gold accents. The fabric canopy was made of cascades of pink silk that matched the comforter, small pillows, and ruffle at the bottom. The bed stood so high that Livvy barely had to bend over.

Claire was wearing a quilted lavender half-jacket, buttoned up to her neck. She was propped up on several pillows into a semi-reclining position. Livvy touched the comforter first, discharging a small spark, and then took Claire's hand in hers.

"Hi there," she said, smiling.

She reached her other hand up to Claire's forehead and lightly brushed it with the back of her hand. Successive facelifts had assured the skin there was smooth. It was hot but Claire wasn't sweating. Livvy gently moved a few strands of Claire's platinum blond hair aside.

"How are you feeling?"

"Like hell," said Claire.

Without any real force behind the words, they hung there like the plain statement of fact they were.

Livvy nodded and heard Min behind her unrolling the mats and getting the goggles ready.

"You've got a helper today," said Claire, though she didn't try to see who it was.

"Soo Min," replied Livvy. "The best of the best."

"I wouldn't have it any other way," said Claire.

Then she coughed—a watery, painful cough. *She'd been lying here too long*, thought Livvy. That would have to stop.

"Have you eaten today?" she asked as Min plugged the goggles into the network box.

Claire made a face.

"We've talked about this before," said Livvy as she gently rubbed Claire's hand. "Mind, spirit, and body. They go together."

Claire only closed her eyes in reply.

Livvy gently released her hand and turned to SK and Min. "Let's get started," she said.

Matthew gave his mother a last look and let himself out, closing the door behind him.

As Min lay down on her mat, Livvy hesitated. Her mother was waiting in the Multiverse and Min was bound to see her. There was simply no way to avoid it. Inwardly, Livvy cringed. Then she thought about the lightning. Aware that SK was watching, she quickly took a seat on her mat.

Just before she put on the goggles, she looked at him. "Back in a bit," she said, trying to sound normal.

Apparently it hadn't worked. Something had alerted him.

He looked directly into her eyes. "I'll be here," he said, a reassuring tone in his voice.

Min already had her goggles on and Livvy heard the snap of the power button and then the mild hum. "See you on the flip side,"

Livvy whispered as she turned on her own goggles and settled back.

CHAPTER THIRTY-SIX

AS LIVVY HAD expected, the Underworld was completely changed. The urban landscape was gone. Nor did Min see the temple in her village. Instead of their normal navigational aids, they both saw the milky white and undulating surface of the true Underworld. It stretched to infinity, blending into the white of the cloudy sky at the horizon. Although it might first appear like it'd be easy to spot a client in the pervasive white, the small hillocks were more than large enough to hide people. Both Min and Livvy knew it was easy to get lost.

"The same," said Min.

"Yeah," replied Livvy.

The last time they'd done this together had been the last time Min had been networked. It had nearly killed her. A combination of the attack by Tiamat, Livvy's wild lightning strike, and the extra effort that it took to be networked had sent Min into a coma from which she had almost not awakened.

Despite knowing this was what they'd find, it was sobering.

Livvy glanced around. *Where's Mom?*

Maybe she wouldn't show up. Could she be that lucky? Thankfully, no ancestor spirits were visible either. In fact, now that she thought about it, she'd never seen an ancestor spirit when the Underworld looked like this.

Min started up a hill to their right. Livvy took another quick look around and then headed up the one to the left.

Maybe her mom had become disoriented in the whiteness. Maybe she ought to be worried about her instead of hoping she wouldn't show up.

A bird cry overhead caused them both to look skyward. Swooping down to a spot in front of Min, her spirit helper landed with a great whoosh. It was Kam, the snowy white owl Livvy had met once before. He had helped to distract Tiamat and saved Min's life in their last joint visit.

Kam furled his wings with a light rustling noise. Min bent over him and gently stroked the glossy white feathers between his ears. Slowly, he blinked his great circular eyes.

"Kam," Livvy said, nodding to him.

He bobbed his head once in her direction, then turned to Min who stood up.

All three turned their faces to the sky.

The clouds had begun to stream away from the fountain in a certain direction. They all knew this was the direction in which the client would be located. Her spirit helper seemed fine.

"Livvy, there you are," came her mother's voice from below.

Livvy felt a shudder down her spine.

Although she had hoped–had almost convinced herself–this moment would never come, it was here. She forced herself to turn and look down the slope.

"What's happened to the Underworld?" her mom asked, as she climbed toward Livvy.

Min had left her hilltop and was approaching from the opposite direction. Livvy swallowed in a dry throat as the two arrived.

Min cocked her head slightly. "I don't understand," she said. "This isn't Claire."

For a moment, Livvy thought of telling Min that this was an ancestor spirit. In a way, it was almost true. But as Livvy watched Min's face and saw the expectant look there, she felt a sudden and unexpected fatigue that pressed her shoulders into a slump. She was so tired of lying.

"No," said Livvy. She paused. "No, Min. This is my mother."

Again Min cocked her head. Kam landed off to her right and was watching.

"Your mother," said Min, as though saying it would help her understand.

Then she looked at Livvy's mom.

"I thought your mother was…" Her head snapped around to Livvy. "Livvy, what have you–"

"She's summoned me," said her mother. "From the dead."

Min stared at the woman.

"See, you can say it," her mother said. "Dead. I've been summoned from the dead."

Her tone was light and conversational and put a weird spin on an already strange meeting. Now Livvy stared at her too.

"Sorry," her mom said quickly. Then she cleared her throat and looked down. "I'm sorry, honey. Just a little nervous."

"That's okay, Mom." Livvy gave her shoulder a little squeeze.

"So," said Min. "This is why you didn't want me here."

There was a rumble of thunder overhead, which they all ignored.

"Yes," said Livvy, looking at the ground too, not able to meet Min's eyes.

"A summoning," said Min as things clicked into place. "You might be one of the few shamans who could do it but, by all the gods in the Multiverse, Livvy, why?"

"Because I had to, Min," Livvy blurted out as she looked up. "I can explain."

Min briefly looked at Kam who had spread his great wings and given a few agitated flaps before folding them again.

"SK doesn't know, does he?" asked Min.

"No, he doesn't. He can't. Please, Min, you can't tell him."

Min glanced from Livvy to her mom and then back again.

"Please, Min, I'm begging you," Livvy pleaded. "Please don't tell SK."

Min's face was grim at the thought and she paused for several long moments. "No, *I* won't tell him," said Min finally.

Livvy breathed a sigh of relief.

"*You* will," Min concluded.

Livvy froze, mid-breath.

"I promise I won't tell SK," Min said. "Now, you promise me that you will."

Livvy saw Min's mouth drawn into a straight line, the forward tilt of her head, and the dark unblinking eyes as Min stared at her.

Livvy looked into her eyes even as she tried to imagine telling SK.

How could that possibly go well?

Min was right, though, and she knew it. In a way, it was a relief.

"I'll tell him," said Livvy. "I promise."

Min nodded. There was none of the condemnation Livvy had

feared, nor any recrimination. Only Min.

"Okay," said Min. "I think we'd better find Claire."

"Right," Livvy said, nodding. "Right."

They both checked the direction of the clouds.

"Mom, you'll have to wait right here where you can see the fountain," Livvy said. "Oddly enough, it's super easy to get lost here."

"I'll come with you," she said. "I might be able to help."

"No!" Livvy said with more force than she'd meant.

She took a breath. If ancestor spirits showed up, they'd be seeking Livvy, not her mom. If Dominique showed up, it'd be the same. The last thing she needed right now was someone else to worry about. The safest and best place for her would be near the fountain.

Her mom must have seen the look on her face.

"That's all right, honey. I'll be here," she said. "You go do what you need to do."

Livvy gave her a brief hug.

"Thanks, Mom. We'll try to be quick."

Her mom gave both her and Min a little smile and then headed down toward the fountain.

"I like her," said Min. "She's nice."

Livvy couldn't help but grin at that.

As Min turned to head toward the client, Livvy put a hand on her shoulder. "Thanks, Min," she said.

Min covered Livvy's hand with her own and smiled with a little nod.

Livvy gave her mom one last look, then headed downslope with Min. In moments, she was on top of the next hill. She waited for Min to jog up and join her.

"When did you start moving so fast?" asked Min.

"I don't know, it just sort of happened."

"Is it part of the lightning?" Min asked as Livvy took up a light jog next to her.

"I think so," Livvy replied.

She felt a little reassured. The clouds overhead were streaming as usual. Her speed seemed undiminished. She hadn't said anything to Min or SK about what had happened with the lightning–for obvious reasons–but everything seemed normal this time. Even so, she wanted to make sure.

"Let me look ahead," she said.

She raced to the top of the next hill, stopped and reached up her hand. "Lightning," she said.

A blistering bolt landed almost immediately, launching multicolored sparks upward as well as raining them down.

"What is it?" yelled Min, topping a nearby hill. "What do you see?"

Kam banked in a tight circle above her.

Livvy dropped her arm immediately and relief flooded through her. "Nothing!" she called back, elated.

Thank all the gods.

She still had lightning. Though she had sensed more than known that she'd never really lost it, she was glad. Something weird had happened that previous time in the Multiverse–to say the least–but it hadn't lasted.

A cry from above made them both look up to Kam. He had spotted something. Min responded by picking up the pace and slightly changing course. Livvy headed in that direction as well. Kam was circling and flew lower.

Suddenly, they were nearly on top of her.

Startled, Claire began to lean backward and was about to land hard on her backside except Livvy quickly caught her.

"Gotcha," she said, as she easily raised Claire to a standing position.

Min supported her by the other arm.

Claire gaped in amazement from one to the other.

"I really can't believe I'm seeing this," she said.

Livvy smiled at her. "Enjoy it while you can because you won't remember a thing," she said.

"Really?" Claire asked, disappointed, as Livvy and Min let her stand on her own.

"Afraid so," said Livvy.

Nor would there be much to remember. Now that they had found her, it was only a matter of taking her wandering spirit through the fountain to the Middleworld and then back to the real world. After all of her journeys with drugs, different rehabs, subsequent overdoses and various hospital stays, Claire had lost her way.

"Too bad," said Claire. "Because this is amazing."

None of them had noticed that Kam had not landed. Above, he gave a short cry that caused them all to look up. A vulture was diving at him and only a frantic tumbling move allowed him to escape the giant bird's grasp.

"Kam!" Min cried.

"Time to go," said Livvy. "We have company."

They each grasped one of Claire's arms and spun in the direction from which they had just come. All of the surrounding hills were now occupied by shamans.

• • • • •

In the real world, SK bent down lower over Livvy's prone body. Her jugular had just jumped from a steady pulse to a quick throb. He shot a look at Min's throat. Hers did the same thing. He looked up at Claire, who seemed the same as before.

He already knew it should be a simple matter of retrieving Claire's spirit. If Min were actually involved–he watched her breathing, which had quickened–then it could only mean one thing.

"Dominique," he said.

He looked back at Min. "Do it, Min," he whispered. "Just do it."

• • • • •

"We've got to make a run for it," Livvy heard Min say from behind her.

They had put their backs to one another with Claire in the middle. Livvy slowly circled, searching for an escape route, and Min matched her movements. More shamans appeared, some of them with their animal spirit helpers.

"Did I say that this was amazing?" said Claire.

"I like what you've done with the place," called Dominique.

She stood on the highest of the hills, to Livvy's left. Her feet spread in an easy stance and her arms crossed over her chest. An enormous raven perched on her shoulder. *She has her spirit helper with her this time*, thought Livvy. *That can't be good.*

"Sort of minimalist with all the white," said Dominique, reaching up to stroke the chest of the raven. "Myself, I prefer black."

The gleaming bird cawed its appreciation.

"Leave my client out of this," said Livvy.

"She can go," said Dominique as though she were dismissing her. "Not that she'll be able to find her way out without you." Dominique stared at her. "And you're not going anywhere."

None of the options were good. Livvy might stand a chance of whisking the client away at top speed but she couldn't leave Min behind.

"Let my friend take her," Livvy called to her.

"Livvy, I'm not leaving you here," said Min.

"No, I don't think so," said Dominique. "Your friend suffers the same fate as you."

There would be no bargaining with her. She was in control and she knew it.

Livvy heard Kam above them and the screech of at least two more birds, but she didn't dare look up. The shamans on the surrounding mounds began to shift their positions slightly.

"Wait for it," growled Dominique, sweeping her gaze around the circle.

"Min," said Livvy under her breath. "I need some separation between us. Make sure Claire doesn't get in the way."

Livvy thrust her hand to the sky. She felt Claire move away from her back.

"Don't make me do this," Livvy yelled, turning around to see all the shamans. There had to be a dozen. Some of them were already readying their attacks. Smoke rose from one, the redhead had her arm upraised for wind. "I don't want to hurt anyone," she tried again.

The clouds above were boiling furiously and a booming clap of thunder split the air, reverberating, and endlessly vibrating. Some of the shamans teetered in place and looked to Dominique.

"Column one," yelled Dominique. "Now!"

As expected, wind poured down from the sky with almost a crushing blow as the ground beneath them began to rumble. She heard Claire scream but her words, if there were any, were quickly whipped away in the torrent of air blowing by. Her whirlwind would have met and held this wind in place but she had decided not to do that.

A quake began to convulse the ground beneath her, almost toppling her, but as suddenly as it started, it stopped. Livvy quickly regained her balance, her arm still upraised. She was going to have to do it. There was no other way.

"Lightning," she yelled.

A searing arc of electricity flashed through the sky and landed on her hand, buzzing, crackling, and writhing as though it were alive. She raised her other arm and pointed it at the heavyset shaman who was creating the quakes.

Then the wind died.

"Livvy," screamed Min. "Look out."

• • • • •

There was a loud knock on the door but SK didn't answer. There was no doubt something had gone wrong.

Electricity danced in the wall sockets like a light show and both Min and Livvy were breathing harder. Their hearts were pounding and sweat was starting to trickle down the sides of Livvy's face.

"SK?" came Matthew's voice. "The lights are flickering out here."

"It's all right, Matthew," called SK as he got up. "Normal part of the process."

He stared hard at Livvy and Min, looking at their goggles and then the network box. He stepped around them and put his hands on the two plugs that led to their goggles. Heat from the electronics had warmed them up.

His mind turned back to a similar situation and he froze. The last time he'd unplugged goggles while they'd been in the Multiverse, Min had gone into a coma. Had severing the connection in the middle of a journey contributed to that?

He glanced up at Claire. Who knows what could happen to the client? Especially if Dominique was there.

There was another knock at the door. "SK, can I come in?"

SK removed his hand from the plugs. No, that was not the way to go. Whatever they were doing, they were going to have to finish.

"No, Matthew," SK called. "Wait there. I'll be out as soon as we're done."

He looked down at the network box and then Livvy and Min. *Let that be soon.*

• • • • •

Livvy had been about to turn at Min's scream when something thudded into her back and sent her flying forward. There was an intense heat between her shoulders. She was on fire. She ripped off the flaming coat and threw it aside. As she did, she reached her hand up again.

"Lightning," she yelled.

Again the arc leapt down as she whirled toward the direction from which the fireball had come.

"Get down," she screamed to Min.

Min dove on top of Claire and flattened them both to the ground as Livvy released the lightning. She aimed it squarely at the shaman who was preparing a second attack. It struck the new fireball in front of her, detonating it, and sending her flying off the top of the mound and out of sight.

Livvy swiveled toward the one who created quakes but a snarling sound from her left brought her attention around. She ducked just in time as an enormous wolf leaped over her.

"Column two," yelled Dominique. "What happened to the quake?"

A thick smoke had drifted down into their depression and Livvy could hear Claire coughing.

The wolf disappeared into the smoke and she heard Min scream. Kam's cry came from directly over Livvy's head, and she glimpsed him sailing by and diving into the smoke.

"Get out of there," Livvy yelled.

She reached up a hand to the sky. If they would use smoke and the redhead wouldn't use wind, then she would. "Whirlwind," she said.

Instantly a funnel descended from the mass of dark clouds over them. The sudden wind whipped her hair and tugged at her clothes but it was also having its desired effect. The smoke was sucked up into the rotating cone. Unfortunately, what it revealed was not what Livvy wanted to see.

Claire was on the ground and Min was struggling to her feet. Kam's talons dug into the back of the wolf's neck, who swung his head from side to side, desperately trying to dislodge the owl. Kam wouldn't let go though. The shaking of an earthquake was starting to rise and Min fell again but as Livvy looked for the source of the quakes, she realized some of the other shamans had fallen too. *Ignore that one*, she thought. *She's doing as much damage as good.*

As Livvy whirled around to find Dominique, a sudden explosion burst around her, throwing her to the ground. The funnel of the whirlwind disappeared.

Dazed, her eyesight blurry, Livvy struggled to her feet.

What happened?

There was a ringing in her ears. She managed to turn toward the shamans closest to her. One of them had her mouth wide open and was taking a deep breath.

A sonic attack, thought Livvy, as a crushing blow to her side sent her skidding across the ground until she smashed into a nearby mound. A giant stag with an enormous rack of antlers backed away from her and lowered its head for another attack.

Livvy raised both arms, one to the sky, one at the deer. "Lightning," she breathed, still on the ground.

The lightning lanced down, out through her hand, and landed with a crack between the deer's eyes. Its head exploded. Flesh and skin vaporized as smoldering antler bits spewed out in every direction. The headless body collapsed.

Without pausing, Livvy rolled up onto her knees and turned around, the arc of lightning sailing around with her and across the shaman with the sonic attack. The woman ducked and dove out of the way, although Livvy knew some of the energy had managed to connect with her when the woman screamed.

"Column three," she heard Dominique yell.

Three?

Was she going to have to keep fighting spirit helpers and shamans until they were all gone?

She glanced at Min's location and saw chaos ruling there. Claire was still lying prone on the ground. Kam dove repeatedly on the spirit helpers who tried to approach Min, while she stood over

Claire and fended off the wolf with roundhouse kicks.

Enough.

With electricity still arcing from her hand, she got to her feet and started to sweep the entire circle of hills. The earthquakes stilled and some of the spirit helpers in the center abruptly stopped their attacks. Shamans dove out of the way as the arc approached them. The prolonged lightning strike was draining her but she strode back to the center of the depression. Shamans and spirit helpers were starting to disappear from view. She was gaining the upper hand.

Then, with a giant whoosh, fire erupted everywhere.

No wonder the attackers had cleared out.

"Claire!" she heard Min scream.

Although Claire had been lying still, she was apparently not unconscious. Her unearthly scream of agony could have torn the Underworld in two.

Livvy thrust both hands above her. "Rain," she screamed.

In moments, a torrent of water poured from the sky, turning into steam as it hit the fire.

"Oh *water*?" Dominique yelled.

Livvy wheeled to face her, breathing hard from the exertion. Raindrops were pelting every shaman and spirit helper in sight. Rivulets ran down Dominique's face. Even so, Livvy could see the exultant look there.

Dominique launched the raven into the sky.

"Water is mine," she yelled. She stretched out her hand into the rain and seemed to squeeze it in her fist.

"Snow," she yelled.

Suddenly, the downpour turned into harmless flurries that floated through the air in the sudden silence.

"Ironic, isn't it?" yelled Dominique, gloating. "A water shaman and a lightning shaman together."

Livvy backed toward Min and Claire. She glanced behind her as Min stepped forward, over Claire's body.

Oh no, why is she leaving Claire?

"You may have the help of a water baby," Dominique called down to her. "But guess what? So do I." She tightened both hands into fists and pushed outward as though she were shoving someone.

"Tidal wave," she yelled.

Livvy backpedaled and then turned, running toward Claire. "Claire!" she screamed.

Min grabbed her arm and yelled, "She's gone!"

Gone?

"No!" Livvy screamed. "No! Let me go!"

She tore herself away from Min. Claire couldn't be gone! She *had* to save her.

A dark blue wall of water suddenly rounded the hill on which Dominique stood and barreled toward them. Its roar was deafening and Livvy had just enough time to see the fine mist that sprayed from the top of the curling wall before it slammed into them. She was only dimly aware of Min submerging with her as the water swept them backward and then down, crashing into the ground as the blow forced the air out of Livvy's lungs. She tumbled amid the eddies and swirling waves with no sense of up or down. Finally, the wave threw her against the side of a hill and dissipated. She fell forward into the vacuum left behind by the receding wave. She landed hard on the wet ground.

She tried to get up but her muscles were slow to respond.

What happened to Min?

She felt weighed down by her waterlogged clothes.

"Really," said Dominique from somewhere above. "I thought this would be harder. Kind of disappointing actually."

Livvy finally raised her head just in time to see the black boot. It connected to the side of her face and she rolled with the blow onto her back, groaning with the pain.

"Come and get a closer look," she heard Dominique say as another kick landed in her ribs, pushing her onto her side. "Liver the Lightning Shaman and her friend what's-her-name. Come on, get a closer look."

"Yes," she heard Min mutter, next to her. "Come closer for a good look."

Min? Where's Claire?

Livvy couldn't focus her eyes.

"Come on, you cowards," Dominique yelled. "Don't be afraid. Look at what we've done!"

"Min?" Livvy managed to say.

There was no response—only the dull sound of shuffling feet

around her.

"A little closer," she heard Min mutter.

Then there was a pause.

"Light!" Min yelled.

An agonizing whiteness filled Livvy's eyes. Screams erupted from all around her. Livvy would have screamed as well, if she could have gotten any breath.

"Dominique!" someone screamed. "I can't see!"

Livvy felt hands on her, jerking her up. "Get up, Livvy," Min whispered into her ear.

"Dominique!" someone else screamed. "Where are you?"

She heard someone groan and fall.

"Oh gods," someone else muttered. "I think I'm blind."

"Everybody," said Dominique, behind them somewhere. "Stay where you are."

"This way," Livvy heard Min whisper in her ear.

Min propped her shoulder under Livvy's arm. "Keep walking."

The confused voices faded into the distance behind them. Dominique was trying to assert control but the shamans were panicking. Like Livvy, they had completely lost their vision.

"Min," Livvy whispered, between labored breaths. "We have to go back for Claire."

"She's gone," she said. "Keep walking."

Livvy heard the splash of the fountain and Kam crying up above. Somehow he was managing to guide them and somehow Min was able to see him.

"Here we go," said Min. "Step over and in. I've got you."

Livvy did as she was told and felt Min's firm grip around her waist as they submerged.

• • • • •

In the real world, it was blissfully dark. Livvy heard SK's voice and then Min's but couldn't quite make out what they were saying.

She blinked inside the goggles. There was only blackness. Maybe she was blind. *That would be okay*, she thought. *Better than the painful white light.*

Suddenly, a lancing pain shot through her forehead from left to right and a coppery smell filled her nose. She tasted salt. The pain ratcheted up a notch. She sucked in a breath but then coughed convulsively. She felt someone remove the goggles. Even though her eyes were squeezed shut against the pain in her temples, she sensed light.

"Liv," said SK. "Liv, can you hear me?"

"SK," she sputtered.

"Bloody nose," Min said.

Livvy struggled to open her eyes.

"She's going to choke on the blood," SK said. "Get her on her side."

She felt hands tug her at her shoulder and hip and then she was on her left side. Warm liquid ran out of her mouth and nose and down the side of her face. She coughed again but was able to get more air. She slowly opened her eyes, but the room was dim. Had her eyesight been damaged? She blinked and inhaled again. It was dim because she was looking toward the underside of a bed. It had to be Claire's bed.

"Claire?" Livvy moaned.

Her vision was clearing and she saw the ornate Oriental rug at the edge of her mat.

"Claire?" she tried again.

No one answered.

What's going on?

Despite the pain in her head, she pushed up on one elbow, still facing the bed.

"Take it easy," she heard SK say behind her and felt his hand on her arm.

"Is Claire okay?" she asked, looking up the side of the bed.

"No," he said.

What? Did he say no?

"Claire is dead," Min said.

Dead?

Grasping the top of the bed, Livvy got to her knees.

"Liv, hold on a minute," SK said as he grabbed her at the waist to keep her from toppling over.

She ignored him and pulled herself to her feet, wobbling, and stared down at the bed.

Claire lay there exactly as she had last seen her, hands folded comfortably over her stomach, eyes closed and face peaceful. Livvy automatically put two fingers to her neck and then quickly thumbed open an eye.

"Oh gods," she whispered. "Gods, no."

She closed her eyes and bowed her head against the pain and also at the awful truth in front of her. She'd lost Claire. She opened her eyes and stared through the tears.

Please no. Not like this.

"Claire," she whispered.

"Can you stand without leaning on the bed?" SK asked.

She felt him at her side, an arm around her waist.

"Yeah, I think so," she said and sniffed.

"Back away from the bed," he said.

She put her hand on his shoulder, gripping the fabric of his jacket, and took a step back. She could see now that she'd left a trail of blood on the bedding.

"Min," SK said. "Help me get her to the ground. You'll have to take the shoulders."

Livvy hadn't realized Min was standing on the other side of the bed until she began to move the bed covers aside.

They were going to attempt CPR.

Rather than be encouraged, Livvy understood it for what it was—standard procedure. In moments, although SK struggled, they had Claire on the floor next to the bed. Min immediately began chest compressions.

"I'll get Matthew," he said, panting as he went by.

"Matthew?" said Livvy, panicking.

"Yes, right away."

Livvy heard the door open behind her followed quickly by Matthew's voice. "*Her heart isn't beating?*" he screamed.

She heard the sound of running feet and then Matthew flew past her. "Mom?" he yelled. "Mom!"

SK came back into the room with the cell phone to his ear. "I'm calling to request an emergency medical response for the following address," he said.

Having finished thirty chest compressions, Min opened Claire's airway by tilting her head back and lifting her chin. She pinched Claire's nose and did two rescue breaths. Claire's chest rose and fell with each.

"She's breathing!" Matthew exclaimed.

Min went back to chest compressions.

"She's not," Min said, breathing heavily. "But her airway is clear."

"But I saw her chest move!"

Min shook her head.

SK stepped forward next to Matthew.

"Emergency help is on the way," SK said.

"Shouldn't someone breathe for her?" Matthew asked, kneeling. "I mean, if she's not breathing? I could do that."

"Min's doing it exactly right," said SK, calmly. "Just let her do her work." He put a hand on Matthew's shoulder.

It was like watching a play from onstage. Livvy saw the fear in Matthew's face, the trembling of his mouth, how he followed every move that Min made.

"Come on, Mom!" he yelled.

Livvy looked at SK—unflappable, in control, but resigned. He knew what Livvy and Min knew—Claire was dead. They were only doing what the paramedics would do when they arrived.

Min did more rescue breaths and went back to chest compressions.

Two maids stood in the doorway, eyes wide, staring. "Is she—" said one.

"She's going to be okay," Matthew yelled. "Where are the paramedics?"

He swung his gaze wildly around the room as if he might spot them and noticed Livvy. He frowned as though he were trying to remember something. The sound of more rescue breaths made him wrench his gaze away and turn back to Min.

Finally, they heard the faint sound of sirens, rapidly growing louder. In what seemed like only moments, heavy running came up the stairs and down the hall.

A paramedic team came into the room and quickly moved to Claire's side. One of the men jumped in and replaced Min. As the changeover took place, the other man immediately felt Claire's jugular and then donned a stethoscope and listened. He checked his watch as his partner waited.

Min stood, still breathing hard, and went to Matthew's side, kneeling down with him. "I'm sorry, Matthew. She didn't return with us," she said quietly.

"But," he said, then shook his head. "This was supposed to be so simple." His face was turning red. "She wasn't even sick."

They could hear more sirens arrive outside.

The paramedic who had replaced Min began chest compressions as the other turned around to Matthew. "Is there a physician in attendance?" he asked.

"A what?" Matthew said, confused.

"No," said SK. "I'm the one who called 911. There is no physician in attendance."

Pounding feet came up the stairway again. Two more men, in slightly different uniforms, came into the room. The paramedic who had been talking with Matthew stood.

"We're going to continue CPR and transport," he said.

The message beneath the words: the patient was dead but there was no doctor present who could pronounce death. Although EMTs and paramedics might make a determination of death and stop CPR, the usual course was to transport the patient to an emergency room.

The two men who had just entered immediately turned on their heels.

Matthew slowly got to his feet. "What's going on?" he demanded.

Even more sirens began arriving outside.

"Sir," said the paramedic. "The EMTs are getting a gurney and we're going to take the patient to an emergency room."

The piercing pain in Livvy's head had subsided, but there was an ache in her ribs and the blood loss was making her nauseous.

SK was at her side. "Liv, you should sit," he said.

"No I'm okay," she said.

The maids in the hallway were crying and more servants had shown up and were hovering outside. The two EMTs pushed past them.

"Stand aside please," the one in front said.

The paramedic who had been talking to Matthew came over to check Livvy. Behind him, an EMT was saying something to Matthew.

"He's right," said the paramedic in front of Livvy, taking her wrist and looking at his watch. "You should sit."

Livvy jerked her wrist back.

Matthew's voice erupted. "I don't understand. What's a medical directive?" he yelled.

It was all happening too fast.

The EMTs had Claire on the gurney. They raised it up with metallic clicks and a locking sound. With one EMT still performing CPR, they started for the door.

Matthew turned in a daze, feeling his front pant pockets, then the back. "Get a driver," he yelled to the group at the door.

The maids jumped and the crowd scattered as the gurney came through. Matthew began to follow but stopped and turned, his glare landing on Min, SK, and Livvy. He looked Livvy up and down, staring hard at something. When she looked down, she realized she was covered in blood. Her silver coat, white blouse, and leggings were heavily spattered with bright red streaks and blotches from the nosebleed.

"I'm going to get to the bottom of this," he snarled.

They could hear the gurney rolling across the marble in the hallway.

"You've got my number," SK said

"Damn right, I do," he said, turning away. "My lawyer will be in touch."

Suddenly, the three of them were alone.

"All right," said SK quietly. "Let's go. Can you walk?"

"Yeah," said Livvy.

Min quickly scooped up the goggles, mats, and bags as SK helped Livvy to the door. On the wide stairs, Livvy gripped the handrail and started down, past the sparkling chandelier. Servants stood aside and gaped at their procession. A siren started up just outside.

It was like a nightmare.

Min passed them, hurrying down. "I'll get the car," she said.

But it wasn't that easy. A police officer met them at the bottom of the stairs and another passed them on his way up. Names, addresses and phone numbers were taken and then a few questions. SK did all the talking, brief as it was, and described their involvement. Seeing shamans at the scene wasn't as rare as it had once been and they were released, pending further questions. Min left to get the car.

Outside, the media at the gate had swollen to ten times its previous size. Every local news channel had a van present and the paparazzi were swarming. As soon as she was out the door, people were screaming.

"Olivia, tell us what happened?"

"How's Claire?"

"Why the police?"

"Olivia, just a word!"

The silver sedan swung around in the circular driveway in front of them. SK opened the door before it had fully come to a stop. Livvy climbed in and scooted to the far side, a little dizzy from bending over. She closed her eyes, heard the door close and then felt the car moving. She fumbled for the door handle to hold on to something.

"Here," said SK.

She felt his hand on her arm and looked over. He'd taken off his jacket and folded it into a small pillow.

"Lie down," he said, gently tugging her over.

"I can do that," she said, barely audible.

Without another word, she slumped over and closed her eyes. The clamor outside was growing louder. As the car slowed for the gate to open, Livvy could hear shouting and then some thumping on the window. The car seemed to be spinning.

"Stay down," SK said, as he rested a hand on her shoulder. "We'll be through this in a second."

She could hear cameras hitting the windows now and even through closed eyelids she could see the flashes.

"Run 'em over if you have to," said SK.

In answer, Min laid on the horn. It must have done the trick. In a few seconds, they were finally moving.

CHAPTER THIRTY-SEVEN

"YOU SHOULD HAVE seen it, Nicole!"

Dominique threw her bag down on the couch, still breathing a little hard from having run up the steps. Nicole stood at one of the easels under the muted light of the windows. Dominique threw her arms around her and nearly picked her up.

"It was glorious!"

Nicole smiled sheepishly but didn't take her eyes off the canvas. Dominique hadn't expected to be acknowledged and immediately released her, too excited to stand still.

"I had her under my boot," she said, striding to the kitchen and turning around. "Under my boot!" She clapped her hands together. "I tell you, Nicole, it was too easy."

Dominique entered the kitchen but then turned around again. "And the dwarf, he had no idea–not a hint."

The dwarf had indeed helped. The tidal wave was perfect, unlike anything she'd been able to do before. It had taken Liver and her little friend completely by surprise.

Dominique paused. Yes, that shaman with the light. She squinted her eyes at the memory. Everyone had been blinded. Their only choice had been to leave the Multiverse. Liver had escaped but only narrowly.

"Except for that little friend of hers, Liver would be dead."

Next time, she'd have her. Next time, she'd make sure no allies came to the rescue. Next time, Liver would be Chopped Liver.

"I'm starving," she said, heading to the refrigerator. "How about you?"

Behind her, Dominique heard something clatter to the floor. She turned around.

Nicole was standing rigid in front of the canvas, her hands in fists, the palette and paint brush on the floor.

Dominique ran to her bag and dumped its contents on the couch.

Where is it?

She shoved the items back and forth.

There!

She grabbed the plastic vial and dumped out two small yellow pills. She took the bottle of water that had been in the bag and dashed over to Nicole.

She put the pills into Nicole's already open mouth and then the bottle of water, holding it for her. "Drink," she said.

Nicole swallowed once, gulping loudly.

The two of them stood still, waiting. Nicole stared at the canvas while Dominique stared at her. More than likely she'd gotten the pills into her in time but it didn't always work like that. Sometimes she'd fall into a seizure.

With all the preparations for the attack, making arrangements with Mayet, all the technical issues with the goggles–she was making excuses. She couldn't remember the last time Nicole had taken her medication.

Slowly, the rigidity in Nicole's shoulders began to slacken.

Dominique breathed a sigh of relief. "Sorry, Nicole," she said, still waiting. "I lost track of time."

Finally, Nicole started to move her arms. She backed up from the canvas and looked down at the palette and brush.

"Let me get those," said Dominique. "You sit down."

Then Dominique remembered the goggles. They had spilled onto the couch with everything else. "No wait!" she said, but it was too late.

Nicole's shriek was ear piercing.

Dominique snatched the goggles up and stuffed them in the bag. "They're gone," she said. "See. They're gone."

Nicole stifled another shriek with both her hands and sat down heavily on the couch, her eyes wide with fear, her nostrils flaring to keep up with her heavy breathing.

Dominique clutched the bag in front of her and shook her head. "By all the gods," she muttered, trying to keep the anger in check.

From the first time Nicole had seen the goggles she had reacted this way. For no known reason, she had been terrified of them.

"Nicole," Dominique said. "It would be so much easier if…if you didn't do that. This is my work," she said, gripping the bag. "This is how I'm going to get us out of this…" Dominique glanced around, "this place."

Suddenly, she heard herself saying those exact same words, somewhere else, far away.

The goggles had been a complete windfall. They had been sitting on the police sergeant's table. The fool had no idea what they were but she *did*, although that knowledge was based only on descriptions. She wanted them and, for a few 'extras' that day, she'd gotten them. When he was finally through with her, she hurried down to the docks, and then to the basement of the bar where she and Nicole had their mattress. She pulled them out of the sack only to have Nicole start shrieking. Dominique immediately wrestled her to the ground and clamped a hand over her mouth.

"Shut up," she whispered harshly in her ear. She glanced up toward the bar. "Shut up! I don't have a new room yet. We can't get kicked out of this…this place."

Dominique blinked and saw Nicole sitting on the couch. She had started to get herself under control, lowering her hands from her mouth. Then she silently put her hands in her lap and stared down at them.

First, forgetting the drugs, then the goggles, thought Dominique. *Two mistakes in as many minutes. Get your head out of the clouds because you don't live there yet. You live here, in this cheap loft under LAX's traffic pattern, and your sister needs your help.*

Suddenly Nicole picked up the sketchpad and crayon from the coffee table and furiously started to draw spirals, one after another, overlapping and sometimes going off the edge of the paper.

"Fine," said Dominique, quietly. "You draw."

She turned away from Nicole, went to the kitchen and put her bag on the counter. Her hands clenched into fists, twisting the heavy canvas, and she bowed her head over it as she tightened her jaw.

This has to end.

CHAPTER THIRTY-EIGHT

"THERE MUST HAVE been at least ten of them, maybe more," Min said as she helped Livvy drop onto the end of the couch.

Livvy had been anxiously listening to Min recount the ordeal to SK. As she had promised, though, Min said nothing about Livvy's mom.

Livvy kept her eyes closed against the spinning room. The pain in her head was almost tolerable. The only problem with keeping them closed, though, was Claire–seeing her body in the bed, hearing her anguished scream in the Underworld.

Min's voice drifted in from down the hall. "It had clearly been planned," she was saying.

Livvy heard the sound of a pill bottle rattling. Soon, Min was back. "Livvy," she said quietly. "Take these."

Livvy opened her eyes to see Min's hand with three ibuprofen. SK was holding out a glass of water.

"I can do that," she whispered and did. Then she sniffed.

"Put your head back," SK said. "Your nose is still bleeding. I'm going to get some ice."

Livvy could hardly keep her eyes open and tried not to let her head thud against the back of the couch. It would only hurt.

"And she said she had a water baby," said Min.

Livvy raised her eyebrows at that but couldn't raise the heavy lids. There were those words again–water baby. *Open your eyes*, she thought. *Pay attention.*

"What is that?" asked Min.

There was silence, although Livvy could hear the ice cubes in a plastic bag in SK's hands. "That's me," he said, quietly.

Then there was another pause.

"Liv," he said. "Lift your head a little so I can put the ice behind your neck."

With great effort and his helping hand, she managed it and then felt the cool ice and eased back onto it.

"You?" asked Min.

"Not me specifically," said SK. "A dwarf."

There was a long pause.

"You're sure that's what she said?" came SK's voice from far way.

No, don't go, thought Livvy. *Please don't go. Don't let me fall asleep.*

"Yes," said Min, also in the distance. "She said she was a water shaman and that she had a water baby."

SK was saying something Livvy couldn't make out. In moments, all was blackness.

CHAPTER THIRTY-NINE

DOMINIQUE DIDN'T BOTHER to block her caller ID.

SK had left Min with Livvy so he could begin the search for Dominique. Instead, she had found him. He almost hadn't believed it was her on the phone. She'd set up the meeting and gotten off.

The small park where she'd said to meet had a sand lot with a slide and swings. A handful of kids were playing there while their mothers stood close by. A couple with a stroller ambled past.

SK sat at a cement picnic table and, except to note that these other people were present, he took little notice of them. Instead, he looked at his phone again. Another minute and she'd be late. He wasn't going to waste a second past that. He looked up. A tall woman with dark flowing hair, dressed all in black, was striding in his direction. He didn't bother standing as she neared.

"SK," she said, swinging one leg easily over the opposite park bench, straddling it, on the other side of the table.

"Dominique," he said simply.

"I'd say it's a pleasure," she said, "but I'm sure it's not. Not after what happened earlier."

He got right to the point of why he'd agreed to meet her. "How are you finding Livvy in the Multiverse?"

"I'm offering you one chance," she said, completely ignoring his question.

He scowled as she waited. "One chance at what?" he finally asked.

"To surrender," she said, tugging down the sleeves of her leather coat. She turned to look him in the eye. "To join me."

He snorted, but she slowly shook her head. "She will lose," she said, her voice level, her eyes glinting in the bright afternoon light. "I will win. It is inevitable."

The woman was calm and exuded a self-confidence that was almost tangible. Whether or not she was right didn't matter. She believed it.

No, more than that. She knew it.

He thought of Livvy's bloody clothes and Claire's death and he realized there was a chance she might possibly be right.

"There's no need to compete," he said. "There's plenty of work in L.A."

"I don't want plenty of work," she said, dismissing the suggestion. "I want you."

He blinked and raised his eyebrows.

"I want the top jobs, only the best," she declared. "I want access to the rich and the famous. You can do that for me. We can do it together."

SK quickly shook his head. "No deal," he said. "You don't pick the intercessor. They pick you."

"Soon, you will have no one else to *pick*," she said. "Not only will the lightning shaman be destroyed but anyone else who gets in the way. This is your one chance."

She was scary in her conviction. If belief in oneself carried any weight, she stood a chance of succeeding on that alone. Suddenly, SK was afraid for Liv.

"There is a hierarchy to things, even in nature," she said. "Non-shamans are right to fear shamans. We have a power they can hardly comprehend. Why shouldn't we benefit from that power? Why shouldn't we take our rightful place at the top? There is *no* reason why we shouldn't. And I can be the one to do that. I can be the one to lead us all there."

Dominique waited, watching his face.

"You live near here?" he asked, trying again to gain any information that he could use to stop her.

In reply, she only stood up, swung her leg back over the bench. "I must say, I'm disappointed," she said, putting her hands in the pockets of the duster. "Not surprised but disappointed nevertheless."

"You must have a big place to network all those shamans," he tried again.

"I want you to remember this day," she said. "I would have treated you right."

"The only reason I'll remember this day," he said, standing up, "is to marvel at how little you understand. A partnership, an intercessor-shaman relationship, isn't negotiated. It's earned."

"Partnership," she echoed. "Tell me, Water Baby, how is deceit part of partnership?"

Now she's going to try some mind games, thought SK, *and she's clearly not going to give up any information.* He'd have to call in every debt and marker in the city, but he'd do it. He'd track her down and all the shamans that were helping her.

He turned to go.

"The lightning shaman has summoned her mother from the dead," she said.

He laughed. Was she really this desperate? He turned back to her.

She removed one hand from the pocket of her duster and tossed something to him. It rotated in the air, glittering like a small star and throwing off rainbows. He caught it with both hands. It was a crystal pyramid.

"Ask her what it's for," said Dominique.

He studied her. Her face was deadpan, completely devoid of expression. Even the confidence was gone–utterly unreadable. Was this who she really was?

"They have lots of uses," he said. "You know that as well as I do."

"They can be used for a summoning," she said, nodding at it.

"You're grasping," he scoffed.

As though she were enunciating a foreign language, Dominique said the words slowly, staring into his eyes. "Elizabeth Lawson."

SK had never heard Livvy's mother's name so he wouldn't have any idea if that was it, but it was too easy to verify. Why would Dominique lie about it? Even so, knowing her mother's name proved nothing.

"They bear a striking resemblance," she said, her voice flat. "Especially when they talk together."

Unbidden, the meeting with Mamacita flashed into his mind, the books Livvy had been stockpiling but that he never saw, her resistance to having Min in the Multiverse. His eyes narrowed and his throat tightened.

"You see it now," Dominique said. She paused, watching him.

"This wasn't a waste after all."

There was a dull stabbing pain in the pit of his stomach. With an effort, he slowly turned away from her as a strange tunnel vision took over.

"Your lightning shaman has summoned the dead, Water Baby. Summoned them right under your nose."

He took a step forward and then another, forcing himself to move. He was almost at the sidewalk when Dominique called out to him. "How's that for partnership?"

CHAPTER FORTY

IN MOMENTS, THE blackness of sleep turned into the harsh white landscape of the Underworld. The city was gone.

"Livvy, there's blood on your sleeve," her mother said, concern in her voice.

Livvy whirled to face her, anxious to see her mom but also afraid of what she might see. Like the last time, though—had that been a dream or the Multiverse, she couldn't remember—her mother was looking fine.

"Mom," Livvy sighed in relief.

"Livvy, you're covered in blood," her mom said, looking down. "Tell me this isn't yours."

Livvy looked down and remembered she hadn't changed. She, Min, and SK had arrived at her condo but she had collapsed on the couch, not even making it to the bedroom, let alone changing. This is what she'd been wearing when Claire had died.

"Are you all right?" her mom asked.

"I'm fine," Livvy said, looking up. "It was a nosebleed."

Her mother frowned. "Nosebleed? That's an awful lot of blood for a nosebleed."

"Yeah, it was a bad nosebleed," Livvy said. She glanced around them. "Mom, what's going on? Where's the city?"

Normally the Underworld only appeared in its true form when shamans were networked together. She wasn't networked with anybody—was she?

Her mother glanced around and then behind Livvy. "I don't know but, more to the point, where's the fountain?"

Livvy spun around. In every direction the rolling landscape spread out, blank and empty. The fountain was gone.

"Wait. How is that possible?" Livvy asked. "How could I have gotten here?"

"You're crossing over without the goggles," her mother answered, as though it were obvious.

Livvy continued to stare at the barrenness of the Underworld. At the horizon, she realized the sky was black and jerked her gaze up. It was pitch black above, no clouds, no stars, no light. The only light in the Underworld seemed to come from beneath their feet, the glow of the milky ground.

Why was that so disquieting?

"Apparently you don't need the city either," her mom continued. "That's probably why it's not here anymore."

"I'm not controlling this," Livvy said. "I didn't even mean to be here."

"You didn't?" said her mother, surprised. "Then you should take a care, young lady."

Livvy turned to her, fear starting to rise. "Why?"

Shamans dance on the edge as it is," she said. "It's all too easy to cross over and never make it completely back."

"Not make it back?" she said, anxiety beginning to overtake the fear.

"You use the goggles to get to the Multiverse and you use the fountain and black lake to travel between the Middleworld and Underworld. If there's no way back, there's no way in. Not even another shaman could help you. You'd be here." Her mother pondered it. "Kind of like me I guess."

"But if I'm here, what happens to…"

Where was her body now? Was she still on the couch?

"Your body?" her mom asked. She shook her head. "You become a vegetable. If you're lucky, that is."

Livvy knew her face must have been asking the question she couldn't make herself speak out loud.

"If you're unlucky," her mother shrugged. "It's a padded white room."

Livvy stared at her for several moments before she could find her voice. "Mom, I'm scared."

Her mother gave her a half-smile, half-frown, and reached out. "I know," she said, pulling Livvy closer. "And you should be," she whispered in her ear.

Livvy stiffened but her mother held her tight.

"So, wake up," her mother said.

"I can't," said Livvy, trying to push her away.

"Yes, you can," said her mother, gripping her harder. "Wake up, Livvy."

"No, Mom, I don't know how," she pleaded.

"Wake up, Livvy!"

• • • • •

Without warning, Livvy felt a sharp stinging pain on the side of her face.

"Wake up!" she heard Min yell.

Livvy's eyes flew open to see Min, her hand pulled back to slap her again. Min stopped herself just in time.

Livvy grabbed at Min's arms as though they were her mother's. "Where am I?" she yelled.

"In your condo," Min said. "You're in your condo."

Livvy looked around, her eyes scanning every which way. Yes, it was the condo.

"Livvy, you're shaking," said Min.

"Is this the real world or the Multiverse?"

"What?" said Min.

"Is this the real world—"

"It's the real world, Livvy," Min said. "It's the real world. Can't you tell?"

Livvy took in a shaky breath.

"I guess if you could tell, you wouldn't have asked."

Livvy slowly let go of Min. She looked around the condo again. *Yes, the real world. Thank the gods.*

Min sat down in one of the chairs. "You didn't move all night or this morning," she said. "Until you started screaming."

Min rubbed her eyes. Livvy realized that they were both wearing the same clothes they'd been wearing yesterday.

"Min," said Livvy, shifting stiffly on the couch to sit forward. "Were you here all night?"

"Yeah," she said nodding. "We didn't think it'd be a good idea to leave you alone."

Livvy realized that SK was gone. Then she remembered what Min had seen. "Min, you didn't tell SK—"

"No," she said quickly. "But remember what I said."

Livvy nodded. She did remember and she knew Min was right. She'd have to tell SK.

"I'm going to get some tea and waffles on," said Min, getting up. "You need to get showered and changed."

It sounded like business as usual but it couldn't be.

"Why?" asked Livvy.

"Because Ursula's on her way."

CHAPTER FORTY-ONE

TRY AS SHE might, Livvy couldn't remember if she'd said anything to Matthew.

With the headache and the nosebleed and the shock of Claire's death, she wasn't sure what had happened.

While she'd been in the shower trying to rinse away the last bits of dried blood, Livvy couldn't help but think of Claire. What Matthew must be going through right now. What he must think of her.

When she came into the kitchen and sat down with Min, she brought out her phone. Min had already laid out their plates, tea, and the syrups.

"I'm going to call Matthew," Livvy said.

Min quickly reached out a hand and put it on top of Livvy's. A small spark popped.

"I don't think you should do that," she said.

"Why not?"

"Well, he's already called," said Min, sitting back and picking up her fork. "Well, not him exactly." She looked at Livvy. "His lawyer."

"Oh," Livvy whispered and looked at the phone.

"Eat," said Min. "It's your favorite."

"What did the lawyer say?"

Min picked up a syrup bottle and squirted some syrup on her waffles and then Livvy's. "Something about a wrongful death," Min said. She put down the first syrup bottle then picked up the second.

"Oh gods," said Livvy.

Min squirted out liberal doses of syrup for them both. "SK is going to handle it," Min said, putting down the second syrup.

"Is that what it was," asked Livvy, not able to look Min in the face. "A wrongful death?" She could hardly believe she was saying the words.

"No," said Min, picking up Livvy's fork and holding it out to her.

Livvy took the fork.

"No, it wasn't a wrongful death. It was murder," said Min.

Shocked, Livvy froze.

"And it wasn't your fault," she said, pointing with her own fork. "It was Dominique's. And those shameful shamans with her." She paused, remembering. "We did everything we could. Hopefully, in time Matthew will understand that."

Min nodded to herself as though that's exactly what would happen, but Livvy wasn't so sure.

"And what is up with all the black?" Min said, picking up a knife. "Someone needs to help that girl with her wardrobe. I mean, even if she's all bad and scary—solid black? Seriously? And those *boots*."

She noticed that Livvy wasn't eating. "Eat," said Min again. "It's not every day I do this." She gazed down at her own plate with some disgust. A round waffle with two colors of syrup swam in the middle of it. "Seriously, Livvy, the things I do for you." Then she smiled that playful little smile and, for a moment, Livvy felt a tiny bit of weight lift from her shoulders.

"I don't know what I'd do without you, Minnie Mouse."

"I know, huh?" she chirped, lifting her shoulders.

"I'm not talking about the waffles," Livvy said. "Not even the light in the Multiverse—which was pretty awesome."

How fitting, thought Livvy, *that Min's shamanic power is light*.

"Thank you for being a friend," Livvy said.

Min beamed and they were quiet for a few moments. Then, she pointed at Livvy's waffles.

"Right," said Livvy.

As she sliced the waffle with the side of her fork, the intercom buzzed.

"Saved by Ursula," Min crowed. "But not you," she said getting up and pointing. "You eat. If you're quick, maybe Ursula won't have to see this."

As the smell of the syrup finally started to seep into her awareness, Livvy realized she couldn't remember the last time she'd eaten. As Ursula made her way up the elevator, Livvy quickly finished the entire plate and gulped some of the Genmai tea. At least that was one thing she and Min could agree on.

As the sugar did its thing, Livvy felt a surge of energy that she hadn't felt for days.

There was a knock on the door and Min let Ursula in. Min hadn't said why Ursula had wanted to come by. Livvy stood and went over only to find herself immediately enveloped in Ursula's hug.

"Ursula," she said in a muffled tone, into the taller woman's shoulder.

"Livvy," Ursula said, relieved.

Livvy felt Ursula rub her back.

"Ursula saw the news," Ursula said. "And wanted to see with her own eyes that you were alive."

Oh gods, the news. It hadn't even occurred to her to check the TV. No doubt, it'd be all over–Claire's death, the lightning shaman's failure, and whatever Matthew was saying. It must have been bad to bring Ursula over like this. Was the news saying she was dead?

"I'm alive," she mumbled into Ursula's blouse.

Ursula eventually let her go but looked directly down into her eyes. "And Ursula wants to know how she can help."

It was starting to feel like old times. Livvy couldn't help but smile. "Thank you, Ursula. That means a lot to me," she said and paused. "But I don't know if anybody can help."

"First," said Ursula, imperiously. "Tell Ursula the problem. Let her decide if she can help."

Livvy, Ursula, and Min drifted over to the living room and Nacho jumped up into Min's lap as Livvy recounted the story.

Ursula alternately shook her head, crossed her arms in front of her, and tsked loudly as Livvy described what had happened in the Multiverse.

Abruptly, Ursula put a hand out to stop her. "Wait," Ursula said. "You had a headache and a bloody nose?"

"Big time," said Min.

"Each time you go to the Multiverse or only when you see this Dominique?" Ursula asked.

Livvy had to think about it. "Maybe only when I see Dominique," said Livvy, slowly. "Yes, I'm sure of it. The headache and bloody nose come after seeing Dominique."

Ursula chuckled, a rich and deep sound that grew to a laugh.

Livvy and Min exchanged puzzled looks and Min started to laugh just because Ursula was. Ursula stopped–though there was still the hint of a smile and a definite twinkle in the eye.

"Ursula knows how Dominique finds you in the Multiverse," she said.

"Ursula does?" exclaimed Livvy and Min together.

"Oh yes. It has nothing to do with networked goggles or goggles at all. This is vodun, pure, simple, and ancient. This is the work of an nkisi nkondi."

"A what?" asked Livvy.

"You might call it a vodun doll," replied Ursula, then held up an index finger. "But it is not."

"Then what is it?" asked Min.

"Although it looks like a person, with a head and limbs, it is actually a container. It is the container, in the belly, that gives it its power."

"Power?" asked Livvy, curious at this glimpse into Ursula's world. "What kind of power?"

"The power to find you, of course," said Ursula, irritated to be interrupted. "Nkisi nkondi means 'the hunter.' Inside there will be powerful medicines and also something of you," she said pointing at Livvy. "Fingernail clippings, a lock of hair, something personal, to give it power, to give it life."

Livvy touched the ends of her hair. She had stopped giving out locks of it almost immediately but had somebody saved some?

"The eyes of the nkondi are made of mirrors, as is the belly. The great magicians of the Congo could use them to look into the world of the ancestors, passing back and forth between this world and the spiritual world, between the real world and the Multiverse."

Fascinated, Livvy didn't interrupt this time.

"The nkondi sees into your world. It keeps a watch on you. It allows the owner, the shaman, to see your world, see what you see, see where you are."

"You make it sound so simple," said Min. "I thought it was going to be something complicated, like with the goggles."

Ursula smirked. "You are exactly right–it only *sounds* simple because of the way Ursula has told it to you. Vodun is never simple."

"And the headaches and bloody nose?" asked Livvy.

"A result of the nkondi," Ursula confirmed. "It is the one way you can be sure someone has used one on you. It is undoubtedly an nkondi 'of the above'–an nkondi of the sky and thunderstorms. Such a one will affect the upper body, particularly the head."

"I've never heard of an nkondi," said Min trying to pronounce the word as Ursula had.

"Oh it is hardly done anymore. Perhaps in the old country," Ursula said shrugging.

"The old country?" ask Livvy.

"Haiti," Ursula said. "Many, many years ago."

Then something occurred to her.

"And now," Ursula started slowly as she looked at Min, then Livvy. "Now there is a new group of Haitians."

Yes, thought Livvy. *That's why Ursula had sought her help earlier—competition from the Haitian refugees. This is starting to make sense.*

The intercom buzzed.

Min looked at it as she got up and went over. "We're not expecting anybody," she said. She pressed the button. "Yes?"

"There's a woman down here who says she needs to see Ms. Lawson," said the doorman.

It had been awhile since the doorman had called because of an unexpected visitor. Livvy had started to get them all the time, which is why she had moved to a secure building.

"She doesn't have an appointment," said Min, a statement and a request at the same time.

But the doorman wasn't through.

"She says she has information about–" He paused and they could hear him asking someone a question. "About Dominique," he finished.

At that, Ursula turned her head toward the intercom, Min looked at Livvy, and the tension in the room jumped several notches.

Who would have information about Dominique? Was it another attack?

Livvy bit her lower lip until Min gave her the 'what should I do?' shoulder shrug.

Finally, Livvy nodded. "Send her up," she said.

CHAPTER FORTY-TWO

"I KNOW YOU," said Livvy, wary.

"Me too," said Min. "You were with Dominique." She left the door open and stepped back a pace.

"I am Tamara," said the heavyset black woman with the short-cropped hair. She stood in the doorway wringing her hands.

Without thinking, Livvy got to her feet and found herself bracing for an attack. Ursula came to her side.

Tamara's wide eyes quickly looked from Min to Livvy and then Ursula. Then she stared at Livvy.

"Why are you here?" asked Ursula, stepping forward.

Tamara wrenched her gaze from Livvy and focused on Ursula. "For help," she said, her voice barely audible.

"Oh!" exclaimed Ursula. "You come here for help?"

"Whatever help you need," said Min. "I think you're in the wrong place."

Tamara seemed to shrink and began to back out the door.

"Wait," Livvy said quickly, holding out a hand. "Wait. Just…let her have her say."

Tamara hesitated and glanced repeatedly between Min and Ursula.

Ursula crossed her arms over her chest.

"Come inside," Min finally said.

The woman stared at her but didn't move.

"So I can close the door," Min said.

Tamara took a couple of small steps forward and lowered her head. Min closed the door but moved away from her to stand on Livvy's other side.

"What kind of help?" asked Livvy.

"I got to be clean," Tamara said, her voice strained. "I got to get clean."

Livvy glanced at Ursula and then Min. Apparently, neither of them had a clue either.

"I don't understand," said Livvy. "Why do you need to be 'clean'?"

"Because it is the only escape," Tamara said, the words coming quicker. "How she controls you."

Livvy shook her head. "I don't understand," she said. "How does Dominique control–"

"The *drugs*," Tamara nearly shrieked. "The drugs," she said again, much more quietly, trying to regain control.

Tamara's outburst had startled them all.

Livvy took a step forward, but Ursula placed a hand on her arm and stopped her. Then she pointedly looked at Min and tilted her head at Tamara.

"Tamara," Min said. "Come in and sit down."

Tamara's eyes squinted at her as though she were having trouble seeing.

Maybe she's remembering Min's light, thought Livvy.

"Here," said Min, indicating the chair next to her.

Tamara looked at the chair almost longingly, as if the one thing she wanted most in the Multiverse was to sit down, but she seemed frozen.

"Let's all sit," said Livvy.

Ursula and Livvy moved slowly over to the couch and sat. Min sat in the second chair and exchanged looks with Ursula.

Finally, Tamara moved to the first chair, reaching out a hand toward it as though she were on a tossing ship. She felt her way along the back of the chair to the arm, came around the front, and sat down heavily. Suddenly, she brushed frantically at something on her arm, but there was nothing there.

Livvy waited and watched. The drugs Tamara had said. If the woman was an addict, they might be watching the initial stages of withdrawal. The advent of goggles had precluded Livvy's use of drugs as an entry to the Multiverse. Even so, from medical school she knew that the hallucinogens preferred by shamans weren't addictive. They could, however, become a gateway drug to others.

"Gods, I want to be clean," said Tamara, looking at the floor.

Clean. As in free of drugs.

"Dominique provides the drugs," said Livvy.

Tamara nodded. "Cocaine," she said.

"She gives you drugs?" asked Min, incredulous. "Even though you're using goggles?"

"I did not start with goggles," said Tamara, still staring at the floor. "It was cohoba. Coke came later."

"Junkies," Ursula said with disgust.

"Yes," Tamara said without flinching as she looked up at Ursula. "Junkies."

"But you're networked through goggles," said Livvy. "You're in the Multiverse with a network." The sudden appearance of all the shamans together made that obvious.

Tamara nodded again.

"So the drugs?" said Min.

"A reward," said Tamara. "A necessity," she corrected herself, shuddering.

"So all those shamans are addicts?" asked Min.

"Yes," said Tamara. "Now, most of them are high. Any drug you want, as much as you want, after the defeat of–" She shot a look at Livvy, aware of what she was just about to say.

"It is an nkondi, is it not?" Ursula asked, her tone a challenge.

Again, the woman only nodded, as though it were obvious. "Ursula knew it," she said.

There were a few moments of silence as they processed what they'd heard.

"So, Tamara," said Livvy. Tamara immediately looked at her, the feverish face searching Livvy's for any hint of what was coming. "You want to be clean," Livvy continued. "And you want help to do that."

Ursula tsked.

"Why now?" asked Livvy.

"In the Multiverse," said Tamara, "you were against Dominique, but you do not want to hurt people. You want to help them–that woman."

"That woman, the client," said Min icily, "she died."

"Yes," Tamara said as she slowly shook her head. "I also do not want to hurt people. I did not but I am sorry."

Livvy remembered the quake that started and stopped and the way it had toppled the other shamans.

"It is Dominique," Tamara said quietly, looking at the floor. "Nothing can stop her."

"You're all responsible," said Min.

"*We're* all responsible," corrected Livvy.

"I hate her," said Tamara suddenly and then louder. "Hate her, hate her, hate her!"

Min jumped a little at the sudden vehemence.

"Then help us," said Ursula, leaning forward. "Give us the nkondi."

Tamara looked up at her as a frown pulled down the corners of her mouth. "You think I did *not* think of that? It is never alone. Never."

"Humph," Ursula grunted and sat back.

"You could tell us where she is," suggested Min.

"She is—"

"So we could what?" asked Livvy.

"Toss in a grenade," said Ursula.

Min actually nodded in agreement.

"Do you hear me?" pleaded Tamara. "She wants control of the Multiverse. She stops for nothing. She can find you there no matter where she is here." Her voice was steadily rising. "The fight is not *here*, it is *there*. I want to help but I do not know how." She was nearly screaming now. "I want her to stop but I do not know how!"

They were all silent for several moments.

"Fight fire with fire then," said Ursula.

All eyes turned to her.

"I will make an nkondi for Dominique," she said.

Tamara's eyebrows flew upward and she seemed alert.

"Can you do that?" asked Min.

"Ursula has not forgotten the old ways," she said, nodding. "It would be a powerful nkondi indeed."

"Wait a minute," said Livvy. It felt like the tide was turning but maybe too fast. "We're not trying to harm anyone," she said. "These shamans with Dominique may not be there of their own free will."

Tamara nodded vigorously at that.

"We don't have to harm anyone," agreed Min. "But if we can see into her world, like Ursula says, maybe we'll know what she's doing, what she's up to. You know, like get the drop on her, instead of vice versa."

Livvy thought about it. The nkondi wasn't a weapon, just a way to see someone, find them. Maybe this could work. Maybe if Dominique knew she had the same ability, the knowledge would be enough to put a stop to this whole thing.

"Ursula needs something of Dominique's," said Ursula, looking at Tamara. "You know what would be necessary."

"Me?" exclaimed Tamara. "I can help you in the Multiverse but I cannot go back there!"

"Yes, you can," said Ursula. "You must."

"You say you want our help," said Min.

"Wait," said Livvy. "Tamara," she said, looking directly at her. "You *will* have our help, no matter what."

"But—" started Min.

"No buts," said Livvy. "We wouldn't refuse to help you. You need to be clean."

Tamara relaxed.

"I know it took a lot for you to come here today and we're grateful that you won't be working with Dominique. But if we're going to try to end this without anybody else getting hurt, or dying, we need you to help us."

Tamara grimaced but remained silent.

"Did you tell her you were leaving?" asked Min.

"No, no, no," said Tamara, shaking her head.

"So, she does not know that you are here?" asked Ursula.

"No!"

Ursula and Min both nodded and exchanged looks. Then Ursula looked Tamara directly in the eye. "Something of her," Ursula urged quietly. "That is all Ursula would need."

Tamara's face screwed up. She had obviously made her choice, had left with no intention of ever going back. Now they were asking her to go to the one place in all the worlds that she never wanted to see again. She looked at the three of them, each in turn, landing finally on Ursula.

She took in a deep breath. "I can try," she said.

CHAPTER FORTY-THREE

"SK, WHAT'S THE matter?" he heard Livvy say as he brushed by her at the front door. Then he heard the door close.

He slammed the crystal pyramid onto the coffee table and wheeled around, unable to stop himself. "You summoned your mother?" he yelled.

She looked as though he'd struck her. She backed up against the door, staring at the pyramid.

"So it's true," he muttered.

Somehow he'd been hoping it wasn't, without even realizing it, until this moment.

"How did you–" Livvy said. "Did Min–"

"*Min?*" he screamed.

Livvy flinched.

"So *Min* knew?"

He threw up his hands before letting them fall to his sides. Of course Min had to know. She'd been in the Multiverse. She'd known and not said anything.

He suddenly laughed and shook his head. "It's like a bad soap opera," he said. "I really *am* the last to know."

"But how–"

"Dominique," he sneered, as though it were obvious. "Oh, of course," he continued, "she couldn't *wait* to tell me."

"Dominique?" Livvy said, her face in complete shock. "But–"

"She called me," he yelled. "Asked for a meeting. Here, all this time I'm trying to find her, and she just calls." He laughed again. "It's too funny."

"No, it's not," Livvy said quietly.

He turned away from her. "Oh, I think it is," he said. "I imagine she's laughing right now."

There was silence. He took a deep breath and tried to fight back the fury.

"SK, I can explain."

He turned back to her. She had stepped away from the door.

"Explain? To me? All of a sudden?"

She stopped. "I want to explain about the summoning," she tried.

"I don't care about the summoning!" he screamed, his hands balling into fists at his side, almost on his tiptoes.

As he said it, the force of that truth hit home. It wasn't the summoning that hurt. It was not knowing–especially when everybody else did.

"Can you imagine how it felt to hear it from her?"

There was silence again.

"No," Livvy whispered at last. "I can't."

Gods, what had he hoped to accomplish by coming here? Especially like this. He should have waited. He should have cooled off.

"That's it," he said, trying to stifle the anger as he turned back to her. "I'd better leave."

She quickly backed up against the door. "But I haven't explained," she pleaded.

"Do you not get it?" he yelled. "I don't care about the summoning. Summon your mother, your father, anybody, everybody!"

"Please, SK. Just let me–"

He took a step toward the door but she didn't move.

"Liv," he said, trying to calm down. "Please. Step aside."

There was a rumble of thunder over their heads and a sudden deluge of rain hit the glass doors. Neither of them looked.

"You won't even let me–"

"Liv," he said. "Step away from the door."

In his peripheral vision there was a faint blue glow.

"No," she said.

The glow grew brighter and he realized without looking that electricity was starting to make its way out of one of the wall sockets.

Was *she* doing that? Without being in the Multiverse?

Thunder boomed overhead. He quickly glanced up and then

back at Livvy. The shock and fear that had been in her face was now replaced with something else. Anger?

"Liv," he said, trying to sound even. "Unless you're going to physically prevent me from going through that door, I'm leaving. I mean it. That's what you'll have to do."

He stood still and waited. She seemed confused now and glanced back at the door. The electricity in the sockets winked off and the rain outside slackened. The room seemed very quiet. Then, she stepped to the side and away from the door.

"SK," she said, still backing away. "I would never–"

He didn't wait for her to finish. He strode to the door, opened it, and slammed it shut behind him. As fast as his short legs would take him, he went to the elevator and hit the call button, glancing back at her door.

When the elevator arrived, he hopped in and hit "Lobby," almost expecting her to appear outside the closing doors. When she didn't and they closed, he exhaled with relief, only to stop the exhale halfway out.

He'd been afraid.

He looked up as though he could see into Livvy's condo. "Gods, Liv," he muttered. "What just happened?"

CHAPTER FORTY-FOUR

IT WAS TWO in the morning and exhaustion was winning. Livvy got up and started pacing again. Every light in the condo was on and Nacho was keeping her company, waiting for her to go to bed.

"Sorry, Nacho. That's the last thing I need to do," she said.

Nacho continued to sit at the beginning of the hallway, watching her.

"No sleep tonight," she told him.

Of course the natural question, if he could have asked it, would have been "Then when?"

She shook her head. She'd have to worry about that later. For now, all she knew was that she couldn't let herself fall asleep. She couldn't let herself wander in the Multiverse, if that's what was really happening.

She might have called Min to come stay with her, but after SK's visit she wanted to be alone.

She stopped pacing, as she always did when she thought of him. She put the palms of her hands over her burning eyes and held them there. She was so tired of crying.

"Maybe there's coffee," she muttered.

She trudged toward the kitchen but stopped next to the crystal pyramid on the coffee table.

'Do you know how it felt to hear it from her?' his voice rang in her head.

She winced and backed away from it, then continued to the kitchen.

Although she didn't own a coffee brewer, she had a vague recollection of instant coffee in the back of a cupboard. She opened the topmost cabinet and looked past the tea.

Min told me to tell him and I promised I would.

There was the coffee. She set it on the counter but didn't open it, though her hand still rested on it.

But I didn't tell him. Dominique did. And now it can't be undone.

Instead of using a spoon, Livvy poured about a quarter cup of instant coffee into a mug. Then she put the water kettle on the stove and set the flame on high. She watched the blue and orange flames lick at the bottom edges of the kettle.

I have to tell him the truth. If I do nothing else, I will do that.

She stared hard at the flames until their ghostlike images began to cloud her vision. The truth wouldn't be easy nor would it change what had happened but maybe he would understand.

"Or maybe not," she said.

There was a reason she'd never told a soul.

The kettle started to whistle.

Livvy poured a quarter cup of water into the dark brown crystals and then added another quarter cup of cold water from the faucet. She downed the entire thing in three gulps and coughed. She had never liked coffee.

CHAPTER FORTY-FIVE

DOMINIQUE HIT THE bell on the counter again, louder this time. Where was that old woman? Was she running a business here or what? Finally, the door to the office opened.

"I'm comin', I'm comin'," said Mamacita as she opened the door.

"I'm comin'," squawked Pete.

When she saw Dominique, she smiled and trundled over. "Dominique," she said, sitting on the high stool behind the counter. "What can I do for you?"

"Actually," Dominique said. "It's what I can do for you."

Mamacita put on her reading glasses, reached for a peanut and began cracking the shell. "That right," she said. "Do tell."

"You—" Dominique said.

"Do tell," said Pete.

Dominique paused and glared at him. The shrill voice was irritating and she didn't like being interrupted. "Shut that thing up," she said flatly.

Without missing a beat, Mamacita put the shelled peanuts in the cage. "Hush now, Pete," she said. "The young lady has something to say."

She turned back to Dominique.

"You were saying."

"You saw the news," Dominique said, less question than statement.

Mamacita only selected another peanut and peered at her over the top of the glasses.

"The news about the lightning shaman," said Dominique.

"Oh," said Mamacita, as she looked down at the peanut she was working on. "I don't know how you could miss it, that kind of news."

Dominique nodded. "That was me," she declared.

"You," said Mamacita. She stopped shelling the peanut and set it down. "You?"

She finally had the old woman's attention. Same way she'd have everybody's attention soon.

"Me."

"And what would you have had to do with that?"

"I met her in the Multiverse," Dominique said. "I met her and I beat her." She paused to let the words sink in. "I'm top shaman now."

"Top shaman," Mamacita nodded, saying the words as though she were impressed. "I didn't know there was such a thing."

Dominique glared at the woman. She didn't have time for games. "There is and you're looking at her."

"Do declare," Mamacita said. "Do declare."

"Do declare," echoed Pete, making the old woman smile.

"And," Mamacita said as she reviewed the bowl of peanuts carefully. "What is it that you can do for me?"

"I'll bring you business," Dominique said. "International business. You could triple this place in months."

"Well," said Mamacita, selecting two peanuts. She set one in front of Dominique. "It would be silly to turn down an offer like that."

"It'd be stupid," said Dominique, pushing the peanut back. "Only one condition."

"Always a catch," said Mamacita quietly.

"Liver the Lightning Shaman isn't welcome here. No more sales to her."

A quick frown crossed the old woman's brown face and then was gone. She smiled placidly. "You might say I have an open door policy," said Mamacita, as she cracked the shell on her peanut. "No shaman is excluded."

She paused and looked Dominique directly in the eye. "Not even you."

Dominique looked right back at her. "You don't know me," she said.

"That may be so," said Mamacita nodding. "But I know my Livvy." Mamacita smiled at the thought.

This was the moment Dominique had been waiting for.

"You think you know her?" Dominique asked.

"Mmm hmm," intoned Mamacita, as she took off her glasses.

"Did you know she's performed a summoning?"

Mamacita's eyes narrowed but never moved from Dominique's face. "That's a serious accusation to make," she finally said.

"Accusation," Dominique said, flatly. "I don't make accusations. I saw it. Me, personally, in the Multiverse."

"I see," said Mamacita, non-committal.

"Do you?" said Dominique. "I seriously doubt that because none of you see her for what she really is."

"And what would that be?" asked Mamacita, sitting back.

"Weak," said Dominique. "She has summoned her own mother from the dead."

Mamacita's eyebrows went up.

"That's right," said Dominique, interested in the small revelation. "Her own mother."

She watched Mamacita's face intently. 'Her Livvy,' she'd said. Mamacita's eyebrows quickly settled back down but with the smallest furrow of worry.

Did the fact that it was her mother matter more than the summoning?

"What?" said Dominique, leaning forward. "Surely you didn't think she thought of *you* as her mother?"

Mamacita sighed and then bizarrely produced a genuine smile for Dominique. Startled, Dominique leaned back, pushing away from the counter.

"I'm going to say this, although I know there's little chance you'll understand," Mamacita said. "She's *my* Livvy because she's dear to me."

By all the gods, were these people blind?

"And she's dear to me because of *who* she is, not *what* she is," Mamacita said. She paused, thinking. "But if there was only one thing I could change about that girl," Mamacita said, looking Dominique in the eye. "It'd be that she was more like you."

Dominique's mouth opened slightly in shock.

"Yes," Mamacita said quietly. "Less compassion, less love. More self-interest, more defenses."

The old woman shrugged and turned away, but not before

Dominique saw that her eyes were glistening.

With a sweep of her long coat, Dominique turned on her heel and strode out. In moments she was on the sidewalk, standing in front of the store.

I know my delivery is effective but...tears?

That's not what she had expected, not from the legendary Mamacita.

Must be getting old.

Even so, a small feeling of disquiet came over her. Dominique shook it off, tossed her hair and readjusted her jacket. She thrust her hands into the deep pockets of the duster and started down the sidewalk. Phase two was complete. On to phase three.

CHAPTER FORTY-SIX

HER HANDS TREMBLED in her coat pockets, but Livvy knew it wasn't the caffeine.

Finally, the door opened. SK stood there, his hand on the knob. He didn't say a word, just looked at her with an expression that almost seemed bored.

"May I come in?" Livvy asked.

He didn't move. For a change, he wasn't dressed for business. The jeans and gray sweatshirt didn't seem like him. She could see she hadn't woken him, but he hadn't yet shaved. The dark circles under his eyes made him look as tired as she felt.

After the sun had risen, she had waited for what seemed like forever. Eventually, she'd just driven over without calling; afraid he wouldn't answer the phone.

"Please," she whispered.

She wasn't dressed for work either–with her army surplus coat, jeans, and orange t-shirt.

Slowly, he opened the door and stood aside.

"Thanks," she exhaled and went in.

She walked into the front room and glanced at the ocean view outside. The thick fog and impending rain made the surf barely visible. Was that a cigarette she smelled? When she turned, she realized SK had closed the door but was still standing next to it. She might not be staying long.

His sullen face held an empty expression that made her chest ache. He was no longer angry but he had retreated, closed himself off. She looked at the floor, unable to look at the grim rewards she'd earned.

Well then, just say it. Say the thing you came here to say. Just do it and have it be over with. He obviously doesn't want you here.

But she had never said the thing that she had always needed to say.

Never.

In her coat pockets, her fingernails bit into the palms of her hands, and her fists thrust down so hard that the jacket tugged tightly at her neck. Her heart was hammering as though she was running for her life. Her lungs burned and she realized she was holding her breath. She squeezed her eyes shut.

"I killed my mother," she blurted out.

She sucked in a sudden breath and opened her eyes. The words rang in the air and for a moment she wasn't quite sure she'd really said them.

"Excuse me?" SK said.

She quickly swung her gaze up to him but the room seemed to tilt.

"I–" she said. "I can't breathe." Somehow her lungs weren't bringing in enough air although they were working furiously now, her chest heaving. She put a hand on the nearest chair to steady herself.

"Here," she heard SK say and realized he was helping her to the overstuffed chair. "Sit down."

She thudded down. "I don't know what's wrong," she exhaled.

"You're hyperventilating," he answered. "Slow your breathing. I'll get a glass of water."

"No, don't go," she managed to get out. "Please. Just let me say this."

He had already turned to go but stopped, several feet away, and turned around. "All right," he said slowly.

Livvy stared at the floor in front of the chair and gripped the arms. "It was an accident," she said, still talking and breathing too fast. "My vision quest, the first time I called down lightning." She swallowed. "She must have been standing *too close*."

Livvy's throat caught and she paused briefly.

"I was in the Multiverse, one of my first journeys. It had seemed so easy," she said shaking her head at the memory–a memory she hadn't permitted herself since that awful day. Yet there it was, as clear as though it had happened only minutes ago.

"Liv, you don't have to do this," she heard SK say but she didn't dare look at him.

She plunged on. "I called down lightning, without a care or a thought, with no clue about what I was doing," she said, grinding the words out as her jaw tried to clench. "I didn't understand what was happening."

She pulled her knees up to her chest and wrapped her arms around them. "I don't know how long I was there, it was only the Middleworld but–"

Oh gods, the image in her mind.

"Liv," she heard SK say.

"But when I came back and took off the goggles," she shut her eyes tight. "She was there, on the floor. I saw right away there was something wrong. Her legs were at a weird angle and I crawled over to where she was." Livvy put her forehead on her knees. "Her eyes were wide open and her mouth looked like it was screaming, the lips pulled so tight. There was a giant blistered burn mark on the side of her head and a deep black hole in the middle of it." She saw it with utter clarity. "Not even one drop of blood," she whispered.

Without warning, a memory of the smell came back–burned human hair and charred bone. Livvy quickly jerked her head up and covered her mouth with both her hands as the nausea rose in her throat. She opened her eyes and saw SK.

His face was twisted in…what? Pain? Disgust?

"Liv, stop," he said.

But she couldn't stop, even if she'd wanted to.

"I had to summon her," she yelled, staring into his eyes. "I *had to,* don't you see? I wanted her to be whole. I needed to tell her I was sorry, that I didn't know what I was doing." She stopped suddenly and looked away. Her voice became a whisper. "I had to tell her it was an accident. Awful. Unspeakable. But an *accident.*"

Now the exhaustion was catching up to her and she felt her entire body trembling. Finally she looked at SK. "I'm sorry I didn't tell you but I couldn't. I was–" She paused. "I *am* so ashamed of what I've done. I couldn't tell anybody, especially you."

She put her forehead tiredly on her knees again.

"I'm sorry," she whispered. "I'm sorry, I'm sorry, I'm sorry."

"Liv, stop," SK said, quietly. "Just stop."

He was right. She nodded against her knees. It was time to stop. There was nothing more to say. She needed to go.

She lifted her head with an effort. "I can do that," she whispered and put her feet on the ground.

SK was standing in the exact same position he'd been in when she'd started, as though he hadn't moved a muscle. He was keeping his distance. She didn't blame him.

"You must despise me," she said lowly, all emotion gone now, replaced by a welcome numbness.

"Never," he whispered. "Not ever."

Then, as though in slow motion she watched him move toward her, his face intent. As surely as if he'd said it, she knew they would kiss.

She slid off the front of the chair and onto her knees just as he was reaching out to her. Unlike their first kiss, there was no hesitation. She wrapped her arms around him and felt his hands on both sides of her face as their lips met.

His mouth was soft but insistent. She felt the gentle pressure of his lips and the stubble on his chin. As he moved closer, she ran her fingers into his short hair and felt his hand behind her neck. Her kiss only became more urgent the more that he responded.

A profound silence abruptly settled on the room and, for a moment, Livvy thought she heard the buzz of electricity. Without warning, a thunderclap boomed around them, inside the room. The windows to their left shattered and small glass shards rained down. She only had a moment to see SK's look of shock before darkness descended on her.

CHAPTER FORTY-SEVEN

"LIV," SHE HEARD someone say. "Liv, can you hear me?"

Couldn't she just sleep? She was *so* tired.

"Liv, can you hear me?"

It was SK. She smiled at the thought. Why is he waking me up? Slowly, she opened her eyes and found she was looking at the ceiling.

"Thank the gods," he said.

She rolled her head toward the sound of his voice. He was kneeling beside her with a small cloth in his hand staring into her face. He tilted his head sideways.

"Can you hear me?" he asked.

Her lips seemed stuck together and she realized they were dry. "Mmm hmm," she mumbled.

"Good," he said.

He dabbed at the bridge of her nose with the small cloth. She felt a stinging sensation there.

She put a hand out to try and sit up.

"Careful," SK said, standing up. "There's broken glass everywhere."

Broken glass?

She looked at the floor around her. It was covered with small, greenish, irregular, pieces of glass that looked like miniature ice cubes.

"I thought when it broke up like this, it was supposed to prevent cuts," he said, dabbing at her nose again.

She looked at his face and there was a fine cut on his cheek. He set the cloth down.

"Here," he said, taking one of her hands in both of his.

As he pulled, she did her best to help and was soon sitting up, staring out into the fog through sliding glass door frames where only jagged edges of glass remained.

"Stay right there," he said, as he crunched his way to the kitchen.

In moments he was back with a glass of water. She drank all of it.

"What happened?" she asked, finally able to speak.

"You don't remember?"

He had been about to set the glass down on the floor in a little clear spot but stopped and looked at her.

She tried to recall something, anything, and looked around. SK was wearing jeans and a gray sweatshirt. She had a vision of him standing in the doorway. That's right. She'd come here to tell him about... Her pulse quickened and she nearly panicked. She saw the chair where she'd sat, recalled the look on his face, and then remembered him coming toward her. She calmed down a little.

"We kissed?" she asked with a little smile.

"We did," he said, also smiling, and took her hand. "And then?"

And then, Livvy thought. *And then what?* She didn't remember anything but the sliding door was broken and there was glass everywhere.

"An earthquake?" she ventured.

"Not exactly," he said.

Puzzled, she looked outside. "An explosion?"

"I don't think so," he said.

She turned to him and his expression had become serious. "Then what?" she asked.

"I think it was you."

"*Me?* What do you mean me?"

He shook his head. "I don't know. We kissed and then there was a deathly stillness."

He paused, watching her, waiting, but her mind was still a blank.

"There was a thunder clap," he continued, "here in the room with us that was completely deafening. My ears are still ringing." He moved his jaw, trying to pop his ears.

"Then," he said, looking at her face. "Your eyes..."

Livvy waited but he was staring at her eyes.

"Yes, my eyes. My eyes what?"

"They glowed a bright white, for just a fraction of a second and then you collapsed."

"*What?*"

She blinked—tried to imagine it, tried to sense anything different—but couldn't.

What in the Multiverse could possibly have happened?

He took her hand in both of his and she stared into his intent face.

"I know," he said. "I know how it sounds but that's what I saw."

She stared at him, looking into his eyes, still trying to understand when she noticed the cut on his cheek again. Gently, she touched his face just below it. "Are *you* okay?" she asked.

"I have never felt better," he said, grinning.

Despite the vague but growing feeling of apprehension that was starting to creep into her consciousness, she couldn't help but smile in return. He was positively beaming.

"Can you stand?" he asked.

"Yeah, I think so."

"All right, let's take it slow and be careful of the glass."

Using SK for balance, Livvy slowly got to her feet. Her legs burned with the effort, as though she'd run a marathon. She realized they were also shaking.

"If you can make it to the car," SK said, holding on to her. "I think we should just go."

"Go?" she said, looking down at him. "Go where?"

"To get some answers."

CHAPTER FORTY-EIGHT

TAMARA HAD KNOCKED on the door to headquarters so quietly that nobody answered. She knocked again, harder this time. Finally, she heard the knob being unlocked. She braced herself for whatever words of derision Dominique would greet her with but it wasn't Dominique. It was Pip.

"Tamara," she said and opened the door.

Relief flooded over Tamara. It was strange to think of how she had never noticed the stress and fear that came with being here until she had made the decision to leave and not come back.

She stepped in and stopped. Pip nearly ran into her back.

"What's wrong with you?" asked Pip, pushing her out of the way.

Tamara took it as a good sign.

As soon as Dominique left, Pip liked to act like she was in charge. Tamara glanced around. It was true. Dominique wasn't here.

"Where is Dominique?" she asked.

Pip headed toward her work area and hooked a thumb toward the windows. "You know," she said over her shoulder.

Dominique was across the alley. At various points during the day she would disappear and they would see her head in that direction.

"Said she'd be right back," said Pip as she sat down at the soldering station with a mess of wires, goggles, and a growing number of network boxes.

I will not have much time. Only minutes.

Most of the shamans were gone now, getting high at home until Dominique ordered them back. Since Livvy had survived, Tamara knew there would be another attack. The next one would be massive by the looks of what Pip was doing. Four more network boxes were being added and the wires that had been duct taped to the cement floor between the mats had been pulled up. The mats were being rearranged, moved closer together.

To make room for even more mats, Tamara thought. By all the gods, it was going to be a slaughter. There were—Tamara quickly counted mats, though they were in disarray—twice as many shamans as before. Dominique would leave nothing to chance. She meant to crush Livvy the next time they met.

Pip had returned to soldering and a couple of shamans were ripping up duct tape. A handful of other women were lying on their mats, oblivious to the noise around them, still riding high from the drugs of the victory celebration.

Tamara looked at the desk.

In the corner, under the windows, she knew what would be on the floor behind it—Dominique's bag. She only took it with her at the end of the day. Unfortunately, no one was allowed in that part of the room. Despite the fact that there was no wall or partition, everybody treated it as Dominique's office. Tamara had already thought of that.

As she approached Pip's place near the front, she searched the floor. "I lost my keys. Have you seen them?"

Pip looked up briefly but didn't remove the magnifying goggles. Her eyes appeared enormous and bug-like. "No," she said. "I haven't seen any keys but, in this mess…"

"Yes," agreed Tamara.

She passed Pip, heading in the direction of Dominique's desk.

"They must be somewhere," she said, as though to herself but loud enough for Pip to hear.

Tamara gingerly picked up a coiled bundle of wire, made a show of checking underneath, and slowly made her way closer to the desk. The bag was behind it. Maybe nothing useful would be in it but it was the one place she could think to look.

Still searching the floor and swinging her gaze from right to left, she came within an arm's length of the front of the desk.

"Hey," Pip said.

Tamara stopped and turned around, trying to keep her face calm.

"You know she doesn't like people over there," Pip said, the magnifiers flipped up onto the top of her head.

Be calm, thought Tamara. Her heart thudded in her chest. Only Pip. Be calm.

"Then do not tell her," said Tamara. "I have no money for new keys."

Pip harrumphed at that. None of them had any money. She flipped her magnifiers back down.

Tamara glanced at the other shamans. Those that weren't drugged were still busy at the far end of the room, ripping up duct tape and wires.

"Dammit!" Pip exclaimed, along with a popping sound. She waved her hand over the electronics to clear a few wisps of smoke.

Tamara whirled around. In a few short steps, she was behind the desk and crouching down. She flipped open the flap of the military messenger bag and looked inside.

It was a mess. Somehow Tamara had expected it to be as organized and squared away as the rest of Dominique's world but it looked like her bag was the same as anybody else's. She reached in and quickly swept her hand back and forth. Her fingers ran across something with a familiar shape. She grabbed it and yanked it out—a small hairbrush with *plenty* of hair in it. Perfect! As she jammed it into the large outer pocket of her robe, something else caught her eye: two bright orange plastic bottles—prescription drugs. She brought one out and saw the name on it was not Dominique's.

"Nicole Durand," murmured Tamara. Who is that?

She picked up the other. It was identical except that it was empty.

Diazepam.

There was no time to think about it. She pocketed the empty bottle and shoved the other back inside the bag.

There was Dominique's wallet, a Velcro enclosure type. Tamara peered quickly over the top of the desk. Pip was still doing damage control and none of the other shamans were looking her way.

Tamara slowly and quietly ripped open the wallet—ID, credit cards, some cash, a packet of drugs—she paused at the packet of drugs. *No*, thought Tamara. *You got to get clean. They said they would help you get clean.*

She jammed the packet back down with the cash and flipped through the photos: a younger Dominique in fatigues with some men in uniform, holding a big rifle at an angle in front of her; an older couple in farm worker clothes in a yellowed color snapshot, probably her parents; and a family shot with Dominique and another young woman who looked almost identical. Tamara bent down for a closer look. Were they twins? And the last photo—a woman who could have been Dominique but there was a strange expression on her face and her hair was cut short. Nicole?

Tamara took the photo out of the plastic sleeve.

"Tam!"

Tamara quickly looked up and saw Pip motioning toward the front door. Someone was unlocking it from the outside. The only person who had keys was Dominique.

In a flash, Tamara put the photo in her other pocket, pulled out her keys, and closed the flap on the bag. Pip was frantically waving her away from the desk. They would both be in trouble if Dominique saw her there.

Tamara jumped up and ran toward Pip. They both froze as the door opened. Pip swung the magnifier lenses down and got back to work while Tamara simply stood there watching her.

Dominique entered and closed the door. She surveyed the room and took stock of the progress that had been made. Apparently satisfied, she crossed in Tamara's direction, toward the desk.

"Come back for more drugs?" Dominique said as she passed behind Tamara.

"No," she said. "I lost my keys."

Pip looked up with the big bug eyes created by the lenses.

Tamara held the keys dangling by the ring for her to see. "Found them," she said.

She mouthed "thanks" to Pip who only looked back down at her work.

Tamara pocketed the keys, felt the other items there, and headed to the door.

"Where are you going?" Dominique said.

Tamara stopped at the door and turned around. "Home," she said.

Keep it simple, she thought. *Say no more than is necessary.*

Dominique waited, which made Tamara wait. And that, it turned out, was the whole point.

"Be ready to come back," said Dominique with a tone of

dismissal. She sat down at her desk.

"Yes, Dominique," said Tamara and then she was out.

As she hurried down the stairs that led to the sidewalk, she put both hands in her pockets to make sure her treasures did not spill out.

Nicole Durand, thought Tamara as she got to the sidewalk. Despite the sweat and light rain that were now trickling off her forehead, Tamara smiled. Dominique had a sister.

CHAPTER FORTY-NINE

AS THEY STOOD in front of Alvina's home, Livvy watched her move the smoldering sage bundle around the edges of the front door, purifying it. The fragrant smell brought back memories of the first time she and SK had come to Palm Springs to see her.

They had come seeking her help against the ancient Sumerian god, Tiamat. Alvina's renown as one of the most adept, knowledgeable and powerful shamans in the area had spread far beyond the Cahuilla reservation where she lived and worked. True to that reputation, she had been instrumental in the victory over Tiamat.

Alvina placed the bundle in the huge ashtray next to the door. Livvy watched her and waited, comforted by the familiarity of the ritual. Alvina looked as though she hadn't aged a day although, to be fair, she already looked fairly aged. Her short straight hair was completely white, combed directly back from her forehead, and tucked behind her ears. Her deeply tanned skin was full of wrinkles, both fine and deep. She was wiry to the point of sinewy, and the skin of her arms had developed that leathery look a lifetime in the desert could create. Although she wore a brightly colored, floral print cotton dress, the beautiful vest she wore over the top of it shimmered in earth tones of tan, gray, and brown.

She held both of her hands in front of her and SK gave her the cigars and scotch. She smiled a brilliantly white smile at both of them and winked at Livvy.

"Welcome, my young friends. Please, come in." Alvina shifted her new acquisitions over to one arm and hugged Livvy with the other. "Livvy. It's so good to see you."

Livvy hugged her back, feeling the taut muscles in Alvina's shoulders and back.

"My how you've changed," Alvina whispered.

Have I? thought Livvy, drawing back.

Alvina's radiant smile had dimmed and there was something about her eyes now that seemed–what was it–maybe a little sad.

"SK," she said turning to him. She placed a hand lightly on his arm. "As always, it's good to see you."

"And you, Alvina," he said, doing the same.

Alvina stood back and took in the two of them. "I take it this isn't business and you have some questions," she said, motioning them to the front room. She closed the door behind them.

Livvy promptly sat down on the couch, grateful she hadn't had to walk far. Whatever had happened at SK's condo, she still wasn't feeling right.

"Tell me everything," Alvina said as she took a seat in one of the chairs.

Alvina's home had a comfortable, lived-in look that reminded Livvy of her grandmother's house. There were framed family photos everywhere. Finely crocheted doilies separated the faintly purple glass bowls from the tabletops. The sheets that had apparently covered the furniture were neatly folded and resting on one of the chairs. Like most shamans, Alvina probably kept her altar in the bedroom. The only clue to her profession was the large wooden bowl of sage bundles on the bottom shelf of the end table.

SK sat on the couch next to Livvy and took her hand. Alvina looked at their hands briefly and then at SK.

He told her everything–about Claire's death, about Dominique, the other shamans, and also the summoning. Alvina had listened, perfectly silent, but turned a disapproving look on Livvy when SK had talked about her mother in the Multiverse. Livvy recoiled inwardly and looked at the floor. Then SK described their kiss and what had happened.

Livvy squeezed his hand during that part. In all of this, it was the one bright spot. She had shared her dreadful secret with him and he had not turned away. In fact, it felt like they were really together now. His voice was even and level, and there was no regret in it.

"I don't understand what's happening," he finished. "We hope you do."

There was silence in the room.

Alvina slowly shook her head and got up. She walked to the front window and parted the drapes to look outside. It had started to rain in giant infrequent drops plopping down on the roof. Alvina watched in fascination.

"Rain in the desert," she said to herself. "Rare, especially this side of the mountains." She gazed upward. "They say it's El Niño." Then she shook her head and was quiet again.

Livvy looked at SK and he shrugged. The silence seemed to stretch into minutes.

"My friends," Alvina finally said, still looking outside. "It can't always be as we wish."

"Is it the summoning?" Livvy asked, afraid of the answer.

Alvina turned around and let the drapes close. "No, it has nothing to do with that," she said. "Although," she fixed Livvy with a serious look from which she could not turn away. "You shouldn't have done it. Summoned into the Multiverse and not the real world? It can't last. It won't."

It can't last?

"It's Dominique," SK said, seething.

Alvina shook her head again. "No, not her either."

There were a few moments of silence until Livvy couldn't stand it anymore. "Well, then what?" she asked.

Alvina tilted her head slightly toward her and there were those sad eyes again. "It's you," she said, pointing at Livvy.

Livvy drew back, pressing into the couch as her hand went to the spot on her chest where Alvina was pointing. She thought for a second about trying to laugh it off but realized that Alvina's face had turned deadly serious.

"I don't understand," SK finally said. "What do you mean it's Livvy?"

Alvina came back to the chair and sat down. She looked SK directly in the eye. "Water Baby," she said quietly. "It's the lightning shaman."

Her words caused SK to tighten his grip on Livvy's hand.

"Okay," said Livvy, afraid now. "What is this water baby? That's the third time I've heard it."

Alvina seemed surprised and then looked back at SK. "She doesn't know about the water baby?"

He was quiet for a few moments and then gave a small shrug. "A little," he said quietly.

Livvy saw something resigned in his face. Suddenly, she felt an odd displacement, as though she weren't really part of this conversation, just an observer.

"What about the water baby?" Livvy asked.

Alvina continued to stare at SK but, when he remained silent, she turned to Livvy. "The water baby is what desert peoples in California call him," she said. "In other parts of the world, he is known by different names: the Master of Animals, the Dwarf of Uxmal, and others. He is the shaman's aid and ally, the go-between, the intercessor, the one who keeps the spiritual world and real world in balance. A shaman who has the aid of the water baby has more power–is capable of doing more and better healing–in the Multiverse."

"The Dwarf of Uxmal," Livvy repeated.

She remembered the first time the Nahual had seen SK. That's what she had called him.

"Not all intercessors are dwarfs though," said Livvy.

"Oh, no, no, no," said Alvina shaking her head. "Only if we're lucky, since dwarfs are the most powerful. In our part of the world, water baby takes his name from the small footprints that he has left in the dark desert rocks of the north. Many, though not all shaman cultures, prize the presence of the dwarf most highly."

Livvy looked at SK and he smiled a little sheepishly at her. "So, you're a rock star," she said.

He shrugged.

Livvy turned her attention back to Alvina. "But what does that have to do with me?"

SK looked at Alvina, also interested in the answer. He'd obviously known about the water baby.

"Many times," Alvina said, "when there is a water baby, he has a perfect match–the perfect shaman to whom he can lend his aid. The Master of Animals is naturally paired with the Master of Fish, a woman who lives under the water." She looked at SK. "The perfect match for the water baby is…" Alvina turned her eyes to Livvy. "The lightning shaman."

"Well but that's good," said Livvy, encouraged. No wonder it felt so right to be with him.

"But not in the way you think," said Alvina. "Not in the way that you want." She gazed down at their intertwined fingers on the couch. "Not in that way."

"Why?" Livvy and SK both asked.

"It is a union in the spiritual sense," Alvina said. "Not the physical."

"What?" said SK, incredulous. "Why one and the not other? They're not mutually exclusive."

Alvina took a deep breath and opened her mouth to begin what seemed like a long explanation but she stopped and addressed Livvy. "Has your menstrual period stopped?"

Livvy blinked and stared at her. "W–What?" she managed to stammer.

How could Alvina have possibly known?

Livvy had been exhausted lately, working too hard, under too much stress. She hadn't had her period for a few months but she had chalked it up to the constant pressure.

"Be honest with me," said Alvina, waiting.

"It stopped a few months ago," Livvy said mechanically.

SK turned to look at her, his eyebrows mounding furiously.

Alvina nodded. "Your child bearing days are over," she said.

SK whipped his head back around to face Alvina. "That's ridiculous," he said. "Livvy's only, I don't know, in her early twenties. There could be any number of reasons–"

Alvina gently held up a hand and quieted him. To Livvy she said, "I'm sorry, my young friend, but I think you sense the truth of it."

Livvy did. Somehow, despite telling herself all this time it was only temporary, she felt the rightness of what Alvina said and now she sensed the futility of arguing it.

"But–" SK said.

"Always there is a balance," Alvina said. "Something lost for what is gained. As shamans, we are sometimes at the center of life and death, the knife edge that separates them."

"SK, you know that as shamans age, we become more powerful. It is the young ones who struggle."

SK could only nod in agreement.

"As we age, we become more and more capable of helping people to live, of sustaining life, but we lose the ability to create it."

She nodded to herself as though she were remembering a different time in her life. "Always the balance," she concluded.

"But," said SK. "You say as you get *older*. Livvy should have years to go."

"No, my friend," said Alvina. "She is the lightning shaman. Her power has blossomed in the Multiverse–grown and grown and grown." She looked at Livvy. "Hasn't it?"

It hadn't been a secret but suddenly Livvy felt caught. Finally she nodded. "I move fast in the Multiverse," she said and glanced at SK, who was staring at her. "Very fast."

"Helped by you, Water Baby," Alvina said. "And also because of who she is–a shaman the likes of which comes once in a generation." Alvina nodded to the window. "I knew you were near when the clouds began to build."

"Shouldn't that only happen in the Multiverse?" he said.

Alvina shrugged. "And yet, here it is," she said. "The wound she carried back into the real world, the weather she creates, and now the speed. Even when we first met–the color of her hair and the electricity during healings. This isn't new."

Suddenly, Livvy thought of the thunderclap when they'd kissed. SK must have been thinking the same thing.

"And...the kiss?" asked SK. His voice was tentative now, no longer the assured tone he'd had when they first arrived.

Livvy found herself dreading the answer, and the tight grip on her hand let her know SK was feeling the same.

"Completely wrong," Alvina snapped, surprising them both. "Completely the wrong direction."

Livvy stared at her and SK shook his head, neither of them comprehending.

"SK," Alvina said sternly. "Water baby aids the shaman, not the other way around. You give your support, your energy to them." She motioned with her hand going from SK to Livvy. "It goes against all nature and the Multiverse if it should flow the other way." Then she motioned from Livvy to SK. "Then you take the energy that she offers. She can't help it. Especially if she..."

There was silence.

"If she what?" Livvy heard herself asking.

Alvina turned the sad eyes on her. "Especially if she loves you," said Alvina. "When you open your heart like that in an unguarded moment, you lose control."

Livvy stared at her without really seeing.

How long had they been here? Fifteen minutes?

"As you change in the Multiverse, you change here," said Alvina quietly. "If you want to stop, then stop."

"What do you mean stop?" SK said.

"To end the changes here, you must bring an end to the transformations in the Multiverse. You can't stop the lightning but you can stop the speed. If you don't, the changes will continue. The more you transform, the more powerful you become, the smaller the possibility of being together. If you stop now, there may still be a chance." Alvina paused and looked down at their hands. "Of course, if you really want to be together, the only true guarantee is to stop being a shaman."

SK inhaled sharply but didn't say anything.

Livvy closed her eyes.

Maybe it'd been thirty minutes, not fifteen. Even so, how could so much have changed in so little time?

Drained of emotion there were no tears. She felt SK's hand on hers.

Don't let go, SK. Whatever you do, don't let go.

He didn't.

"I'm sorry," she heard Alvina whisper.

CHAPTER FIFTY

"IN AN EXCLUSIVE interview, Channel 8 Morning News is the first to bring you an in-studio interview with shaman Dominique Durand."

The morning news anchor was the station's up and coming reporter, Mike Chambers. With only ten years in Los Angeles, he was a relative newcomer. He had been covering the lightning shaman almost exclusively for the station and had used that coverage to land the desk spot.

"Welcome, Dominique," he said, turning to her.

In her softest, smoothest, and most appealing of tones, she tilted her head and smiled her best smile. "Thank you, Mike. It's a pleasure to be here."

"Dominique, let's get right to what everybody's been wanting to know: What has happened to the Lightning Shaman, Olivia Lawson?"

"Honestly, Mike," said Dominique sadly. "It's not really for me to say what's going on with another shaman. I can tell you, though, that I've seen Olivia and spoken to her."

"Well then, you're the only person I know to have done that."

Dominique knew he'd probably been calling every phone number he had, anyone even remotely connected to Liver, and they had all refused his calls.

"Can you tell us how she is?" he asked.

"I'm happy to say that she's doing as well as can be expected," Dominique replied.

"As can be expected," he echoed. "So, not quite business as usual then?"

"I think that's fair to say," said Dominique coyly.

"It's probably a forgone conclusion after Claire Stockard's

242

death," he said and turned to the camera. "I'm sure most of our viewers are familiar with the circumstances surrounding the death of Claire Stockard, two days ago. For those who aren't, this reporter was at the Stockard compound that day."

Dominique watched a monitor that was built into the long and angled desk at which they sat. The video had been shot from the gate and focused on the silver sedan.

As it drew closer, the camera was jostled and Mike's voice was almost lost in the clamor. "Mike Chambers here with Channel 8 News," she heard him say. "Here comes Olivia's sedan. We saw Olivia, Soo Min, and SK hurriedly enter the vehicle at the front door only minutes after the ambulance arrived. From this distance it was hard to tell but it looked like Olivia had blood on her shirt and jacket."

Then the sedan rolled slowly by. Dominique recognized Liver's little friend who'd blinded them all. In the back seat, the tinted windows made it difficult to see. Dominique had seen this footage before, as anybody who watched the news anywhere had.

"We can just make out Olivia and SK in the back seat as they're going by. It looks like Olivia is actually lying down, though whether it's because she needs to or she wants to be out of camera view, we can't tell."

Shouts and calls to Liver drowned out Mike's voice and the footage ended. Dominique was careful not to smile.

Mike looked at the camera again.

"Channel 8 news has also learned that Ms. Stockard's son Matthew has been in touch with his attorneys and that a civil suit in the matter of a wrongful death is being considered."

He turned back to Dominique. "Is there any light you could shed on that aspect, Dominique?"

"No," she said, shaking her head and flipping her hair a bit at the end. "I'm afraid not."

"Is there anything you *can* tell us?"

"Mike, I think shamanism has come a long way in Los Angeles and I'd hate to see that trend reversed. I want to reassure your viewers that there are other shamans here who can help them."

"Shamans such as yourself."

"Actually, no," she said, giving her pre-calculated laugh. "Honestly, Mike, I'm completely booked up."

This was a lie, of course, but Dominique had seen with Liver that when something wasn't available, people seemed to demand it all the more.

He raised his eyebrows and nodded once.

"Although I'd try to make an exception for any of Olivia's clients," she added, as though it were an afterthought.

"Oh really," he said. "So, you don't think Olivia will be working for her clients anymore?"

As though she'd let the cat out of the bag, Dominique frowned a little. "Oh no, no. I'm sure she will be. Eventually."

"Eventually," he echoed.

Dominique only smiled and nodded.

"Well," said Mike, wrapping up the four-minute spot, "Thank you, Dominique, for coming to the studio in a shaman first."

"Mike, it has truly been my pleasure."

CHAPTER FIFTY-ONE

LIVVY HAD ALWAYS assumed she'd have children. She adored them. In what seemed like a different life, back in medical school, she had intended to specialize in pediatrics. Of course, she'd never had to make a decision about kids. She'd never met the right guy—until SK. They'd have to talk about the genetics of dwarfism but…

Nacho was rubbing his face on her ankle. She blinked and slowly came back to the moment. She was still standing in the middle of the living room, goggles in hand.

"Hey, Nacho," she said quietly.

She crouched down and he put his front paws on her knees as though he were going to climb up, desperate for affection.

"I know," Livvy said, scratching the top of his head and behind his ears. "I've been pretty scarce."

He purred and she kept moving her fingers but her eyes unfocused again. She heard Alvina's voice: 'Your child bearing days are over.'

She and SK had hardly said a word on the drive back from Palm Springs. She had been too shell-shocked to put together a coherent thought, let alone a sentence. She knew that he had glanced at her several times but he'd kept quiet also.

Their first kiss hadn't been right, she thought suddenly. Besides not remembering much of it, she realized that she'd probably sat in the chair long after SK had left because she hadn't been able to get up.

Or maybe *he's just a great kisser*, she thought, smiling a little to herself. *Because he is that.* They *had* to be together. It just felt too right. Maybe Alvina was…

Nacho was meowing.

Livvy blinked at him, the half-smile quickly fading. "Look

Nacho, I've got to go for a while but there's fresh food in the bowl." She leaned forward and kissed his soft forehead before standing up. "I've got to see Mom," she said. "It's time to have that talk."

The words didn't have the dread she was used to feeling when she thought of her mom and the summoning. Maybe because SK knew now. Maybe because she knew the summoning wouldn't last. Maybe because she was past feeling anything.

Whatever it was, it was a relief. She went to the bedroom with the goggles and shut the door behind her.

• • • • •

"Mom," said Livvy, "I'm sorry it's taken me so long."

Without a goggle network, the downtown cityscape of the Underworld was restored. Livvy glanced around before hugging her mom. Although she didn't see any of them, the crowd of ancestor spirits might be restored as well.

"That's all right, honey," said her mom, hugging her back. "You're here now. That's all that matters."

Livvy backed away from her so that she could see her face. "I wish it were that simple," she said.

"I don't understand," said her mom.

There was no good way to say this.

"I can't stay in the Multiverse but neither can you."

"What?"

"You can't stay in the Multiverse, Mom. It just doesn't work that way."

Even as she repeated what Alvina had said, she started to put the pieces together.

"Everything here seems to work against it," she continued. "The ancestor spirits last time…"

Her mom nodded, tentatively at first, and then with more force. "You must be right," she said.

A brief look of confusion quickly changed to one of resignation. It was as though she'd heard a death sentence and already resigned herself to it–a death sentence that Livvy had delivered.

Livvy hugged her. "Mom, I'm so sorry," she said.

They swayed together for a few seconds; Livvy did her best not to cry.

"Wait," said her mom. "It won't last in the Multiverse." She held Livvy at arm's length. "What about the real world?"

Suddenly, they swayed again, but this time it was unintentional. Livvy grabbed her mother's arms and managed to keep them both upright.

"Livvy, what's going on?"

If Livvy hadn't known better, she'd have said it was an earthquake. Even as she thought it, though, she knew it wasn't. There was no rumbling, no sound, no vibration, nor did the glass of any of the surrounding buildings move. Even so, she and her mother were having trouble staying on their feet. In fact, they were starting to slide toward the fountain.

"Mom," said Livvy, still holding on to her. "It's gotta be the Multiverse."

The ground was tilting noticeably now.

Livvy looked up to the sky but wondered how lightning would help. Wind? Maybe a whirlwind? She reached a hand upward but the ground tilted wildly in answer.

Her mom's arm was wrenched out of her hand. "Livvy!" she screamed.

Then Livvy lost her footing and slid.

Below her, she saw her mother tumbling out of control, heading toward the fountain. But like a giant game where they were the marbles, the angle of the tilt changed and Livvy's mom just missed it. No sooner was she past it, though, then the tilt changed again.

Alvina was right, Livvy thought as she careened toward the waiting water. This was never going to work–not in the Multiverse.

CHAPTER FIFTY-TWO

MAMACITA SEPARATED THE books from the incense and candles, sliding them into two neat piles on the counter. Livvy hardly noticed as she shelled a peanut for Pete and tossed it into the cage.

"Not a conjuring," Mamacita said.

Livvy's head whirled toward her faster than her hair could keep up and it washed across her face.

Mamacita sat back on her stool. "Don't try it, baby," she said. "You don't know what you're getting into."

Livvy felt her face flush. "I don't know what you're talking about," she said quickly.

"Huh uh, no," said Mamacita, shaking her head. "Not with me. You know better."

"Are you going to sell me the books or not?"

Mamacita ignored that. "I know about the summoning, child. There's no point in pretending."

Gods, did everybody know? Had SK told her?

"Dominique was here," Mamacita said, answering the unspoken question.

"Dominique!" Livvy said, her voice rising. "I'm sick of hearing about Dominique!"

"You'll get used to it," Mamacita said, all mildness.

What? Was that a threat? From Mamacita?

Outside, lightning flashed.

Mamacita peered over her glasses toward the front window and then back at Livvy. "Livvy, honey," said Mamacita. "I'm not saying this to cause you pain. That's the very last thing I'd want to do. I think you know that."

Livvy didn't reply. What was she leading up to?

"I'm saying this because I love you, child, and don't want to see you get hurt."

Mamacita patted the books on the counter between them. "Leave these here."

Livvy glared down not even seeing them. Dominique had been here. She must have tried to turn Mamacita against her. Had maybe succeeded.

Gods, not Mamacita.

"I can't," said Livvy through clenched teeth. "I have to have them."

"No," replied Mamacita, looking at her over the glasses. "You don't."

Was everybody going to tell her what she could and couldn't do? Who she could and couldn't be? Who she could and couldn't be with?

There was another flash of lightning and the sound of thunder.

"You can't help everybody," Mamacita said, shaking her head. "You can't fix everything, though you might try. By all the gods, how you try."

"Are you going to sell them to me or not?"

"No," said Mamacita. "But I'll—"

Livvy inhaled deeply. "*No?*"

"Let me finish, child—"

"*No?*" Livvy yelled as rain lashed the window. "Well as everybody is *so* fond of reminding me, I'm the freaking lightning shaman. The once in a generation shaman, lucky me," she yelled, unable to stem the frustration. "How about if someone trusts me for a change? Didn't question everything I do? Even the *shopkeeper* is going to question me now!"

"Livvy—" Mamacita said, a warning tone in her voice.

"No, Mamacita! I didn't ask for this. I *never* wanted to be the lightning shaman! And now I can't even—"

Livvy thought of SK and stopped. What was the use?

And now Mamacita and Dominique?

"Why, Mamacita?" Livvy moaned. "Why would you believe her but doubt me, after all this time?"

"That's exactly why," said Mamacita. "Because after all this time, I know you, honey." Mamacita shook her head slowly. "After all this time, don't you know me?"

Livvy shrank back at the real hurt in Mamacita's voice. A sudden pang of regret pushed down the rage she felt for Dominique. Tears stung her eyes.

Mamacita pushed the books toward her.

Livvy stared down at them.

"You're going to sell–"

"I'm not going to sell them to you, I'm going to give them to you," said Mamacita. "No charge. You should have let me finish."

Livvy reached out and took them in shaking hands.

"But, for your own sake," said Mamacita. "Don't bring a spirit into this world. Don't tamper with that kind of power."

Livvy tucked the books under her arm and avoided Mamacita's gaze. "I don't have a choice," she said, her throat tight with the effort of not crying.

She headed to the door and raised the collar of her coat against the rain outside.

As the bell above her tinkled, she heard Mamacita's soft voice from the counter. "There's always a choice, baby. You'll see that one day. Don't–"

Livvy quickly opened the door but paused.

"Don't be a stranger," Mamacita said.

CHAPTER FIFTY-THREE

URSULA WATCHED AS Tamara entered through the draperies, backing into the room as was proper. She turned around only when she was completely through the door and it had closed. According to the rules of Ursula's loa or patron vodun spirit, the entire world was inverted: right was wrong, up was down, and backward was forward.

"You will be pleased," Tamara said, stopping at the doorway.

In response, Ursula rose from her chair and stepped toward the crackling fire. On the mantle above it, two glass bottles waited–one large, one small. She took them both and, in only a few graceful strides, stood in front of Tamara, holding them out to her.

"These will help you…" Ursula paused, trying to remember the phrase that Tamara had used. "These will help you *get clean.*"

Tamara stared, her eyes grown impossibly wide, and slowly extended her hands to receive them.

Ursula gave her the large bottle first. "To help your body rid itself of toxins."

Tamara took the bottle but her eyebrows knitted together in worry. Ursula watched as she silently mouthed the word 'toxins.'

"Toxin," said Ursula. "Poison." She waited. "Pwazon."

"Pwazon!" Tamara said. "Yes. I must be rid of the pwazon. Um, toxins."

Ursula nodded.

"For sleep," she said, as she gave Tamara the smaller bottle. "For the dreams, the tightness in the chest, the sweating."

Tamara took the bottle but stared up at Ursula with a look of wonder. "You know?"

"Yes, Ursula knows. Ursula remembers."

There was quiet understanding in Tamara's face. She clutched the bottles to her chest.

"Mési anpil," she whispered. "*Thank you very much.*"

Ursula slowly nodded and then indicated a small, high, glass-top side table, just left of the fireplace. "Show Ursula what you have brought."

Tamara gingerly set her bottles down and dug into the pockets of her robe. She brought out a brush and laid it down.

A brush with hair. *Excellent*, thought Ursula. *Excellent.*

Then Tamara brought out a wallet-sized photo and an empty prescription bottle and laid them there as well.

Ursula came closer. "The hair will be more than sufficient for—"

"Dominique has a sister," Tamara burst out, grinning.

"What?" said Ursula.

"I found these in her bag," she said, picking up the photo. "This is her."

"A sister?" asked Ursula, taking the photo.

"I know," said Tamara, almost giddy. "They can be twins."

"*Could* be twins," Ursula corrected.

"Could be twins," Tamara repeated.

Ursula looked at the photo, puzzled.

"Yes," said Tamara. "You do not know Dominique. If this woman had long hair, she *could* be Dominique."

"How do you know it is not?"

"In her wallet there is a family photo, two girls together, who look like little Dominiques," said Tamara. "Anyway, the one photo Dominique has of herself is from the army."

Ursula raised her eyebrows but then scowled. The Haitian military had been disbanded years ago—*good riddance*. Dominique would have been too young. Maybe Tamara had meant the National Police. Even that was nonsense. The only women they tolerated were prostitutes.

She examined the photo again and picked up the empty prescription bottle. "Nicole Durand. Diazepam," read Ursula. "What is it for?"

Tamara shook her head. "I do not know."

Ursula placed the photo on the table and put the bottle on top of it. She moved the hairbrush on top of it too.

"Sisters," she said.

"A *secret* sister," said Tamara. "She does not talk about her but…" Then Tamara realized where the sister had to be. "She goes across the alley. That is where she is." Tamara regarded the bottle. "Something is wrong with her and she is a secret."

Ursula nodded.

Practicing the type of shamanism Dominique did it was no surprise she kept her family hidden. Eventually someone was bound to take revenge, probably by targeting someone close to her. Dominique should have divested herself of all such connections long ago but perhaps her sister wasn't capable of being on her own.

"One nkondi," said Ursula, nodding at the items on the table. "For both of them."

CHAPTER FIFTY-FOUR

THERE HAD BEEN just a hint of a swagger as Mayet had entered Mamacita's office, then he saw SK. Now, he looked apprehensive. Apparently Mamacita hadn't told him that he'd be here.

Good for you, Mamacita.

SK stood but didn't offer his hand. "Mayet," he said, looking down on him as much as their difference in height allowed.

"SK," answered Mayet.

As they took their seats, Mamacita closed the door to her office and then she joined them.

"I was surprised at your message, Mamacita," said Mayet.

"I don't doubt that," she said, settling down. "But I think we need to get all our cards on the table."

"You said," began SK, "that we might be working at cross-purposes."

"Well, I like it better the way you say it," she said. "But, yes, I think we might be pulling in opposite directions."

"In what way?" asked Mayet, glancing at SK.

SK had also been surprised to get Mamacita's call. In all the time he'd known her, she had never called *him*—only the other way around. He had been less surprised to hear of Mayet, though not pleased. Los Angeles was easily dense enough for more than one shaman intercessor, even more than one water baby, but Mayet was clearly out to expand his territory. It took some nerve to come here unannounced. Intercessor etiquette would have dictated that Mayet contact SK first—not to ask permission, necessarily, just a polite heads-up. Mayet had already known the reception SK would have given him.

"Well, first, let's talk about Dominique," said Mamacita.

SK nodded.

"Dominique?" said Mayet. "What about her?"

"I'm sure you didn't know," said Mamacita soothingly, "but she attacked Livvy in the Multiverse and was responsible for the death of Claire Stockard."

Mayet quite literally sputtered, even coughed a little. "What? When?"

"Two days ago, in the afternoon," said SK.

Mayet's eyes flicked to the floor remembering.

"No," he said. "No, I was there."

"Yes, I know you were," said Mamacita.

There was an awkward pause.

"No," said Mayet. "No, you can not possibly think—"

"I said that you didn't know," said Mamacita, holding up a hand.

"I did *not* know," Mayet insisted.

"I'm sure," said Mamacita.

Mayet glanced at SK. Everyone knew he worked with the lightning shaman. They had apparently been working against one another.

"She was clever," Mayet implored. "She lied."

SK ignored him. "Tell us what you saw," he said.

"But how was I to know?" Mayet asked Mamacita, almost whining.

"By being an intercessor," SK shot back at him.

"Gentlemen," said Mamacita. "Please."

Mayet swallowed as SK continued to glare at him.

"Mayet," said Mamacita. "Tell us what happened."

Tiny beads of sweat had appeared on his forehead and he licked his lips. "She had a client," he said to her. "No doubt someone just pretending." He studiously avoided looking at SK. "The network was huge. I'd never seen one before. Everything was home-made."

"So you were at her home?" asked SK.

Mayet shook his head, still not looking at him. "No, I don't think it was anybody's home. More like a workplace."

"But you know where it is?" asked Mamacita.

"I do," he said.

SK looked at Mamacita. They could get to Dominique.

"Fine," said Mamacita, nodding. "That's just fine. We'll leave that for later."

There was a brief silence and Mayet took out a handkerchief and wiped his brow and head.

"I know *you* don't know..." Mamacita said.

SK realized she wasn't talking to Mayet. He turned to see her looking at him.

I don't know what?

"Livvy is going to attempt necromancy."

Mayet jumped down from his chair. "By all the gods!" he said.

"*What?*" said SK, hardly hearing Mayet.

"Now calm down, the both of you," said Mamacita. "Let's just everybody calm down."

"It can't be permitted," exclaimed Mayet.

"I know that, I know that," said Mamacita, holding up both hands.

"It's insanity," he continued.

"Mayet, please, sit down," said Mamacita.

Mayet looked at her and then at SK but took his seat.

"Did she tell you that?" SK asked, his calm voice surprising him.

"She didn't say it in so many words," said Mamacita. "But the pattern in her purchases was clear. So, yes, you could say she told me."

Necromancy. SK shuddered at the thought. The room had become very quiet and they all remained silent for several seconds.

"Do you know anything about it?" SK finally asked Mamacita.

She slowly shook her head. "Same as you," she said. "It seems like every religion back to the Stone Age had their conjured spirits, welcome and unwelcome. I've heard it said that a shaman who conjures a spirit risks being possessed by them. They say a shaman who uses necromancy gives a bit of their own life."

SK nodded. It went against the very structure of the Multiverse and yet there were those for whom it held a macabre fascination—maybe *because* it was so dangerous. Liv wasn't one of those.

"I know something about it," Mayet said.

SK shot a look at him. *Well that figures.*

"No doubt you have heard," Mayet said to Mamacita.

"There is little that I don't hear," she confirmed.

Mayet took a deep breath. "A mistake of youth," he said sadly. "Of pride. It nearly ended my career before it began." Mayet paused, remembering. "At the bedside, right after the death of the client. The shaman would not give up, would not come back to the real world. There was something personal between them. When I realized what might be taking place, I…" He glanced at SK. "I decided to lend my aid."

SK held his face rigid.

Mayet looked at his hand as he tentatively extended his arm in front of him. SK couldn't help but stare at it as well, knowing the power that a water baby could add.

"It was not enough," said Mayet. "*I* was not enough. For just a moment, the shaman's eyes opened and she stared at me, but I knew instantly it was not her."

Mayet fell silent.

"What happened then?" Mamacita asked.

"She died," he said quietly, grimacing at the memory. He shook his head and looked up at Mamacita and then SK. "By all the gods, what would ever make her attempt it?"

SK knew what. It was her mother, particularly the way she had died.

Had she kept this from him as she had the summoning? No, he couldn't believe that. She had poured out her soul that day. Of that, there was no doubt. Something must have happened since he'd last seen her. Was this the result of hearing Alvina's news?

"Who knows what a lightning shaman could call forth," said Mayet. "She has to be stopped."

Mamacita nodded.

"That's why I bring it up," she said. "But I'm not sure we can."

"I do not understand," Mayet said.

Mamacita recounted the weather, a phenomena SK recognized all too well. Then there was the electricity, all around her. The power of the Multiverse practically overflowed from her.

"She is the lightning shaman," she concluded.

Yes, that's for sure, thought SK.

Mayet sat back in his chair.

"Even so, I've been doing some thinking," said Mamacita.

SK regarded her silently. Mamacita–always thinking.

"Mayet, if you will," she said to him. "I'd like you to tell me where Dominique's workplace is."

"Yes, of course," he said eagerly.

"SK," she said turning to him. "Could you–"

"I'll talk to Liv," he said.

"What will you do to Dominique?" asked Mayet.

"I intend to help her," said Mamacita.

"What?" said Mayet.

"You said yourself that it can't be permitted. I agree but not for the same reasons. I don't really care what's right or not right."

Mayet seemed about to protest but Mamacita continued on.

"I don't give a fig about necromancy," she declared, "but I won't see Livvy hurt. I just won't. If I have to use an enemy of hers to put a stop to it, that's what I'll do. The only thing I need you to do is give me her address and stop working with her. Not that you would, I know, but I need to make sure that I have her all to myself. Best to keep this simple."

Mayet only nodded.

Mamacita was starting to worry SK now.

"Dominique will kill Liv if she has the chance," he said.

"Oh I don't think so," said Mamacita. "If Livvy were to unleash her full power, no one could stand against it."

"You don't know that for sure," he said.

"I think I do," she replied. Over the tops of her glasses, Mamacita fixed him with the patented Mamacita stare. "Would you prefer she try necromancy?"

The prolonged silence in the room was her answer.

CHAPTER FIFTY-FIVE

LIVVY CLOSED THE last book and set it on the shelf with the others. A conjuring into the real world would probably be easier than a summoning into the Multiverse. She shook her head a little. It was ironic.

Do I always pick the hard way?

The answer was no, of course. Somehow, seeing her mother's spirit in the Multiverse had seemed okay. She knew it wasn't right, had tried to keep it a secret, but it hadn't seemed like actual... necromancy.

According to these books, it wasn't. The main difference was that, in the Multiverse, they dealt with each other strictly on the spiritual plane–spirit to spirit, as it were. The living and the departed interacted regularly there.

In the real world, Livvy would need a protective circle for her physical body. She trusted her mom, of course, but a soul returned from the dead might be disoriented, try to enter whatever body was at hand.

Then there was the blood. At least she knew how to draw a sample. It didn't need to be much since she didn't intend the conjuring to be permanent–just give them a little time.

There was a buzz from the intercom.

Livvy shut the cabinet doors. She hadn't been expecting anybody. She hesitated before turning off the light in the walk-in closet and glanced back at the cabinet.

"Hold on, Mom," she muttered.

There was another buzz as Livvy jogged over and hit the answer button. "Yes?"

"Ms. Lawson," came the doorman's tinny voice. "Ursula and Tamara are here to see you."

It must be about the vodun statue.

"Send them up," Livvy said.

She quickly scanned the living room for any books or artifacts and then went and closed the closet.

A light knock came from the front door.

"Ursula," said Livvy as she opened the door. "And Tamara."

They stood together, a complete contrast despite their similar backgrounds. Tamara was short, round and nervous, her dark shaman robe a bit tattered and dirty at the hem, her callused feet in thin sandals. Ursula was tall, slim, and regal, with her bright headwrap and burgundy robe immaculate. Her feet were fashionably ensconced in high-heeled boots.

"Come in, come in," Livvy said.

Ursula carried a small bundle and a black canvas tool bag. The bundle was wrapped in heavy brown shipping paper sealed with packing tape.

"Thank you," said Tamara as they both passed into the living room.

Ursula gently set the package on the coffee table.

"So you were successful?" Livvy asked Tamara.

"Yes," Tamara nodded.

"*Very* successful," said Ursula.

Livvy looked down at the package. "May I open it?" she asked.

In reply, Ursula motioned to it as she took a seat.

Tamara took a seat as well.

Livvy carefully peeled back the brown packing tape. The one side and both ends were pretty much covered in it.

"Rip the paper," said Tamara, impatient.

Impatient herself, Livvy did. As she tore it and folded it back, she found herself looking at a lump of black leather that was studded with several nails. She looked at Ursula, puzzled.

"Turn it over," said Ursula.

Gingerly, Livvy lifted it off the paper and started to turn it over. Something rattled inside—a hollow sound. She stopped.

"The treasures inside," said Tamara. "Turn it over."

Livvy turned it over. "Gods!" she said, holding it away.

The grim face that stared at her from the front of the large wooden head wore long skeins of shiny black string nailed into place. Livvy now realized it was wearing a black leather coat.

"Dominique," Livvy whispered.

"Dominique," agreed Ursula.

The eyes immediately drew her attention. Two small almond-shaped mirrors reflected the surroundings. Livvy realized she was actually looking into her own eyes.

"It's amazing," Livvy said.

Ursula smiled.

"Open the stomach," said Tamara.

A circular piece of cardboard was taped to the spot where the stomach might be. Livvy took up the tape and the cardboard came with it. The stomach was hollow and now she could see what had made the rattling sound.

Inside she saw what looked like a hairball, an orange prescription bottle with a white cap, and a small photo. She picked up the bottle and then turned a quizzical look to Ursula. "Who is Nicole Durand?"

"Her sister," said Ursula, smiling. "Look at the photo."

Livvy picked up the small photo and turned it over. She cocked her head. "Dominique?" she asked.

"No," said Tamara. "Nicole."

Livvy stared at the woman with the short hair. "They could be–"

"Twins," said Tamara.

Livvy set the wooden statue in a standing position on the paper. Its diminutive arms were flexed at the elbows and the hands rested on its hips.

"Her sister is a secret," said Tamara, "so Dominique does not seem weak."

"Seem weak?" Livvy asked.

"What does that drug do?" asked Ursula.

Livvy re-examined the bottle. "Diazepam," she said. "It's used in lots of different ways–everything from controlling anxiety and panic attacks to convulsions."

"What kind of convulsions?" asked Ursula.

Livvy shrugged, considering. "It's impossible to tell from this," she said, putting the bottle on the table and taking a seat. "It could be anything from epilepsy to drug overdose."

"She has a disabled sister, possibly a twin," said Ursula. "And she keeps her a secret because she is a liability."

"I don't understand," said Livvy. "Why is she a liability?"

"Because Dominique is a dark shaman, she must always guard against revenge. No doubt she can protect herself but this Nicole may be another matter."

Livvy studied the photo of Nicole. Something about the expression on her face didn't seem quite right. Whatever her problem might be, it wasn't strictly physical.

"So," said Livvy, as she replaced the photo and sat back down, "how does this help with Dominique?"

"They are tied together," said Ursula, "if only by blood, though I suspect by something more based on their resemblance. By using an nkondi based on both of them, you cannot fail to find Dominique."

"You can find Dominique before she finds you," said Tamara.

Livvy nodded. "And then what happens to Nicole?"

Tamara looked at Ursula and Livvy followed suit.

Ursula shrugged. "Unknown," she said. "I am not aware of such an nkondi ever having been constructed."

"It is good," said Tamara, excited. "It is more powerful."

Livvy stared at the macabre figure. Even without knowing how it worked, she had to agree. The nkondi was horrific.

Ursula stood and set her small tool bag on the coffee table next to it.

"What are you doing?" asked Livvy.

"It is time to complete the nkondi," said Ursula.

She picked up the statue, laid it on its back on the area rug surrounding the coffee table, and knelt down next to it. The prescription bottle and photo went back into the cavity but instead of placing the cardboard over the circle, Ursula brought out an irregular candle the color of dark honey and a circular mirror. As Livvy and Tamara both watched, she lit the candle and waited. Although smoky, it gave off a pleasant pine smell.

"Resin," said Ursula as she watched the concave top of the candle fill with liquid.

She held it out over the nkondi and dripped the liquid around the cavity, making several circular passes. Before the drippings could harden, she bent low over the stomach, blew out the candle in the direction of it, and quickly laid the mirror on it, sealing in the contents with some smoke.

She sat back and nodded, apparently satisfied.

"Is that it?" asked Livvy. "Is it ready?"

"Not yet," said Ursula. "The next part is to be done by you."

"Me?" asked Livvy. She hadn't the first clue about vodun.

"Come here," said Ursula, pointing to a spot on the floor next to her.

Livvy did as she was told and knelt next to Ursula, who was putting the resin back in the bag. She heard a metal clanking sound and, when Ursula turned back to her, she held out a small hammer and several nails.

"Drive in the nails," said Ursula.

Livvy tentatively took the tool from her and then the nails. "Just hammer the nails in?"

"Yes," said Ursula. "But for each one, make an oath. Declare your intention for the nkondi and what you hope to achieve. Be careful of the mirrors but put nails in the face and the body."

Livvy stared down at it: the black hair, the leather coat, and its gaping O-shaped mouth. It just didn't seem right to pound nails into something that looked almost human.

"You need not say the oaths out loud," said Ursula, seeing her hesitation.

"It is necessary, to give the nkondi power to help you," said Tamara.

"Okay," said Livvy, still unsure. "But I don't want to see her killed or hurt. I just want to stop her."

"Then," said Ursula, sounding disappointed, "let that be your oath...such as it is." She nodded down at the nkondi.

Livvy placed a nail on its chest, raised the hammer, and paused. *Find Dominique*, she thought and brought the hammer down.

"Good," said Ursula. "More."

One by one, Livvy pounded more nails–into the face, into the torso–and for each she gave a variation of the first oath: to find Dominique and to defeat her.

Finally finished, she gave the hammer back to Ursula, who replaced it in the bag.

"Dominique will stop at nothing," said Ursula as she stood the nkondi on the coffee table. "You must use everything at your disposal. You must acquire every ally that you can. You know Ursula will stand with you."

"And me," said Tamara.

Livvy smiled and realized it was something she hadn't done in a while. "Thank you," she said. "Thank you both."

She gazed at the nkondi again and pictured the surprised look on Dominique's face when Livvy was able to find her.

"The nkondi that Dominique uses is tied to the network box," said Tamara.

Livvy snapped out of her reverie. "What?"

"How she finds you," said Tamara.

Suddenly Livvy pictured her own nkondi and looked at Dominique's. It would have white hair instead of black and it wouldn't have the black leather but…

The thought made her shudder.

"You must tie it to your network box," Tamara concluded.

Livvy nodded, still thinking of a nail-studded version with white string.

"When?" asked Ursula.

That's just like Ursula, Livvy thought. *Straight to the point. No reason for delay.*

But Livvy *did* have a reason. First, she needed to perform the conjuring.

"Tomorrow," she said.

CHAPTER FIFTY-SIX

THE POWER OF television is shocking, thought Dominique. Awesome but shocking. She looked out on her legion of shamans, all of them sitting cross-legged on their mats, except for the one who was lying down and wearing goggles.

They had flocked to her, as had new clients. Even so, she had chosen carefully. Not just any shaman would do. Addicts of the old school were preferred, but they had to be comfortable with the shadowy side of shamanism. Even with those restrictions, she had managed to expand the ranks considerably.

She nodded as she did the math. Four columns by twelve rows, except for the one empty spot where Tambourine should be. Forty-seven shamans.

It was an army.

The hum of their chatter, crackling of water bottles, and the occasional squeak from a rubber mat added up to a good amount of noise.

Dominique clapped her hands twice. "All right," she yelled. "Quiet down and listen up."

The decibel level dropped immediately and all eyes turned to her–all except for Pipsqueak who was still working frantically to incorporate the new arrivals.

"For those of you who haven't been with us before, I'll expect you to get with those who have to learn the details." She walked to her left, hands clasped behind her back. "Suffice it to say, this will be a pre-planned and coordinated operation and you'll need to know which column you are in."

She nodded to the one at which she had stopped. "This is column one." She strode in the opposite direction.

"Column two," she said passing. "And so forth."

She came to a stop, front and center. "We don't have an exact ETA this time, so I'm ordering everyone restricted here until further notice."

There was some grumbling in the back.

Dominique strode down between the columns. Heads whipped around as she passed and the shamans in the back looked as though they wanted to melt into their mats.

"Have I made myself clear?" she said.

"Yes, Dominique," they said.

She glared at each of the shamans in the last row, not sure where the grumbling had come from. None could hold their gaze with her and each looked down at their mats.

She turned and strode back to the front. Her boots thudded on the cement with an echoing sound in the silence. Front and center again, she turned around smartly.

"Keep lots of water nearby. And, as usual, there'll be plenty of drugs, anything you want, when we're through."

There were nods and exchanged looks.

"This is it," she said "We're going to do it this time. You follow me and I will lead you to the top. We will claim not only victory but we *will* have what is rightfully ours—respect for our power and the rewards that are fit to match it." She paused to drink in the eager looks on their faces. "You follow me and we cannot lose."

That she knew with certainty because, despite the overwhelming odds this number of shamans represented, she still had her secret weapon. Only a fool would keep using the same tactic if it didn't work.

And she was no fool.

CHAPTER FIFTY-SEVEN

WHATEVER IT WAS, Livvy knew it couldn't be good. Min and SK both wore serious expressions. They had called from the lobby although Min had a key.

"We know about the necromancy," said SK.

"We're here to ask you to stop," said Min.

Min had taken a seat in one of the chairs. SK was standing next to her, hands in pockets. Both watched her carefully as she sat on the couch.

Stop the conjuring, she thought, looking at them. *Oh, is that all you want? Sure, why not. It was just a whim.* She sighed and rubbed her eyes. She started to laugh quietly, though she didn't smile.

"It's not a joke," said Min.

"Well, you've got that right," Livvy said. She let her hands drop into her lap. "Say what you have to say."

Who had it been this time? Dominique again? Maybe Mamacita?

"Liv, don't be like that. We're here to help," said SK.

"Be like what? Do I seem upset?"

"Yes," they both said.

"Well, if you think this is upset—"

"Livvy," said Min, beginning a count on her fingers. "It's wrong, it's unnatural, it's forbidden—"

"Thanks for the top ten list."

"Liv, stop it," said SK, his voice strained.

The more upset the two of them got, the more calm she felt.

"It's dangerous," said Min, finishing.

"Oh no," said Livvy, mocking. "Really? Well then, never mind."

SK folded his arms over his chest and she could see his jaw muscles working.

"Yes, never mind," said Min. "Just stop it. Let your mother go."

Livvy looked her in the eye but Min didn't back down. "You have no idea what you're talking about," said Livvy, a cautionary tone in her voice.

She glanced at SK. He hadn't told Min about how her mother had died, had he? The thought of it made her back go rigid.

"Everybody loses a parent, eventually," said Min. "We're all going to go through it if we live long enough."

So SK hadn't told her.

Which is worse? she wondered. SK, who knew exactly why she needed to do the conjuring or Min, who was clueless? Livvy shook her head.

"We can't help you on this," said SK. "We won't."

"Did I ask you?" said Livvy.

"I can't be there to watch your back," said Min, her voice rising. "What about Dominique?"

Livvy glanced at the nkondi on the table, as did Min and SK.

"I can handle Dominique," said Livvy.

"I don't think you can," said SK.

Was that a challenge in his tone? Did he really think her not capable?

"You'll be distracted," said Min. "Someone has to watch your back."

"I guess that'll have to be my mom," said Livvy.

"You need another shaman," declared Min.

Livvy sighed and felt her shoulders sag. It wasn't like she wanted to conjure her mother's spirit permanently. She was only doing it because they couldn't be together for more than a minute in the Multiverse. It wasn't what she wanted. It was what she needed, just for a little while.

"Can't you guys trust me?" she muttered, looking from one to the other. "Even just a little bit?" She shook her head, tired.

"It's not about trust," said SK.

"Really?" said Livvy. "Cause it sure feels like that."

"We're worried about you," said Min. "Because we care about you."

"We don't want to see you get hurt," said SK.

We, Livvy thought. *What about you?*

"Well, unless you're going to forcibly retrieve my goggles…"

The impasse had been reached and the room was quiet. There

was no thunder, no lightning, not even any rain. The evening outside was black and still.

Min seemed at a loss for words and sat staring. Finally, she looked at SK and shrugged. He shook his head and looked at the ground before looking up to Livvy.

Their eyes met but no words were exchanged. Then he turned to Min. "Could you give us a minute?"

Min glanced from one to the other. "I'll wait in the car," she said and got up. She looked down at Livvy and the nkondi but didn't pause. In a few moments, Livvy and SK were alone.

CHAPTER FIFTY-EIGHT

"WILL YOU AT least sit down?" Livvy said.

SK looked at the chair as though the decision took a lot of thought. "I shouldn't," he said.

Since their meeting with Alvina, they hadn't talked about them. Except for the silent car ride back from Palm Springs, they hadn't even seen each other.

"I guess we do a lot of things we shouldn't," she said. "Why stop now?"

He just shrugged and stood there.

"How's the window?" she tried.

"Liv, I don't think we can continue seeing each other," he said quietly.

"Oh," she whispered.

So that was it.

"Don't I have some say in it?" she asked.

"Do you think it's what I want?" he shot back.

There was a long silence.

"Then let's try to work it out," she said.

He shook his head. "You heard what Alvina said."

"I won't use the speed. Only my spirit helper."

"It may not be enough," he said.

Alvina's last words seemed to hang in the air between them. The only guarantee was for Livvy to give up shamanism.

"I'm not going to ask you to do that," SK said.

"We're not even there yet," said Livvy quickly. "Let me stop the speed, stop the changes in the Multiverse. I can do that."

He deliberately shook his head.

"Can't we even try?" she said.

"Liv, I won't risk hurting you," he said. "Even without the flying glass, you hit the floor and were completely unconscious. Who knows what could happen?"

"Maybe Alvina is wrong," Livvy said, but even as the words came out she knew how weak they sounded, even to her.

"I can't risk it," he said with finality. "And I won't."

"So that's it?" Livvy asked, though she knew the answer.

"Not exactly. I don't think we should see each other…at all."

"What?"

Not at all?

"You mean like–"

"Like not working together anymore," he finished for her.

"But why? Alvina said we were the perfect team. The water baby and the lightning shaman."

"Yeah, look at us." He shook his head. "We crossed a line," he said quietly. He stared at the floor as though he could see it. "A line we didn't even know was there."

He looked up at her. "Can't you feel it, Liv?" His eyes searched her face.

She did feel it. She'd felt it at Alvina's but couldn't bring herself to say it–not then and not now.

"It's a point of no return, isn't it?" he continued. "How could we go back to what we were before? Pretend there's nothing between us?"

No, thought Livvy. *This can't be happening.*

"Gods, I wish I could do that but I can't," he said. "I don't have it in me."

Say something. He's about to leave. Say something!

There was nothing to say, though. She couldn't pretend either.

"I'm sorry, Liv."

Then he turned and left, without a moment's hesitation or a look back.

He was gone.

"I'm sorry too," she whispered.

CHAPTER FIFTY-NINE

REALLY, I SHOULDN'T be so surprised, thought Dominique.

"Let's talk outside," she said.

Mamacita looked past her into the large expanse of the loft. Shamans milled around everywhere and Dominique could hear whispers of "That's Mamacita" and "Look, it's Mamacita."

Dominique closed the door behind her.

"Other than Liver or SK," said Dominique, standing on the small landing with Mamacita, "you're the last person I'd expect to see here."

"Mayet gave me the address."

Mamacita was taller than Dominique would have imagined. Maybe it was the lack of that enormous counter or the fact she was standing.

"He won't be back," Mamacita said.

Dominique had always assumed he wouldn't be.

"It's not like we need him," said Dominique, leaning back against the railing.

"Oh I can see that," said Mamacita, nodding at the door to the loft. "And that's why I'm here."

"You're wasting your breath. This operation is going forward."

"Oh, I'm sure," said Mamacita. "And you're going to win." She paused. "Because I'm going to help you."

Dominique scowled at her. "Really," she said.

"Mmm hmm," Mamacita hummed and opened the canvas tote bag for Dominique to look inside.

Instead of the knitting needles and yarn she had expected to see, there was a sleek, shiny, black box. On its front panel were several indicator lights and switches and on the top were rows of input jacks. It was a goggle network box—a sophisticated one.

"What is this?" Dominique asked slowly, squinting at it and then at Mamacita.

In answer, Mamacita closed the canvas bag. "I have one condition," said Mamacita.

A network box like that would mean Pipsqueak, the entire shaman squad, could be ready in less than an hour.

"Wait a minute," said Dominique. "Yesterday you declared your undying love for Liver and today you're going to help me destroy her?"

"You haven't heard my condition," said Mamacita. "I'm not going to help you destroy her. You," she said pointing at Dominique, "are going to help me save her."

"Really," said Dominique. "How do you figure?"

"You know what she's trying to do over there and so do I. Well, I want it stopped."

"You want *me* to stop the conjuring," Dominique snorted.

"And that's all," said Mamacita. "I want it stopped and I don't want any harm done to Livvy."

The old fool.

"If I have this," she said, pointing at the bag. "And I have them," she said pointing at the door. "What's to stop me?"

"Well, you might start by offering your word. You'll stop because in exchange for this, you'll give me your word that no harm will come to Livvy and the conjuring will be prevented."

"Okay, sure," said Dominique, reaching for the bag. Mamacita let it go. "You have my word."

"Now, I know you don't take Mamacita for a fool," she heard Mamacita say as she peered at the new box. "So let there be no doubt that if anything should happen to Livvy, you and the other vermin in there won't find a rock big enough."

Dominique finally tore her gaze from the box. *Vermin? A rock? Did I hear her right?*

Mamacita was smiling at her and Dominique cocked her head.

"You see, Dominique," Mamacita continued. "You are playing in my sandbox." Mamacita's smile slowly disappeared and her upper lip curled into something feral as she stepped forward. Suddenly the landing was too small as Mamacita's girth loomed.

Her voice dropped an octave. "You don't know my world. You couldn't possibly. But now that you're here, I want something clear.

The *only* thing that need concern *you* is *me*. You are one step away from crossing a line. It separates my good side from—let's just call it the other side. I can promise you that the other side is a place you do not want to be, even in the tiny amount of time you'd have to think about it."

Dominique automatically leaned back and felt the door behind her but couldn't take her eyes off Mamacita's face. If she didn't know any better she'd say Mamacita was about to pull a knife. She blinked.

Mamacita withdrew slowly. Then her smile was back and her eyes had their familiar shine. "Mmm hmm."

She moved past Dominique to the stairs and put her hand on the rail. "I'm so glad we understand each other."

CHAPTER SIXTY

NO MORE GUILT, no more nightmares. It would be such a relief.

Livvy stood in the living room staring down at the leather pouch on the coffee table. She'd need the same artifacts for the conjuring as she had for the summoning. Then she looked at the goggles in her hand, gazing into the bulbous silver lenses on the front.

"Everybody loses a parent," she murmured, echoing Min, *but not everybody kills their mother.*

The small candles in glass holders ringed the protective circle and cast a calming, almost meditative light. There were twelve, stationed at equidistant intervals, with thin red arcs of powdered ochre between them. In the center was her mat and small pillow.

She became aware of the quiet of the room–and the emptiness. There'd be no one to help with this. Mamacita had tried to stop her, and then Min and SK.

Then he had left.

She imagined him standing where she was standing now.

"I can't go back either," she said, picking up the pouch.

She felt its taut contours. With the syringe of blood added to it, it was nearly full.

Livvy moved over to the nkondi and crouched down in front of it. The unearthly eyes seemed to flick toward her as she glimpsed her reflection moving by. She lightly skimmed her fingers across the tops of the nails.

Yes, it would help to know what Dominique was doing and where she was in the Multiverse but…Livvy recalled the photo of Nicole. Tamara had called her Dominique's weakness but, in truth, she was an unknown–except for the fact that she probably wasn't well. Not even Ursula knew what effect her belongings would have on the nkondi except that it would be stronger. It made Livvy uneasy but it would be good to have the advantage for a change. She looked into the horrific face.

"Stronger how?" she asked it, but there was no answer.

She hadn't expected one.

CHAPTER SIXTY-ONE

"YOU WON'T BELIEVE this, Nicole," said Dominique.

She closed the door behind her. Nicole was painting at an easel and didn't turn to look, though Dominique hadn't expected her to.

"Mamacita has thrown in with me," she continued, almost breathless.

She rushed over to the broom closet, opened it and fetched a few plastic bags from the floor.

"I gave her my word I wouldn't harm Liver," she said, setting the bags down on the kitchen table. "For what that's worth!"

The old woman couldn't be serious about threatening *her*.

"Pipsqueak is almost done, so I've got to hurry."

She searched one plastic bag after another. *Here we go*, thought Dominique. *This pair of goggles ought to do nicely.*

She snapped on the power button and they buzzed to life, though the pitch was too high. Right, these weren't the best pair. She shut it off and picked up another pair out of the same bag and turned them on. They sounded better.

"Somebody's goggles went bad–" She stopped when she realized what she was saying and jerked her head up to see Nicole.

Nicole had frozen, with her brush still on the palette. She was staring at the goggles. Dominique quickly thumbed off the power switch and jammed them back down in the bag. Nicole went back to painting.

"Hey," said Dominique. "Are you finally getting used to them?" Nicole didn't look over. "Maybe you are."

Everything is going right today.

"Look, I've got to go," Dominique said, transferring the goggles to her bag. Nicole paid no attention. "But I'll be back soon."

She strode back to the door and turned around. "This is it,

Nicole. I'm going to crush Liver this time. There's no way I can lose."

She watched Nicole painting for a few moments.

"I wish you could see it," she said quietly. Then she nodded. "All right," she said. "I'll be back soon and, when I'm back, it'll be a new shaman world in L.A."

CHAPTER SIXTY-TWO

SK SILENTLY SLID the key into the lock and turned it.

Min had left more than an hour ago. He had waited in the lobby and then dialed Livvy. After a few calls with no answer, it was time to come up.

The entry was dark but he knew she had to be home. He'd have seen her go through the lobby if she'd left. *It would have been better if she had*, he thought. The fact that she didn't answer her phone only meant one thing: she'd gone to the Multiverse.

The light from the candles caught his attention, and he closed the door. She was lying on her mat, goggles on. Nacho sat on the floor next to her but immediately ran over, meowing the entire way.

"You keeping watch too?" he asked, scratching him behind the ears.

Nacho answered by trying to move his head back and forth under SK's hand.

SK turned his attention to Livvy and approached the circle. He gazed around at it but never even paused. He'd already made that decision. He stepped over and in and then sat on the floor next to her.

She was lying comfortably, her breathing normal, as though she were in a deep sleep. He gently moved a lock of hair away from her neck. Her jugular was pulsing steadily but not overly strong. Everything seemed to be all right so far. Some tension released from his shoulders.

"Not that I don't trust you," he whispered. "But I had to make sure you were all right."

He paused, his eyes lingering on her lips, though he hadn't expected her to speak. He looked at the small leather pouch grasped in her hand.

"I know what you're doing over there and you know I don't approve," he continued. "But," he stroked the hair at her temple. "I'm not going to leave you, Liv. I love you."

He gave her a little smile.

"I know you can't help trying to be with your mother." He lightly brushed the back of his fingers along her jaw line. "But I also know you can't defeat Dominique," he said. "Not because you don't have the power but because you just don't have it in you to hurt people. It's one of the things I love about you the most."

"But—"

Wait a minute. He stared at her goggles. They weren't connected to the network box.

He straightened and turned around, startling Nacho who leapt away. The network box and nkondi were on the coffee table. She had decided not to use them. She would not be able to avoid Dominique in the Multiverse nor would she have the advantage of surprise.

Dominique would.

He took out his phone and did a quick dial. An eternity seemed to stretch for each ring. He glanced at the network box and considered hooking her goggles up to it but there was no way to know what effect that would have while she was in mid-journey.

"SK?" answered Min, finally.

"Go," he said. "She's already there."

CHAPTER SIXTY-THREE

"LIVVY!" EXCLAIMED HER mom.

As Livvy landed in the plaza of the Underworld, she gave it a quick check. Her mom was here but, other than that, they seemed to be alone. Before the plaza could tilt or do whatever else the Multiverse might throw at them next, she intended to get in, get done, and get out.

"We've got to hurry," Livvy said, giving her a brief hug.

She knelt next to the fountain. "I think I've got this figured out."

She arranged the items as she had for the summoning but on the ledge of the fountain instead of the ground.

"I'll call down lightning on the pyramid but instead of you being summoned forth in the beam of light that comes out, we'll both step into the light together. I'll take you through the fountain and then into the real world."

"Ready when you are," said her mom.

"Okay," said Livvy, stretching her hand up. "Give me some space. You don't want to be standing too close when the lightning strikes."

Her mom nodded and took several steps back.

Livvy turned her face up to the whirling clouds, as did her mom. "Lightning," she said.

Nothing.

Gods no, not now!

Her mom waited expectantly and Livvy reached her hand higher, glaring at the sky. She had been about to try again when she saw that same strange pattern in the clouds. They were swirling and bubbling with patches of gray, white, and black that flowed into one another. In the center, though, was what looked like an enormous globular cell just before it divided, with a faint line down the middle.

"Livvy?" said her mom, approaching. "Is there something wrong with the conjuring?"

The outlines of the globular gray cell suddenly stood out more, as did the line that divided it. Livvy looked at her mom and held up a hand.

"Mom, stop." She stopped.

"Now back up." She backed up.

As Livvy watched the clouds, the blob wavered and its outlines disappeared. Soon, the usual churning and whirling had replaced it and lightning bursts lit the entire mass from within.

"Okay, Mom," Livvy called. "Just wait there."

Her mom stopped backing up and looked to the sky.

Livvy reached up her hand again. "Lightning," she said.

The snaking band of white energy struck Livvy's hand with a loud crack as the voltage traveled down her body and into the ground beneath her feet. Her hair rose in the static field and sparks showered down from her hand.

Relieved, she looked over at her mom, who took that as her cue to come back.

"No wait," Livvy yelled over the buzzing and crackling.

Somehow the nearness of her mother had something to do with the lightning. A dozen images flashed through her mind. Had she ever called down lightning when someone besides a client was standing close? She tried to remember all the times she'd been networked.

"Is there a problem?" yelled her mom.

"No," yelled Livvy. "Just wait there."

There was no time to wonder about the lightning. It was here now and it was time to use it. She looked down at the pyramid and pointed her other hand toward it. A smaller bolt leapt to its tip and it started to glow. Livvy waited as the charge built up and the pyramid glowed brighter but the beam of light didn't emerge.

"What are you waiting for?" her mother yelled.

"Nothing," yelled Livvy. "I don't know why the beam doesn't appear."

"More lightning," her mother yelled.

Livvy closed her eyes, bowed her head and concentrated. She

pulled from somewhere deep inside and called down even more energy. She felt it surge through her and slowly opened her eyes. She saw the sparks beginning to swirl around her as though caught in their own slow whirlwind. She stared down at the pyramid. Though it glowed brightly, it still hadn't produced a beam. It was starting to drain her.

"Don't stop now!" her mother yelled.

She didn't want to stop but soon she'd have no choice. Heat was building up in her chest and the ground around her feet was starting to blacken.

Suddenly, she realized the problem.

"The ring!" said Livvy as she dropped her arm and the lightning disappeared.

Breathing heavily, she looked at her mom and waved her over. "The ring, Mom. I forgot we need the ring. You're wearing it."

Livvy bent down, trying to catch her breath, and thought about sitting.

Gods that had been hard.

She wiped sweat from her forehead but instead of sitting, she raised her head and glanced around the plaza. It was still empty but something seemed amiss.

The sky was full of clouds, as usual, and the windows of the tall buildings reflected them like mirrors. Without the lightning being channeled, you could have heard a pin drop.

Wait, she thought. *The plaza is empty.* When she'd arrived, she'd been relieved not to see Dominique, the other shamans, or a crowd of ancestor spirits but now she realized there was no spirit or ancestor traffic at all. None. It was deserted.

Still breathing hard, Livvy looked back at her mom, who was grinning at her. With an effort, Livvy stood up straight and looked down at the pyramid but the ring was still missing.

"Mom, what are you doing? We need the ring and we don't have much time."

Her mother held up the hand where she wore it, showing it to her.

"Mom, you've got to take the ring off so I can use it."

"Well, that's the problem," said her mom, still grinning. "It's not that easy to take off."

"What? What are you saying? You haven't even tried. Please,

Mom, Dominique could be here any second."

"Oh, I know. I'm counting on it."

"What?"

The woman in front of Livvy broke into a chuckle. As though she were made of rubber, her face and body began to stretch and deform and then, starting from the top of her head, she began to open.

"Mom!" Livvy screamed but she took a shaky half-step back.

The split opened like a zipper, down the front of her mom's face, then her body. Something was emerging from inside. It was… her mom. Without the support of the outer body, she fell back and hit the ground with a thud.

"Mom?" Livvy said, starting toward her.

The amorphous outer body hadn't stopped moving, though. As Livvy watched, it stepped away and zipped itself up. The body was shorter and thinner and the young face that finally appeared had a sharp weaselly look to it. She peered at Livvy and smirked.

A movement at the lip of the fountain caught Livvy's eye. A small green lizard that looked like an iguana was creeping among the paraphernalia. Its head was huge compared to its body and its eyes swiveled independently at both her and the other shaman. As it hovered over the amethyst heart, its color changed to a light purple.

A chameleon.

It was this shaman's spirit helper. This shaman had impersonated her mother. But why?

She crouched next to her mom, who was starting to get up. "I was trapped inside," she said, her voice trembling. "I tried to—"

"What a touching reunion," said a voice from the other side of the fountain. Livvy didn't need to turn to know who it was.

As she rose, Livvy helped her mother up with an effort and whispered in her ear. "I need you to run."

"And you've also met my secret weapon," Dominique continued.

Livvy turned to face her. Dominique nodded toward the chameleon shaman.

"Part decoy, part flypaper," Dominique said. She motioned to her right and left. "The ambush you've seen before."

Dozens of shamans, in twos and threes, were starting to enter from the surrounding buildings. The air was filling with the sounds of their animal helpers, who began to filter in from between the buildings.

"It's win-win for me," Dominique said. "She takes up your time and energy while you attempt a conjuring and fail. Or, if you succeed, she comes back with you and possesses your body. She's very good at that, you know."

The weaselly-faced woman chuckled.

Livvy half-turned to her mother. "Run now. Get inside a building," she said under her breath.

The chameleon shaman joined the others with Dominique. They *kept* filing in. So many.

Her mom put a hand on her arm. "Livvy, I can—"

In a blur of motion, Livvy grabbed her mom around the waist, spun around, and launched her toward the nearest building. "Run!" she screamed and whirled to face Dominique.

"Let her go," Dominique said to the chameleon shaman, who had started to give chase. "We're done with her."

Livvy glared at Dominique across the fountain. *We're done with her?*

A sudden fury built inside and a crashing peal of thunder exploded above them. The shamans and spirit helpers in the plaza all stopped. For many of them, it was their first time in the presence of the lightning shaman. The water in the fountain rippled in concentric circles.

Livvy thrust her hand toward the sky. "Lightning," she said, bringing the bolt down on her hand in a shower of sparks.

She raised a hand toward Dominique and yelled, "Leave now."

Dominique looked at the fountain and the sky but didn't flinch. "Torrent," she yelled.

She extended one hand down toward the fountain and the other up toward the sky. Then she quickly brought them together in front of her as though she were closing the jaws of a crocodile.

A column of water jumped up from the fountain and joined one that was descending from the clouds. The two forces slammed into one another as Livvy unleashed a lightning bolt. It hit the column of water creating a screeching and hissing explosion of steam. The bolt of electricity punched through it but was fractured into three tendrils. Two landed on nearby buildings, carving craters in their facades and raining down debris. The third landed in the plaza, scattering the shamans who had been nearby.

Livvy dropped her hand, breathing hard. Dominique turned her head toward the great raven and said something to it. With two great scoops of its wings, it was skyborne. An eerie wailing caw seemed to hover in the air. A group of shamans off to the left, behind Dominique, were now moving forward.

Livvy ran straight at her, leapt over the lip of the fountain, blasted through the column of water, and crashed into Dominique's chest. She had a moment to register Dominique's shocked expression as she grabbed her by the lapels of the duster, carried her with the momentum, and then landed on top of her, pinning her to the ground.

"Is this what you want?" she screamed.

In the next instant, Livvy felt a crushing weight hit her back that slammed her against Dominique and then the heat of a fireball. She ducked and rolled sideways.

"Rain," she yelled, reaching to the sky.

The rain put out the fireball and, as she rolled to her feet, she saw another fizzle about four feet away.

"Icicles," yelled Dominique.

In midstream, the rain turned to small white pellets of ice that rapidly grew larger. Elongated chunks were starting to land as Dominique ran for the nearest building. Livvy looked up just in time to see a large icicle descending directly above her. Only a desperate twisting motion kept her from being impaled as it grazed the front of her shoulder and clipped the outside of her thigh.

In the distance, she heard shrieks of agony and realized Dominique didn't care if her own shamans got hurt. Enormous cones of ice were landing now, shattering like bombs all around. Plumes of water splashed up from the fountain and sloshed down into the plaza.

As she dodged and kept an eye on the sky, Livvy raised her hand to the clouds. "Whirlwind."

An enormous funnel, almost black in its density, swirled above the plaza. Large and small icicles alike stopped in midair and then rushed up into the whirlwind with a great whoosh. When Livvy looked back to the building, Dominique was gone. She spun back toward the plaza.

In front of the fountain, three shamans were coming together. They faced her, interlocked their arms behind their backs, and opened their mouths simultaneously.

Livvy barely had time to cover her ears. The sonic blast rattled her vision. Everything vibrated—the ground, the air, her eyes—but Livvy didn't wait for it to stop. Hands still over ears, she charged them. They had only just realized what she was doing when Livvy launched herself into a horizontal position and barreled into all three of them. She heard their grunts and exclamations of surprise as they flew backward and into the fountain. Livvy flung out a hand and gripped the rim to keep from flying in after them. As the swirling water covered the other three and drew them down, Livvy clawed with both hands to get a purchase on the stone lip.

Not yet! Mom is still here somewhere.

The water pulled on her legs, downward and to the side but, with a final heave, she hauled herself over the wide ledge. Back on the pavement again, she pushed herself up to a standing position. Without warning, a pressure wave burst on her left side, sending her sailing to the right, almost skating along the ground until her foot caught on something and she tumbled. Pain from the blow radiated from her left hip down to the knee. Ignoring the throbbing Livvy rolled into a kneeling position and raised her arm. This time the pressure wave came from the opposite direction, hitting her on the right side.

Two pressure shamans, she thought, panting. *One on either side.*

As she hit the ground and skidded, she heard the raven caw above.

The wind began to pick up and quickly grew to a howl. Livvy raised her head. Her hair whipped in the gale as she searched for the shamans responsible for these new attacks but a looming form in her peripheral vision got her attention—a wolf loping toward her. Buoyed by the wind, it made an incredibly long leap. Its fur rippled in waves as it sailed through the air. Not able to dodge, Livvy did the only thing she could. She raised her arm up between them. The gaping maw of glistening white teeth opened wide just before it clamped down in a sickening chomp. Livvy screamed.

CHAPTER SIXTY-FOUR

IN THE REAL world, Livvy sucked in a sharp breath.

"Liv?" said SK.

She let the breath out.

The beads of sweat he had watched forming on her temple coalesced into a trickle. Her jugular was pounding. When he looked toward her diaphragm, which seemed to be in overdrive, something on her arm caught his eye.

Blood?

He reached out his hand and, careful to avoid the small wounds that were appearing, gently grasped her arm.

"Lightning Shaman, Water Baby is here."

• • • • •

The animal snarled in response to Livvy's scream. Only inches from her face, the gray wolf pressed forward with her forearm in its jaws, black lips curling, the snout wrinkling and quivering with its low growl. The white teeth glistened with a faint red that Livvy knew was her blood.

Suddenly, the pain in her arm dropped a notch and she felt new energy flow into her.

Still kneeling, she did the unthinkable. She pushed, forcing her arm further into the back of its mouth. For a moment, their eyes locked. Its yellow irises blazed with the excitement of the kill.

Livvy slapped her free hand over the burning eyes. The wolf's immediate response was to begin shaking its head, but Livvy's intent hadn't been to hide herself from view. Instead, she squeezed.

The beast's growl gave way to a high-pitched whine. She pressed her fingers into the eye sockets, and felt the soft orbs deforming, then a sickening wet pop as her thumb penetrated the left eye. Her middle finger continued to push inward on the other eye. Its jaws gaped open as the wolf yelped and tried to back away.

Behind her, Livvy heard a new sound bearing down, growing rapidly louder–something with hooves, something galloping.

With her forearm now free, she rose up and tightened her grip on the wolf. The other eye gave in to the pressure but her thumb punched past the eye and into the brain. As though the wolf's high-pitched whine had simply been shut off, the noise ceased and its body went slack.

The galloping behind her grew louder.

Still gripping the wolf's head by the eye sockets, her newly freed hand grabbed it by the scruff of the neck. The pounding hooves were nearly on her now and, without looking, she spun and swung the flaccid body of the wolf in an arc.

As she came around, Livvy saw a bighorn ram thundering toward her. The wolf collided solidly with it even as her partnered spin with the wolf moved her out of the ram's line of attack. The massive head, with its gigantic, almost circular horns, jerked sideways upon impact and there was a distinct snapping sound. Carried by its momentum, the ram sped by her but hit the pavement and skidded on its chin, its haunches doubling up behind it. Livvy let go of the wolf and it landed behind the ram, neither of them moving.

She tried to catch her breath as she clutched her wounded forearm.

Where is Dominique?

Where is my mother?

She caught sight of the fountain just in time for her vision to go instantly gray.

In every direction, a thick mist had materialized in the plaza. *It has to be Dominique*, Livvy thought. Even the fountain, though it had only been several yards away, had completely disappeared. Livvy felt outward with her hands and saw the moisture-laden air swirl around them. Up above, only the dimmest outlines of the tallest skyscrapers were still visible.

Well, if she couldn't see them, they couldn't see her, but it was going to make finding her mother all but impossible. Time to summon wind.

The raven cawed above her. She looked up to see it circling. Suddenly, she felt a hand on her left arm, then her right. A sharp blow behind the knees sent her straight down as more hands grabbed her neck, her shoulders and her hands. The fog slowly sank to only inches from the ground.

She was surrounded.

Livvy struggled but there were too many. Hands reached out to her from every direction. The shamans crowded in on her and even jostled one another to stake a claim. They jerked her in different directions with their frantic jockeying. Someone was tugging on her hair.

"Leave her for me," she heard Dominique order.

The pushing and pulling stopped immediately, leaving Livvy frozen in place, gasping. Dominique shoved people aside as she made her way through the crowd, her boots swirling the heavy mist at ground level. She elbowed past the inner circle and came to a stop directly in front of Livvy. Livvy could only move her eyes to watch her.

Dominique favored her with a joyless smile. "Really, I should make this slow," she said as she reached down and grabbed Livvy's neck with both hands. "But I've seen too many movies."

Despite Livvy's labored breathing, the airflow stopped. In seconds, her lungs were burning. She tried to turn, twist, or move in any direction, but the only thing she managed to achieve was an even greater need for air. Dominique's face loomed close and her hands squeezed tighter.

Livvy sensed her own lips parting but no sound escaped them. Blood hammered in her ears, pounding crazily. Each beat throbbed in her temples and pulsed in her swelling eyes. Again, she jerked but barely managed any movement at all. Dominique squeezed harder. The roaring in her head that had been unbearable gradually started to dim. She couldn't feel the other shamans holding her, only Dominique's hands on her neck. Her tortured lungs wanted to scream, but Livvy didn't control them. They seemed to belong to someone else. She tried to look away from Dominique, but her eyes no longer responded.

The throbbing started to slow. It was getting quiet.

Mom?

There was no answer.

SK?

She briefly saw his face.

It's getting dark.

Then, her vision went painfully white.

Screams and cries rang out all around her. One by one, she felt hands release her as she sank down, her head finally coming to rest on the cool pavement. Her chest heaved in great wheezing breaths. She gasped over and over, desperate to fill her lungs until someone grabbed her arm.

"Livvy, it's me," said Min. "Get up."

The white light! Min!

Livvy tried to reply but only coughed spasmodically.

Chaos had erupted around them. Dominique was shouting, trying to maintain order.

"Tasha," she screamed. "Tasha now."

Livvy felt Min's hands help her to her knees.

"Min," Livvy managed between coughing fits, trying to find Min's arms.

Livvy felt her lean close. "I'm right here," she heard Min say in her ear.

They were both getting jostled by shamans as they stumbled and groped their way.

"Tasha," Dominique screamed.

Other voices called for her as well.

"Darkness!" screamed a voice over the din of the rest.

As though the white light had been switched off, Livvy's vision returned.

"Uh oh," said Min.

CHAPTER SIXTY-FIVE

IN THE REAL world, SK finished taping off the gauze he'd wrapped around Livvy's forearm. She gave no indication that she was aware of the bandaging. As he worked, though, he saw that her breathing was becoming more regular and her heart wasn't working so hard.

Good. Min must be there now.

• • • • •

The rumbling noise reached them first. Then, the buildings in the plaza shook. Windows shattered and shards of glass fell. The water of the fountain looked as though it was boiling, leaping up in chaotic spouts.

Min jerked Livvy up.

"Let's go!" she said, pulling Livvy backward.

Livvy turned and ran, limping slightly as she and Min dodged around the other shamans. As the quake intensified, shamans around them teetered and those further away couldn't keep their balance. They fell to their hands and knees all around them in the plaza.

Min ran in the opposite direction, toward calmer ground, half-supporting, half-dragging Livvy until they were across the plaza and through the revolving glass doors of one of the buildings.

"Min, how did you get here? I mean, how did you find me?"

"An nkondi," said Min. "But we can get into that later. Tamara can't keep up the quake forever."

"Tamara?" said Livvy. "Tamara is with you?"

"She's in the one of the buildings, for a better view of the plaza."

The quake was fading.

"If you go *now*," said Min, looking out a large window next to the revolving door, "especially at your speed, you can get to the fountain."

Speed, thought Livvy, remembering Alvina's words. There could be no speed, not any more. Not if she wanted to be with SK. No matter what he'd said, she wasn't ready to give up.

"You've got to leave through the fountain," Min said. "But we don't. Once you're gone, we'll meet you back in the real world."

"I'm not going," said Livvy.

Min stared at her. "What do you mean?"

"I've got to find my mother."

"Oh, Livvy, no, not—"

"It wasn't my mother before!" Livvy said. "*She* didn't want the conjuring. It was one of Dominique's shamans."

Min shook her head, not understanding.

"A chameleon," said Livvy. "She was impersonating my mom." Livvy recalled her mother's nervousness when she'd met Min. Had that already been the chameleon? "Anyway, my real mother is still here but I've got to get rid of Dominique."

They both looked toward the plaza. Dominique was easy to see with her long hair and black leather duster. The other shamans were rallying to her. Various spirit helpers roamed and hovered nearby. The raven circled overhead.

Livvy turned to Min. "I don't want you to stay," she said. "You've done enough already, you and Tamara. You should go. I have to stay."

"What? And miss all the fun?" Min sneered.

Livvy stared at her. That didn't sound like Min.

Min giggled.

"I always wanted to say something like that," she said.

Livvy couldn't help but smile at her. "Don't ever change, Minnie Mouse."

"I know, right?"

In the plaza, shamans surrounded the fountain. Dominique was pointing at one of the buildings to their left and a small group of four shamans took off at a trot. She was beginning a search.

"There's fewer now," said Livvy. "Maybe a third are gone. Some probably ran away and I launched some into the fountain. I think

Dominique might have even injured some with an icicle attack."

"Okay," said Min, getting serious. "I think someone named Tasha and I need to have a meeting."

"There's no way I'll be able to deal with Dominique if these other shamans are around," said Livvy. "Luckily, they've decided to guard the fountain."

Livvy watched as the majority of the remaining shamans gathered around it while a handful hung back with Dominique. Whether they were truly guarding it or not she had no idea. But if she could force them into it, they'd be gone.

"You'll find that shaman who controls darkness," Livvy said, "and I'll head toward the fountain. Ready?"

Min nodded in answer.

"Let's go."

CHAPTER SIXTY-SIX

NICOLE STARED AT the goggles Dominique had left on the kitchen table.

'Are you finally getting used to those?'

Dominique? She looked around the room.

Dominique was gone.

Nicole stared back down at the goggles.

Buzz?

Without touching the goggles, she collapsed the plastic grocery bag down around them, like a shallow dish. There they sat in their polished black shininess.

Buzz?

She held up a closed hand in front of her and slowly extended the index finger toward the ceiling. Then she bent her wrist, pointed at the power button, and slowly lowered her hand toward the goggles. She watched as the reflection of her hand grew larger and more distorted in the curved black plastic. Her finger finally came to rest on the small rocker switch. She felt its smooth edges.

'Are you finally getting used to those?'

Dominique? Her finger still on the button, Nicole looked around the room. Dominique was gone.

When she looked back down at the goggles, she accidentally depressed the switch.

Click!

She snatched her hand back, clutching it to her chest.

Buzz, buzz, buzz.

She cocked her head and watched as the light from the interior projectors lit the insides of the lenses.

Buzz, buzz, buzz.

There was orange there, and red, and yellow. Orange, red, and yellow. Orange, red, and yellow.

She bent down low and peered into them.

Pretty.

She smiled and picked them up.

• • • • •

With Min behind her, Livvy ignored the pain in her left hip and stepped out onto the sidewalk. She reached her hand skyward and focused on a spot over the fountain. "Whirlwind," she said.

A funnel cloud descended as she strode forward. Min flanked out to her left. The group of four shamans who had been heading to the next building stopped, unsure of what to do. They looked toward Dominique but she was too far away.

Kam swooped down at the group with a sharp cry as Min changed course and headed toward them.

Livvy concentrated on the whirlwind and kept walking toward the fountain. She'd need to be closer.

Some of the shamans there were holding up their hands against the wind, trying to see what was going on but hadn't spotted her yet. Livvy looked up to the sky. She expanded her hand, stretching her fingers apart. The funnel cloud continued its ferocious spin and descent, but it widened and became hollow in the middle.

A fireball erupted from the group of shamans that still stood with Dominique, but they were too far away. It smoked and fizzled, hitting the ground short of Livvy. A small pressure wave buffeted her but wasn't nearly enough to topple her. She continued walking. The shamans around the fountain spotted the funnel cloud.

It stopped descending.

Someone else was using wind.

No, thought Livvy. *Not this time.* She reached up both her arms, brought her hands together in a loose circle and then quickly lowered them.

The funnel cloud descended with such velocity that it hit the ground with an explosion. Small chunks of asphalt flew upward in a perfect circle around the fountain, obscuring the shamans within like a fence.

Out of the corner of her eye, she saw Dominique's group running at her with Dominique pointing and yelling. Another fireball erupted.

Livvy constricted the circle of her hands and the funnel cloud contracted to just within the stone rim, sweeping the nearby shamans along with it.

The fireball in her peripheral vision grew larger. Livvy more sensed the fireball to her right than saw it as it blocked out everything with its fiery glow. Dominique's group was within range. This fireball was not going to peter out. With no time to summon wind or dodge, she turned her back to it and prepared to hit the ground rolling.

Livvy felt the fireball's heat beginning to build as she tightened her hands together and thrust them at the ground, palms down. The funnel cloud narrowed and crashed down into the fountain, sending up a single plume of bright blue water two stories high that then rained back down. The shamans who had been there were gone.

Before she could react, an explosion behind her lifted her off her feet and sent her hurtling forward. She struck the pavement with a grunt, but she got her arm under her head first, saving her from a cracked skull. She rolled completely out of control, watching pavement and cloudy sky swirl past. Another fireball passed by and she finally came to a stop on her back. She tried to sit up.

Gods, what hap—

"Stay down!" someone yelled.

She obeyed. Another fireball shot by only inches above her. Livvy turned her head as best she could and saw a sideways view of the plaza, but even sideways she recognized Ursula and Alvina. They were running towards her.

Livvy watched as Ursula created one fireball after another and leapt over her. She was neutralizing the incoming fireballs with her own. Concussive explosions were detonating where the fireballs met.

Alvina came to a stop and readied a pressure attack, compressing her hands in front of her. "Ursula," she yelled.

Ursula immediately crouched down as Alvina pushed the pressure wave outward and over the top of her. A sonic boom sounded in the distance and the shamans in front of Dominique were shoved backward into her. They had underestimated how far

Alvina's attack could reach.

Livvy slowly got to her feet behind them, as Ursula glanced back at her. "The fountain," she yelled.

Livvy shook her head. "No," she yelled back. "Dominique."

Livvy frantically searched the plaza and then remembered the raven. It was circling behind the fireball shamans. There she was behind them.

"What is happening?" yelled someone from behind. Livvy whirled to see Tamara running toward them.

"I've got to get to Dominique," she yelled. She turned and pointed at her.

As though she had heard Livvy, Dominique looked at her. Then she looked up at the raven. He circled tightly for a few turns and flew away between the buildings.

"How about a quake?" Livvy yelled, starting to move in the direction of Dominique.

Tamara shook her head. "It starts in front of me," she yelled. "Best when I am far away." That's why she'd been in the building on the other side of the plaza. "But I can try," Tamara yelled, following Livvy.

Ursula fell in beside them, ready with a fireball between her hands. "No wind," she yelled to Livvy.

The four of them passed the fountain and headed toward Dominique. Livvy could see Ursula's spirit helper, the rooster Kuku, hoisting a writhing snake into the air. Alvina's coyote sprinted ahead on their flank, zigzagging and drawing the attention of the other spirit helpers. A galloping sound from behind made Livvy turn to look.

"Kochon," yelled Tamara. "He is mine."

A wild boar rushed by them and toward Dominique's dwindling group.

Tamara stretched out her hand and the ground began to shudder.

The boar charged, head low. At the last moment, it veered right and picked off the shaman on the end, lifting her in the air as it thrust upward with its tusks.

Despite her shrinking numbers, Dominique wasn't intimidated. She seemed to be waiting for them.

"Give me some distance," Livvy yelled and stepped in front of

Alvina, Tamara and Ursula.

She raised her hand over her head. "Lightning," she said.

The bolt seemed to appear out of nowhere, crashing on top of Livvy's hand. Both Ursula and Tamara cowered away as the sparks rained down.

A few shamans in the periphery of the ranks responded by winking out in flashes of light. Dominique rushed up behind the ones in front of her saying something into the ear of each one in turn. They stood their ground.

Livvy pressed forward, her other arm extended in front of her, aiming at what was left of Dominique's squad–a half-dozen shamans at most. One of the shamans reached a hand upward as well. A howling wind ripped at their clothes and neutralized all the fire shamans.

"I think Tasha's gone," Livvy heard Min yelling from behind.

Livvy glanced back to see that she had joined Alvina, Tamara and Ursula. If Tasha was gone, they could use light.

This is going to work.

She turned back to Dominique. She and her group were backing up over the shuddering pavement, but they were staying together and the wind shaman was keeping up the wind. Every one of them was staring at Livvy and her outstretched arm.

One giant bolt, on the pavement right in front of them, Livvy thought. *That's all it would take.*

She pointed at the spot as an explosion rocked the Underworld.

Livvy watched the plaza tilt at a wicked angle. Dominique and her squad were replaced with the blur of buildings flying by and the pavement rushing up. Livvy collided with it and then felt weightless. Then she collided with it again and came to a rest.

Up, she thought, *get up*, but her body was moving slow. *Gods, the pain in her left ear.* She turned her head to see what had happened to everybody and felt warm liquid running out of it.

On the ground next to her, Ursula was lying face down.

"Ursula," Livvy said. She slowly sat up and crawled to her. She carefully turned her over. Ursula groaned at the movement and opened her eyes. Alvina sat up next to Ursula and shook her head to clear it.

Min and Tamara lay tangled together slightly further away. Min started to move which made Tamara suddenly cry out in pain.

Thank the gods, thought Livvy. *At least they're still alive.*

Though maybe not for long.

Beyond them, Dominique was approaching with an enormous new group of shamans behind her.

More? Where had they come from?

The raven cawed overhead, its malevolent sound echoing in the sudden silence.

Livvy forced herself to stand. Either she'd have to use lightning and kill them or she and her friends were going to die. Now, there was no choice.

Livvy looked to the sky, wavering in place. The clouds were already churning and swirling. Lightning lit them from within, the power there bursting to be let loose.

Dizziness made her vision swim but she raised a hand up to that energy.

CHAPTER SIXTY-SEVEN

IN THE REAL world, Pip heard it before she saw it—a tiny crackling sound.

Once Livvy had thrown her into the fountain, she was done. She would need an excuse ready when Dominique got back, but she was glad to be out of it. There was no way she was going back.

Many of the shamans had returned. They were exhausted, drinking water, panting heavily, and staring into space. To see the Lightning Shaman in person, in the Multiverse, while networked—it had all been too much. One was already putting her goggles in her bag.

Pip looked toward the crackling sound.

It was the network box Mamacita had given them. The reserve squad was hooked up to it. Dominique had taken no chances this time. She had split off some of the best shamans into this separate group as a fallback. From their labored breathing, it seemed as though she'd needed them, but something was wrong.

Pip got up from her mat and approached the sleek black machine. The crackling sound grew louder and then there was a pop. A thin wisp of smoke rose up from under the box.

It was burning!

"Fire!" Pip yelled.

She hit the power button and ran to the wall and unplugged it. The shamans attached to it started to make noises and move. They were returning to the real world—no choice.

Pip checked the box and waved a hand in front of her face to move the smoke, which was pouring out now. Before a fire alarm went off, she dashed to one of the large windows and cranked the glass open. The reserve shamans sat up on their mats and looked around, confused.

Pip went back to the box as the newly returned shamans watched her.

"The box," she said, pointing at it. "It caught on fire."

"The one from Mamacita?" someone asked.

Yeah, thought Pip, eyeing it. *The one from Mamacita.*

• • • • •

Instead of lightning coming from the sky, an incandescent bolt suddenly flashed in from the side and struck the ground in front of the approaching group. Livvy reflexively shielded her face against the sudden explosion.

Most of the shamans with Dominique were blown off their feet, but now many of them were winking out in muted bursts of light. Dominique swiveled her head from side to side as her forces disappeared.

Livvy looked down at her hands. Had she called down lightning without channeling the strike?

Wait, it didn't come from the sky.

She searched the direction from which the lightning had come and had to blink at what she saw. She knew her mouth must be hanging open. Was it another trick?

Next to the fountain, her arm still upraised, stood her mother with a bolt of lightning channeled from the clouds and sparks raining down. Her mom turned her head to face Livvy and smiled.

"Mom?" Livvy said, taking a tentative step toward her.

Without warning, a brilliant flash of light and a small booming sound came from Dominique's direction. Livvy and her mom both looked over.

A shaman appeared in the middle of the burst.

Livvy raised her hand upward preparing to strike but something about this woman was familiar. She stared at her trying to remember. Yes, it was the woman from the picture, the one in the nkondi. It was Nicole and she looked surprised.

Then, time slowed.

To Livvy's left, lightning erupted from her mother's outstretched hand.

To her right, Dominique began to open her mouth.

Nicole was turning toward her sister, oblivious of the deadly energy bearing down on her.

In her mind's eye, Livvy suddenly flashed on Alvina in Palm Springs. 'Stop the speed,' she had said.

Livvy saw the bolt of electricity begin to move inevitably forward. There would be no taking it back and no stopping it.

'There may still be a chance,' Alvina had warned.

Livvy glanced back to Nicole. There was no way the strike would miss. When it landed, it would be lethal.

Alvina's voice rang in her head. 'Stop the speed.'

But if I don't get to her, she'll die.

Livvy surged forward. She watched as Nicole continued her slow-motion pirouette. Dominique had not moved but her mouth was opening wider. The incandescent bolt from her mother steadily approached from the left.

As Livvy looked at it, she realized it wasn't just one bolt but four. The shafts themselves were tiny, barely there, following one after another. The first one superheated the air around it to produce a glowing purple tube. Even as it slowly blinked off, the one behind took its place in the luminous channel. The effect was like a sluggish and eerie strobe, although no one could see it except her.

Livvy's eyes began to sting from the wind rushing into them. It rippled her skin and tugged furiously at her hair as she squinted, pressed her lips together, and leaned forward.

She glanced at her mother's determined face. The sparks around her seemed to fall like lazy flakes in a snow globe, clearly reflected as tiny points in her eyes.

The lightning strobed again and Livvy turned back to Nicole.

Almost there.

The brightness of the approaching electricity lit Nicole's back and reflected off her hair. It made her seem as though she were wearing a bright purple wig.

Almost there.

Nicole had nearly completed a half revolution, her eyes on Dominique now, and her smile radiant, positively lovely. The lightning slowly went off and then back on.

Almost there.

The tip of the supercharged lightning was a deep but intense shade of violet. It was more beautiful than any color Livvy had ever seen, but she had to turn her face away from it as time snapped back into place.

· · · · ·

In the real world, SK used a damp hand towel to dab Livvy's forehead. He nearly dropped it when he realized Livvy had made a sound.

"Thank the gods!"

They must be done and coming back. It was hard to know without being with Min and the other shamans.

He stood and looked at Livvy's face, but as the seconds ticked by he realized that wasn't the case. Though Livvy's expression hadn't changed, her lips had parted slightly and a quiet but anguished moan escaped. The muscles in her neck became taut and her diaphragm stopped moving.

"Oh gods, no," he muttered.

He snatched up his phone and dialed emergency help.

· · · · ·

What began as a sensation of cold numbness built rapidly to a searing and sizzling burning in her side. The lightning strike crashed into her full force, knocking her toward Nicole, who she instinctively grabbed. Livvy hugged her close but they were moving too fast. The ground impact forced the air from them both in sharp grunts and broke Livvy's grip.

Sapped of all strength, her arms flopped uselessly as she skidded on her side. Launched by the collision, Nicole flew away from her and started to roll.

At last, Livvy came to a halt.

Without enough energy to moan, Livvy simply closed her eyes to the excruciating pain in her side, the side she was lying on. She lay perfectly still, hyperaware of the silence—until she heard Dominique.

"Nicole!" she screamed. "Nicole!"

Was Nicole okay?

Livvy slowly opened her eyes to see Nicole several feet away from her, also lying on her side, looking directly at her. Her eyes seemed alert. In fact, she was beginning to smile.

Then someone's feet cut off her view.

"*Livvy*," her mother gasped. "Oh gods, Livvy!" She felt her mother's hands on her. "Gently," her mother said. "Roll her onto her back."

The pain doubled and Livvy couldn't help but scream. Finally, she was on her back, breathing hard, eyes closed.

"Is she okay?" Min asked.

"Oh gods," said her mom, now that she could see her left side. "I don't think so."

"SK is in the real world," said Ursula. "She only has to get to the fountain."

"We can carry her," said Tamara.

"Absolutely," said Alvina.

Livvy opened her eyes. "Nicole?" she said, weakly.

"I'm here," another voice said.

Livvy turned her head in that direction. Nicole was standing behind her mom. Dominique was there as well—the twins, side by side.

"I'm right here, Livvy," Nicole said again as Dominique gaped at her. She knelt down next to Livvy's mom. "You saved my life," she said.

"Good," Livvy managed. "Good."

"Livvy, honey," said her mom, her voice trembling. "I didn't mean to—"

"I know, Mom," Livvy whispered.

Her mom looked up at Min, Alvina, Ursula and Tamara. "I was aiming for Dominique and then she appeared." She nodded toward Nicole. "But it was too late."

"I have never seen anyone move so fast," said Ursula.

"Not fast enough," Livvy whispered. She tried to laugh but it hurt.

"Fast enough," said Alvina as she and Livvy made eye contact. Alvina knew what it had cost.

They were all silent for a few moments.

"Why?" Dominique said quietly. All faces turned to her. "Why would you do it?"

"You," said Ursula, "deserve to die."

There was a rustling of feet.

"Ursula," Min warned.

Dominique looked away from Ursula and back to Livvy, the question still on her face.

"Because she's the lightning shaman," said Min simply.

"You waste your breath," said Tamara.

"Are you going to be all right?" asked Nicole. She sounded exactly like Dominique and yet not.

"I'm going to be..." Livvy said quietly but paused. She had meant to say 'fine.' Although the burning pain in her side had already begun to subside, it was being replaced by a strange tingling sensation. "Actually, I don't know," she finished.

"The first thing will be getting you to the fountain," said Min.

"Let me handle that," said her mom.

"What?" said Ursula.

"We can help," said Alvina.

"No," said her mom. "Livvy and I–we have some unfinished business."

There was an awkward silence.

"Don't worry," said her mom. "Just some mother daughter talk. It won't take long."

"Nicole?" said Dominique.

Nicole looked at her and then back at Livvy. She bent low over Livvy and kissed her softly on the cheek. "Thank you," she whispered.

Then she rose and stood next to Dominique, like mirrored images except for the length of the hair. Dominique looked at her sister and then down into Livvy's face. She took in a breath and seemed as though she had something to say. Instead, she slowly exhaled. A brief look of puzzlement turned into outright confusion.

Nicole took Dominique's hand and tugged it. Dominique turned to follow her and they were gone.

"Are you sure we can't help?" asked Min.

"Yes," said her mom. "We won't be long."

Livvy looked over at Min. Tamara, Ursula, and Alvina stood around her. "It's okay," Livvy said, her voice stronger.

The four of them exchanged looks and then Min nodded. She turned back to Livvy with a little smile. "All right," she said. "I'll see you on the flip side."

In moments, Livvy and her mom were alone.

"Here honey," said her mom.

Livvy felt her head being lifted up and settled back down. She gazed up into her mother's face, her head resting in her lap. Above them, the tall buildings of the plaza no longer seemed so high. Cotton ball clouds slipped by beyond them.

"So, you're a lightning shaman," Livvy said.

She recalled the strange pattern in the clouds when her mother was near and the inability to call down lightning. Maybe lightning didn't work when two lightning shamans were present. Maybe it got confused or couldn't split. Maybe…

"Well," her mom said, touching Livvy's hair and then moving her hand to the side of Livvy's face. "You can see how good I am."

Livvy laughed and then winced. Her mother's face became serious. It was also getting dim around the edges.

"It wasn't your fault that I died," she said.

"Oh Mom," Livvy started to protest.

"No, just hear me out." She scowled and took on a stern tone. "Do not make me use my mother voice for this entire thing." Then she smiled.

"Okay," said Livvy.

"It wasn't your fault that I died," her mom said. "And I'll tell you why. It was your fate."

Livvy's mom paused to let it sink in but it didn't. "What?" said Livvy.

"Your fate," said her mother, looking directly into her eyes. "The fate of every lightning shaman."

Livvy tried to raise her head.

"Hold on," said her mom. "Hold on. Let me finish."

Livvy stopped and settled back down.

Her mom took in a deep breath and gazed out at the plaza. "I never wanted to be a lightning shaman," she said. "Though I imagine none of us do. Honestly, I was unsure of shamanism to begin with but especially when my mentor told me what I just told you."

Livvy still didn't understand and shook her head slightly. Her mom gazed down at her and Livvy looked intently into her green eyes, though they had started to fade.

"Only once in a generation, right?" her mom said. "That's

because the old lightning shaman has to die so the new one can come into their power."

"*What?*"

"Well," said her mother, looking away, "I couldn't do that. I wouldn't. Besides," she said, smiling and looking at Livvy while stroking her hair, "I wanted to have kids."

"So you never became a lightning shaman?" asked Livvy.

Her mom shook her head. "No, I never did. Not a lightning shaman, not any kind of shaman at all. My mentor and I parted ways. I met your father. And the rest you know."

Once in a generation, Livvy thought, *and not always then.*

"I knew the old lightning shaman would have to die for the next one to come along but I wasn't really sure if that was me or my mentor," said her mom. "I had managed to put it from my mind, until you were born."

"Because then you had a family to worry about," Livvy said.

"No, honey," she said. "No, not really."

Livvy waited, watching her.

"No," she said, sounding sadder than Livvy had ever heard her mother be before. "No, because the minute I laid eyes on you, I knew you were the next lightning shaman."

Livvy searched her mother's face, her eyes moving back and forth between her mother's eyes. *She knew?*

"My mentor knew it would be me," she said. "She knew I was the next lightning shaman. She told me I would know the next one as well, even if I didn't acknowledge my own power."

"You knew?" asked Livvy. "From the time I was born?"

"It's hard to explain," said her mom. "I knew you were the next lighting shaman because it was kind of like seeing my own grave."

"And you didn't tell me?"

"Livvy, honey," she said, caressing Livvy's face. "That's a hell of a thing to tell your daughter, especially if you're not sure. It's not like there's a rulebook somewhere. It's more an intuition."

Her mom slowly shook her head. "I don't know how often a lightning shaman goes from mother to daughter," she said and shrugged. "Maybe never. A lightning shaman doesn't usually have children."

Livvy didn't know what to say. Her mother's voice was growing dimmer and her entire body was starting to lose its color.

"Livvy, I can't explain to you in words how happy I was the day you were born, even when I realized who you were," she said, almost glowing with the memory, her eyes glistening. "I treasured each and every day with you and, if I had to do it again, I wouldn't change a thing. I…"

She started to choke up.

"Oh Mom," Livvy said, reaching up to her.

Her mom leaned forward and hugged her, rocking gently. "I love you, honey," she said into Livvy's hair.

"I love you too, Mom," Livvy managed between the tears.

They hugged and rocked, and occasionally sniffled until, finally, they were quiet. Livvy's mom slowly straightened up and wiped a tear from Livvy's face.

"All right, my girl," said her mom. "It really is time for you to go, before there's not enough of me to help you."

Livvy could only nod.

"Can you stand?"

"Let's try," Livvy said.

It was tricky and painful. Livvy realized she couldn't bend her left leg or put any pressure on it but, with her mom's help, she managed to stand.

"I think you should keep this," said her mom.

Livvy looked down as her mom held out the engagement ring. Livvy extended her hand.

"It's yours," her mother said, placing it into her palm.

Her mom propped a shoulder under Livvy's left arm and they hobbled to the edge of the fountain.

"Livvy?" her mom said, smiling. It was getting difficult to hear her.

Livvy turned to her, watching her lips.

"I'm proud of you, honey."

Livvy hugged her tightly as she tried to burn this moment into her memory–her mother's touch, the sound of her voice, and that smile. Reluctantly, she let her go.

Her mom looked at the fountain and nodded at it.

There was no point in trying to talk now.

Livvy slowly sat down on the ledge. Her mom helped lift her legs over the lip and into the water, though Livvy could barely feel her hands. She watched in silence as her mom sat next to her, facing the opposite direction.

She was almost gone now.

Her mom looked into the distance as though she recognized something there and then turned back to Livvy.

"Love you," she mouthed as she disappeared.

"Love you too, Mom," Livvy whispered and reached out.

But she was gone.

CHAPTER SIXTY-EIGHT

"I GUESS I thought maybe we could talk," said Dominique, but Nicole seemed not to have heard.

Dominique had come back to the real world to find headquarters deserted. Not a single shaman remained. Empty water bottles were scattered everywhere. The desk and all the cabinets were open, their contents spilled out. She knew they'd been looking for the drugs. It looked like they'd found everything.

There was a note on her stomach when she'd taken off the goggles. It was from Pipsqueak. The box from Mamacita had burned up. That would have accounted for her reserve squad disappearing the way it did.

Mamacita.

There was no time to think about her, though. Dominique had run down the stairs and across the alley to see Nicole–this new Nicole she'd seen in the Multiverse.

Dominique watched her squeeze various colors of paint onto her palette.

"Nicole?" Dominique tried again.

She'd heard her speaking so clearly in the Multiverse, as though she'd been talking all her life. Now that they were back, it was as though nothing had changed. She hadn't uttered a word. She'd been painting when Dominique arrived.

Something on the kitchen table caught Dominique's eye.

The goggles were on.

She went over to the table and picked them up. The symbols of the entrance to the Multiverse were still playing inside. She turned them off with a little clicking sound and looked back at Nicole, who took no notice.

Dominique remembered how she'd popped into existence, like

any other shaman–how Nicole had smiled and turned toward her as though she were actually seeing her. It was the first time she could remember thinking that Nicole recognized her.

And then had come the lightning.

Dominique had barely had time to realize that the bolt was on its way before Liver... She paused. Before *Livvy*...

"Saved Nicole," murmured Dominique.

She put the goggles back on the table and looked over at her sister, who was painting furiously on a huge canvas. Dominique slowly walked over to try talking again. Nicole had seemed so lucid, so at ease in the Multiverse.

For once, she had dared to hope.

"Nicole," she said. "Please try. Please–"

She stopped as she came around the canvas and could see it.

It wasn't the symbols of the Multiverse. In all her life, she'd never seen Nicole paint anything but the abstract icons.

And now this?

Dominique stared with her mouth open. It was a portrait of Livvy.

The plaza of Livvy's Underworld, the surrounding tall buildings, the sky full of clouds lit from within. It was the Multiverse in extraordinary detail, almost lifelike.

And there stood Livvy, looking right at them, her feet apart, one hand on her hip, one hand held out as though waiting for someone to take it. Her green eyes smiled and it was as though you knew you could take her hand and everything was going to be all right. Her white hair was swept to the side in a breeze and the effect was so realistic that Dominique almost felt her own hair moving.

Without knowing it, Dominique began to reach out her hand to the sparkling water, but something stopped her. She stared down and saw Nicole's hand on hers. She jerked her head up to see Nicole staring steadily into her eyes. There was no disapproval there, nor the frantic expression she was used to, only a calm gaze that seemed to be waiting. Dominique looked back at the painting and abruptly felt a sudden wave of cold realization.

She dropped her hand.

Nicole returned to painting.

Dominique hugged herself as the reality of what Livvy had done flooded over her. She stood silently as Nicole deftly added minute detail to the stonework of the fountain. She felt the tightness in her chest lessen the more she watched Nicole work but something wasn't quite right.

"The water," said Dominique, so quietly she almost couldn't hear herself. "It's more blue than that."

Nicole stopped and cocked her head, looking at the fountain.

She went to her palette and mixed two different blue dabs with a bit of white. She began to touch up the water, adding highlights here and there and then she stood back. Dominique cocked her head to the right and Nicole to the left and then, together, they nodded.

CHAPTER SIXTY-NINE

LIVVY STOOD OUTSIDE the door, leaning on the cane, and tried to look through the dark glass. Although the sky was barely light, she knew Mamacita would be there. She reached a hand toward the knob but stopped.

What would she say?

Thanks for everything, Mamacita. Sorry I doubted you. Sorry I acted so terribly, and then lied, and also tried necromancy.

Gods.

She shook her head.

Mamacita would have every right to tell her to get out. Stay away. Never come back. After what she'd said? Mamacita ought to—

Suddenly the door opened, the little bell tinkled on its spring, and Mamacita appeared.

She stood there, hands on hips.

"Now how are we supposed to hug if you just stand out here all day?" She opened her arms and smiled.

Livvy dropped the cane and wrapped her arms around Mamacita so fast and so fiercely that she thought she'd break her. To her surprise, Mamacita did *exactly* the same thing—squeezed her hard, like she wasn't ever going to let her go.

After several moments, Livvy realized that's precisely what she was doing. Mamacita knew. Livvy smiled a little and hugged her even tighter.

Time passed, though Livvy had no idea how much, and Mamacita finally let go. They looked at each other and Livvy felt understanding pass between them.

Mamacita bent over, picked up the cane, and handed it to her.

"Mmm hmm," she intoned lightly, reaching for the door. She paused in the opening and looked over her glasses.

"Don't you be a stranger," she said and waited with a smile.

Livvy nodded and then watched as Mamacita quietly closed the door.

CHAPTER SEVENTY

LIVVY SLOWLY LOWERED herself into one of the high-backed cushioned chairs in the lobby of her condo. Leaning heavily on the cane and keeping her left leg straight, she still dropped that last little inch.

Ouch.

"I wish you'd wait for all the test results," said SK. He pushed her rolling luggage in front of him and then out of the way as he stood in front of her. "What would it be, another couple of days?" he asked.

It had been like this since she'd said she was leaving.

He took her hand and held it. He'd done a lot of that too. She smiled down at their hands and then at him. The sun was to her back and the very first rays of morning were streaming in, lighting his naturally brown eyes to almost hazel. He was wearing blue today; his hair was perfect, his beard flawlessly trimmed at the jaw line.

This was how she wanted to remember him.

"Seriously," he said. "What difference would a couple of days make?"

"None," she said.

"Well then?"

"The test results won't make a difference either."

The puncture wounds from the wolf attack had vanished. The deep purple and black bruises on her left side remained though. Despite the fact that x-rays had confirmed her left hip, thigh, and two ribs had been broken, the bones were almost completely knit back together. No cast necessary. It was the rigidity and weakness of the leg that had everybody puzzled. There seemed to be no cause.

"This," she said glancing at her leg. "I have a feeling this is going to take a while, and I'm not sure conventional medicine is going to help."

"All the more reason to stay. Where else are you going to find as many shamans as here?"

"I can't stay," she said quietly.

They'd been over this too.

He regarded her silently for a moment before he looked down at her hand, running his thumb gently over her fingers.

"I know," he finally said.

He was right. There was no place with more shamans than L.A. but it was all the more reason for her to leave. He needed to work with them, be in the middle, and regain balance. Even more so after Mayet had decided to leave. She knew her clients would be in good hands, not only with SK but also Min and Ursula.

The civil suit with Matthew had ground to a standstill. Lawyers on all sides were still trying to come up with legal codes that addressed anything in the Multiverse. With a bit of luck, SK had said, Tamara might be convinced to give a statement that would corroborate Min's. They would likely settle out of court.

He looked up at her. "If not a couple days, how about a couple hours?" he asked.

She smiled at him. "What would a couple of hours do?"

"I could pack a few things, make a few calls—"

"This is something I need to figure out on my own," she said gently.

The meeting with Alvina, the revelations from her mother—Livvy couldn't shake a persistent feeling that it was time to understand her place in the Multiverse. It was past time.

Too much had happened. So much had been said. Some bridges had been crossed. They were silent for a time, content just to hold hands.

The sound of a car door behind her said that Min was there. She'd brought up the silver sedan from the garage below. Livvy heard the door to the lobby open but neither she nor SK took their eyes off one another.

Min cleared her throat.

Livvy looked up at her and smiled.

Min had already started to cry.

Livvy put both hands on her cane and pulled herself up as SK put a hand on her good hip to steady her.

She wrapped Min up in a big hug. "Minnie Mouse. Come on, now. I'm counting on you."

Min nodded.

"Not so many treats for Nacho," Livvy said, rubbing Min's back. "I think he's putting on weight."

Min nodded again, hugging her tightly, and sniffed.

"Okay," said Livvy, pulling back. She reached into her jacket pocket, pulled out the amethyst pendant, and looped the long chain over Min's head.

Min stared down at it.

"Thank you, Min," Livvy whispered. "For everything."

Min sobbed now and held her hands to her mouth.

Livvy hugged her briefly this time and then turned, took hold of the suitcase and headed to the front door of the lobby. Even though she leaned on the cane, she still had to limp. SK held the door and then stowed the suitcase in the trunk.

With some difficulty, she lowered herself into the car and SK shut the door. She lowered the window.

"Still no idea where you're headed?" he said.

Livvy shrugged. "East, I think. Maybe there'll be more sun."

SK looked in that direction for a few moments and then nodded.

"About us," he said, turning back to her.

She waited for his eyes to find hers.

"I haven't given up," he said, smiling a bit.

She grinned in return and even laughed a little. "I think I knew that."

They paused and looked at one another, their smiles slowly fading.

"I may not know where I'm going," she said. "But I know I'll be back." She paused and held out something. "This is yours."

He held out his hand and Livvy laid the amethyst heart in the center of it. "You'll wait?" she asked.

He leaned forward and, as she closed her eyes, he softly kissed her forehead.

"I can do that," he whispered.

After several long moments, she opened her eyes for one last look at him but found her tears had made him blurry. She turned the key in the ignition and the engine started. Before she could think twice, she checked the mirrors, eased down on the gas, and pulled onto the street.

She knew better than to look back. The road ahead was open, and the sky was crystal clear.

ABOUT THE AUTHOR

M. Terry Green is a full-time writer, former archaeologist, and budding minimalist. For more information about her and Livvy's Techno-Shaman Multiverse, please visit her web site at mterrygreen.com, or chat her up on Facebook or Twitter.

If you'd like to know about new releases and *only* new releases, then the M. Terry Green Newsletter is for you. I loathe spam and will never share your address. Plus, the unsubscribe button is always just a click away.

LETTER FROM THE AUTHOR

Dear Wonderful Reader,

I hope you enjoyed *Shaman, Friend, Enemy*. Honestly, I wasn't sure if I'd continue the techno-shaman series. But when the first book began to win both readers and critical acclaim, I felt like I was onto something. From this second book onward, I knew there would be a series, and I even knew how that series would end.

Although *Shaman, Friend, Enemy* is a darker tale than Book 1, it remains a reader favorite. I think there might be a few reasons for that popularity, but one stands out to me more than the rest: Livvy's compassion. From the start, I wanted her heroism to be fueled by her desire to help others.

But that's just how I see it. I would dearly like to know how you see it—or even if you feel the same! If you have a few seconds, I'd really appreciate hearing your thoughts. Feel free to tell me what you found appealing, what left you cold, and even what you disliked. I'd adore hearing from you. You can write me at terry@mterrygreen.com and visit me on the web at http://mterrygreen.com.

Once again, I also have a favor to ask. Reviews are the life blood of a book and just as precious because they're often so few. If you're at all inclined, I would very much appreciate your review for this novel, whether you liked it or not.

Thank you so much for reading *Shaman, Friend, Enemy*, spending your money on it, and most of all spending your time!

Take care and see you on the flip side,

Terry

BOOKS BY M. TERRY GREEN

THE CHRONICLES OF WHITE WORLD SERIES

Iced (Book 1)

Trapped (Book 2)

Book 3 - Coming Soon!

Be notified of the release by signing up for my newsletter!

THE OLIVIA LAWSON TECHNO-SHAMAN SERIES

Shaman, Healer, Heretic (Book 1)

Shaman, Friend, Enemy (Book 2)

Shaman, Sister, Sorceress (Book 3)

Shaman, Priestess, Pawn (Book 4)

Shaman, Lover, Warrior (Book 5)

OLIVIA LAWSON TECHNO-SHAMAN AUDIOBOOKS

Shaman, Healer, Heretic (Book 1)
Audible | Amazon | iTunes

Shaman, Friend, Enemy (Book 2)

Audible | Amazon | iTunes

Shaman, Sister, Sorceress (Book 3)
Audible | Amazon | iTunes

Audiobooks Four and Five Coming Soon!

23280928R00194

Made in the USA
San Bernardino, CA
11 August 2015